DAMAGED Crowns

STILL Shine

LATWAINA KELLEY

EMPOWER OUTLOOK LLC
DETROIT, MI

DAMAGED CROWNS STILL SHINE

This is a work of creative nonfiction. The events are portrayed to the best of the author's memory. While all the stories in this book are true, some names and identifying details have been changed to protect the privacy of the people involved. Everything here is true, although some events have been compressed and/or embroidered. The conversations in the book all come from the author's recollections, though they are not written to represent word-for-word transcripts. Rather, the author has retold them in a way that evokes the feeling and meaning of what was said. Thus, in all instances, the essence of the dialogue is accurate.

DAMAGED CROWNS STILL SHINE © 2022 LatWaina Kelley

Paperback ISBN: 978-0-578-80984-7

Empower OutLook LLC
Detroit, MI

Printed in the United States of America

First Edition, July 2022

Cover Design by Make Your Mark Publishing Solutions
Interior Layout by Make Your Mark Publishing Solutions
Editing by Make Your Mark Publishing Solutions

DEDICATION

This book is dedicated to my husband, Stephen Kelley, who is my rock and strength and the apple of my eye. I want to thank him for his love and support over the years as well as during the process of writing this book. Thank you for pushing me and believing in me. Thank you for tolerating the late-night work sessions in such a selfless manner. You have been such an inspiration in my life from day one. You're a great husband, father, compassionate counselor, a great teammate and team player, and coach. You're my number one cheerleader, my homie, my lover, and my friend. I love you, Husband.

This book is also dedicated to my baby doll, my daughter, Lakiya Neal, a God-fearing, smart, courageous, young lady. From the day you were born, my world changed forever. You gave me a renewed sense of purpose, a desire to live my best life. Your love for God and family is amazing. A lover of academia, it's no wonder you graduated high school valedictorian and graduated college with high honors. You are my inspiration. I thank God for blessing me with you. I am beyond proud of everything you have achieved so far in life. If you put your mind to it, you can have anything your heart desires. I love you with the whole of my heart. Thank you for pushing and supporting me while writing this book. I couldn't have done it without your love and support.

This book is also dedicated to my handsome son, my baby boy, Travon Tyler. If anyone knows how to fight, it is you. You defied the odds as a child and overcame a multitude of illnesses that were meant to cripple you and keep you bound to sickness and disease. But you fought … hard. You astounded the entire medical staff who was your provider of care. You're my special miracle. You are clothed with so many unique gifts, one of them being a public influencer. Your love for God's word is captivating. Your ability to learn quickly is awe inspiring. Go for it all. You're the CEO. A relentless pursuer of knowledge and wealth. Keep God near, and you'll go as far as your little heart desires! Remember, God is faithful and just. Thank you for your support during the writing of this book. Mommy loves you eternally.

ACKNOWLEDGMENTS

First, I want to thank God for being the head of my life and for giving me a clear mind and a healed heart to pen the words in this book. Without Him, this book couldn't have come to fruition. Thank You, God for giving me the courage to tell the story of my life. While I had moments of flashbacks, God carried me through. It is only by His loving mercy and grace that I am still standing today. He has never once guided me in the wrong direction. I trust His plan for my life, even when things appear to go wrong. God always shows up and shows out, demonstrating His power of love and care.

To my loving mother: Mama, I thank God for you. Thank you for giving me life. Without you, I would not be the woman I am today. I love you!

In loving memory of my dad: Daddy, not a day goes by that I don't think of you. You were my best friend, the first man I've ever loved. I wish you were here to see the woman I've become today. I wish you were here to see your grandchildren. You'd be so proud of who they've become. Rest on in Christ. We'll meet one day. Please continue to shine down on your baby girl, Latwaina. #girldad

To my stepfather: Thank you for being an inspiration in my life.

I would also like to thank Monique D. Mensah, the baddest self-publishing coach in the industry. Working with you has made the process of writing and publishing my book seamless. Your knowledge about the industry and the inner workings of book writing is unmatched. I cannot thank you enough for guiding me in the right direction and placing me in the hands of those who could grasp the vision and help make it a reality. Thank you! Thank you! Thank you!

I would also like to thank D'edra Y. Armstrong, my writing coach, for sticking with me during this journey. Thank you for the pep talks, the encouragement, and even the difficult conversations. You helped me expand the scope of this book tremendously. Thank you for believing in me and my ability to "tell my story unabashedly." I am forever grateful to you for your professional genius and your services.

Margie Lindsay: You were an angel sent to me for more than twenty years. You were like a mother to me and grandmother to my children. We will never forget you for your loving kindness and generosity bestowed upon us while you lived. You've earned your angelic wings for sure. The kids and I miss you so much! Your spirit lives on.

To my grandmothers: Thank you for your praying hands. There's no love like the love of a grandmother. I try to remember to live by the principals you taught me. You were a role model in more ways than you realized. It is because of you that I know God, His Word, and how to pray. You instilled faith and trust in me. You showed me that the power of love can restore brokenness. It is because of you that I am still standing. Rest well. I love you and miss you both!

CHAPTER 1

Beginnings

Mama thought Tyrone was the spice of life. Like my dad, Tyrone was light skinned, tall, and extremely handsome. I guess you could say that my mother, a dark-skinned woman, had a thing for this prototype of a man, if you will. For my mom, Tyrone brought joy back into her life. Tyrone was a local electrician and was known as Mr. Fix It, able to fix just about anything electrical. He often worked on big projects as a contractor, making his days long … sometimes, fifteen and sixteen hours. With all of this going for him, I could see why my mother fell for him.

If you didn't know any better, you would've thought Tyrone was our biological father. He was attentive, brought us to school almost every day, paid us plenty of attention, and even showered us with gifts. He treated my sister Ebony, my brother Daniel, and me as though we were his biological children, even though we all had different fathers. And Tyrone even got along well with my biological father, Samuel. Tyrone couldn't fool Grandma Lily, though. She knew he didn't "have all his marbles," as she would say.

One night, after all the company had left, Grandma Lily and Mama were in the kitchen having "grown-up conversation," when I overheard things I probably shouldn't have.

"Grace, where's that man of yours at?" she said to Mama as she reached into the kitchen cabinet and retrieved a large container.

"He's doing a job," Mama said, helping Grandma Lily put some of the leftover dinner in a large container, so we could take it home with us.

"You sure he's working and not spreading himself around town?" Grandma Lily said.

"Mama, not in front of the kids," my mother said.

"Well, since he's at work, I'll put enough food in this here container, so he can grab a bite or two. You know I ain't too fond of him, right?"

"Mama, Tyrone's a good guy. Give him a chance, will ya?" my mother said, "defending her man," as they would say.

"Grace, the man just ain't got all his marbles, okay? You can love on him all you want, but you'll see what I mean one day," Grandma Lily cautioned.

"Oh, Mama, please," my mother defended once again, fanning her hand in the air as though she was fanning the comment away. He ain't no worse than your favorite son-in-law upstairs," Mama said, rolling her eyes and sucking her teeth simultaneously.

"The two of them are peas from the same pod," Grandma Lily said almost with a sly grin on her face.

"No, Mama, he ain't like Mike. You worship the ground Mike walks on. But he might just be the reason we all get caught up in legal trouble."

"Don't be talkin' up no trouble. I mind my business down here in my own home. Long as they paying their share of the mortgage, ain't none of my business what they doing up them steps."

I didn't know what "trouble" Mama was referring to … not until about three weeks later when the police broke down Grandma Lily's front door and made us all get on the floor.

"Don't move," Mama whispered to Ebony and me as a female police officer held Mama's hands behind her back. Ebony and I lay paralyzed on the living room floor.

"Any drugs in here?" the lady officer said to Mama.

"I said, I don't live here!" Mama lashed out at the officer.

"That's what they all say, lady," the officer said, sucking her teeth. It was obvious she didn't believe Mama. It was also obvious that she seemed to have something personal against Mama—like Mama stole her breakfast that morning or something.

"This is my parents' house, and I came to get my kids."

"Lady, you know what's going on in this house. If we find what we came looking for, Department of Children and Families is coming for the kids," the officer threatened as she ferociously chewed on a piece of bubble gum.

Mama began to sob. That is until a Spanish-speaking male officer whispered something into the lady officer's ear. The last thing she said was, "You're lucky. And if I were you, I wouldn't bring my children back around here."

As children, we didn't see in Tyrone what Grandma Lily saw in him. Mama loved Tyrone, and until their relationship turned upside down, she was that ride-or-die chick.

As a nurse, Mama worked a lot. She was very much an atypical woman. Although she gave birth to three children and was not married, she was educated. She liked the finer things in life and worked hard to obtain them. And when it came to her children, she was a mother hen—she would kill to protect us, if it were in her power. Life was good, for the most part … in the beginning. I remember when things began to change.

Too young to put two and two together, I just remember awkward things. The sorts of things that make you stay paralyzed in fear … afraid to move because somehow you think that things may go from bad to worse if you do. That was me. Recluse. Shy. Timid. Nervous. I was protected when I was around my immediate family because they knew me … saw me grow in a shell and not out of one.

Tyrone wasn't home when we got back from Grandma Lily's house that night. Mama made him a separate plate from the container of food we took from Grandma Lily's and put it in the oven for him.

"Get ready for bed, guys," Mama yelled out to us from the kitchen.

"We are," my sister Ebony confirmed.

Daniel jumped in the shower first. He didn't like taking baths as much as Ebony and me. His showers were quick, so that was good.

"You can go after Daniel," Ebony said, retrieving her earplugs from her purse.

"Okay," I said as I opened my drawer to grab a pair of pajamas. And that's when we heard the front door slam.

"Grace …" he called out to her. But his voice was different. "Grace," he called out again.

Ebony and I crawled into the hallway and peered around the corner. We could see Tyrone standing behind Mama in the kitchen.

"Thank you," Tyrone said as Mama pulled his plate from the oven and handed it to him.

"But that's not what I want right now," Tyrone said, putting the plate on the counter and grabbing Mama around the waist.

"Stop it, Ty. The kids are still up."

"Come on, let's go to bed … now," Tyrone said, trying to lead Mama toward their bedroom.

"What is wrong with you tonight?" Mama said as she tried to stand firm.

"Come on, woman," Tyrone begged.

Mama had sensed correctly—something was wrong with Tyrone. And when they went in the bedroom, whatever it was that was going on with Tyrone intensified.

We could hear Mama's frail body bang against the walls in their bedroom. Then we heard a final thump … then silence. By this time, Daniel had emerged from the bathroom. Ebony pressed her index finger against her lips.

"Shh," she cautioned Daniel. "I think Mama and Tyrone just had a fight."

"He better not be hittin' on my mama," Daniel said as he attempted to storm past us.

"Don't go. Stay here. Wait … I *think*," Ebony clarified, not wanting things to escalate.

Reluctant, Daniel backed up and leaned his body against the wall.

Without even knowing it, Ebony, Daniel, and I were complicit in hiding the abuse going on behind the walls of Mama and Tyrone's bedroom. We went to bed that night without further discussion of what we witnessed by way of "hearing" and not necessarily "seeing." The next morning, it was B.A.U. (business as usual) in the house—Mama left for work in the wee hours of the morning, and Tyrone saw to it that Ebony and I got to school.

As the youngest, I stayed under my mother, at least as much as I could. As a nurse, my mother worked the typical twelve-hour shifts, often leaving us with Grandma Lily or at home with Tyrone. She trusted him. And luckily, her judgment did not fail her. Tyrone never *physically* abused us.

I would often wonder why Tyrone would be sitting in the living room in the same clothes that he wore the previous day. But my mother would always make excuses for him.

"Mr. Tyrone came home late last night. He was over there doing the electrical work on that new building downtown." She was proud that Tyrone made good money. And with the money she made as a nurse, we sure weren't hurting for anything … well, not at first.

Christmases were fun, and we had plenty. But one Christmas season, however, things took a dramatic turn. The thirty-plus beautifully wrapped gifts that were under the Christmas tree were stolen.

"Mama! Mama! The gifts are gone!" Ebony and I screamed as we ran to my mother's bedroom.

"Oh, my goodness!" Mama said as she eyed Tyrone.

"Yeah, baby, some rotten scoundrel stole the Christmas gifts," Tyrone said, nervously stroking his soft head of hair as he returned the suspicious look at my mother.

"Now we can't have Christmas," I yelled as tears cascaded down my plump cheeks.

"I promise you … we're going to make it up to you guys," my mother said almost apologetically.

"Yeah … we're going to make it up to you guys," Tyrone echoed. "We're going to get even more gifts and put them under the tree … just wait and see," Tyrone promised, patting Ebony and me on our backs.

Every day, we waited to see whether new gifts were going to replace the "stolen" gifts. The day never came. And if it had not been for the gifts my dad and my grandparents gave us, we wouldn't have had a Christmas that year. Well, it wouldn't have stopped Christmas from coming, but we would have had a "giftless" Christmas. Incidents like this went from rare to very often, because either somebody loved the little stuff we owned, or we had the worst luck in the world. One morning, we woke up and someone had stolen all our electronics. Someone even started stealing our food … at least that's what we thought. So, most days, my sister Ebony and I had to go to family and friends' houses to eat. Out on the streets doing his thing, Daniel fended for himself.

It was easy for Mama to disguise the abnormal things going on in the house because she always hid behind her profession—she worked long hours and would get home too late to do this or that … from cooking to helping us with homework, attending parent–teacher conferences, church, and the like. But I made the mistake of telling Grandma Lily that Mama hadn't bought groceries in a while. And that's when I learned that "what goes on in the house is supposed to stay there," that is, if you don't want outside interference. But it was too late. My grandparents put us in the car and drove us home.

Pretending to be engaged in conversation in the living room with our grandpa, we could hear the conversation between Mama and Grandma Lily.

"Grace, I want the truth," Grandma Lily said, standing in front of the pantry entryway.

"Mama, I just ain't been shopping … that's all," Mama said, trying to close the pantry curtains.

"There's barely anything these kids can eat in here … without them having to be Julia Childs," Grandma Lily said, letting her hands fall from her hips.

"These kids ain't hungry, Mama," my mother defended.

"Of course, they ain't, 'cause they eatin' everybody else out of a house and a home. Look, I don't know what's going on over here, and I don't wanna know. But you better think long and hard about whatever it is. You'll lose your job, your house, and these kids if you don't watch it."

"I know," was all Mama said.

"Now come on. Your daddy and I will take you grocery shopping," Grandma Lily said.

Mama went into her bedroom and came back out moments later with her purse. "I'm ready," she announced, clasping the handles of her clutch purse.

Later that night, after Grandma Lily and our grandpa left, Mama gave us the "What goes on in this house" speech. "Let me tell you this one good time. What the hell goes on in this house stays in this house, all right? If you don't like it, you can get your ass out!"

"Grandma Lily asked me what we ate," I said, oblivious that I had broken some golden rule.

"You ain't starving around here."

"But why can't we tell Grandma Lily the truth?" I said, puzzled.

"Because I said so," Mama said. The "because I said so" explanation was so common and rarely challenged back in the day. Although we heard what my mother had told us, we were so close to our grandparents, that it didn't feel as if we were violating our mother's trust by merely answering our grandparents' questions. We were too young to try to hold Mama and Tyrone's secrets … the fighting *and* the drugs.

As children, we didn't know what was truly going on behind their bedroom door. On the opposite side of the door was a different story. We'd sometimes see Tyrone stretched out on the sofa where he'd fallen asleep the night before. He'd still be wearing the dusty, dirty clothes from the day before. We'd try to tiptoe past him to the kitchen. But sometimes, he'd wake up, mumble a good morning greeting and then roll back over or get up and stumble to his and Mama's bedroom.

Things in the house began to change. First, it was the Christmas toys being stolen. Then it was the electronics. Then what used to be a house stocked with food became a house in which food was scarce. Then, Mama began to change. Mama was always very well kept. Neat hair. Well dressed. Manicured nails. Pedicured feet. And a beautiful smile to complement it all. That all changed too. We'd see Mama come out of her room with her hair all over her head as if she'd been in a boxing match with the world's heavyweight boxing champ. And it was one of these days that Grandma Lily and our grandpa happened to make a surprise visit.

"Grace!" Grandma Lily said in a stern voice.

"What, Mama?" my mother said, not really making eye contact with Grandma Lily.

"What is going on around here?"

"What do you mean?" my mother said, stupefied by both the surprise visit and the question itself.

"You know what I mean. Something ain't right here, and I want you to tell me what's going on," Grandma Lily said, her eyes scanning the room.

"Everything's all right, Mama," my mother lied. "Right, honey?" she said, expecting me to concur.

"Leave her out of it," Grandma Lily said. "Now, I asked you what's going on in this house."

"Mama, we're all right over here. What do you want me to say?"

"I want the truth."

A single tear escaped its duct and trinkled down Mama's left cheekbone. It confirmed what Grandma Lily had suspected. Grandma Lily looked up at the ceiling and closed her eyes for a moment. I think she said a quick prayer for Mama … and us—Daniel, Ebony, and me.

"You want me to take Daniel and Ebony again?"

"Mama, don't take my kids. They're all I got," my mother pleaded.

"I'll take Daniel and Ebony … you'll still have Latwaina," Grandma Lily said, making her intentions very clear—she had no plans on taking me.

Mama burst into tears and collapsed on the living room floor. My grandpa went over to help her up, while Grandma Lily ordered us—Daniel, Ebony, and me—to our rooms. "I'll be in there in a minute. Just go on and grab a few things for a few days. You, too, Latwaina," she added.

"Me too?" I asked for confirmation. Just moments ago, she had suggested that I was staying with my mama. Besides, it wasn't out of the norm for me to be left behind.

"Yes, you too, Latwaina," Grandma Lily confirmed.

Ebony and Daniel were used to staying with Grandma Lily for long periods of time, but I was not. Our family dynamics were different. Although Grandma Lily and my grandfather were married, they lived in separate households. My grandfather lived in the house he and Grandma Lily had purchased. Because she was the caretaker for her parents, my great-grandparents, Grandma Lily lived with them. My grandpa didn't mind living in a separate household, so the arrangement worked for him.

I'm not sure whether my young mind could fully grasp the severity of what was going on at the time. As we packed, we could hear the faint sounds of Grandpa talking to Mama in the living room. I packed several articles of clothing, some toys, and things for school. And although I had packed up what I thought belonged to me, I left a piece of my soul in that house that day. Tucked away and hidden was a fragment of my being … something that would cause me to unravel day by day, week by week, month by month, and year by year.

CHAPTER 2

Keeping Secrets

Detroit neighborhoods had what were called two-family flats. Grandma Lily and Aunt Lisa each occupied a flat. Aunt Lisa and her husband, Mike, lived on the top level and Grandma Lily lived in the downstairs unit. We had a large family, and we were very well known. In the 1980s, we almost made the Guinness Book of World Records, for the largest family in the world. In 1985, my great-grandfather turned 117 years old and was the second oldest man in the world. My great-grandparents celebrated more than seventy-five years of marriage. Many of our relatives lived close by. This type of notoriety is what made our family well known. Plus, Grandma Lily and her sisters were great cooks. They'd cook big dinners often, and the likes of people like the Four Tops, the Temptations, Aretha Franklin, Jesse Jackson, and Stevie

Wonder would stop by to have dinner. So, Grandma Lily's house had a revolving door. You'd never know what famous person was going to stop by. It happened more often than not. Pictures of Grandma Lily and many celebrities were in picture frames all over her house. Most of the children loved the fun and excitement at my grandparents' house … all except for me. In my eyes, the constant commotion from laughter and celebration was just what I didn't need. I felt drowned out by stardom, a hunger for attention, and a host of other problems.

Ebony always tried to get me to enjoy the parties at Grandma Lily's house or upstairs at Aunt Lisa's house. Dance. Play with other kids. Anything. While these wild parties went on, we were instructed to go outside until it was just too late to be hanging out. We had our share of looking into the eyes of strangers often, some of whom tried to win us over with a warm smile. Uncle Mike was always the life of the party. And if Aunt Lisa didn't like hosting those wild parties, she sure did a hell of a job faking it. She pranced around the house with glass of wine after glass of wine, showing off her body in the scantily clad apparel she wore.

Sometimes, things got a little heated, like the time when Ricky, the neighbor from across the street, and Uncle Mike got into an argument.

"Where's the rest of my money?" Uncle Mike said, getting up from his chair.

"That's it. That's all of it," Ricky said, backing up. Uncle Mike was not one to be played with.

"Don't try to play me for no fool. You tryna short me. I've been in this game for a long time now. I know when somebody's tryna play me for a fool. I want the rest of my money or there's gonna be some problems," Uncle Mike said, getting into Ricky's face.

"All right. All right, man!" Ricky said, tossing a crumbled-up dollar bill in the air. It landed on the table in front of Uncle Mike. A white powder-like substance escaped the folded bill.

"Let's go back down to Grandma Lily's," Ebony said, sensing things were getting ready to get even uglier.

"What was in the dollar bill?" I asked Ebony as we jetted down the back steps to Grandma Lily's.

"A special powder they like to eat," Ebony said.

"Powder? Who eats powder?" I said.

"Stop asking questions, and don't tell no one what you just saw. No one. Ever," Ebony instructed.

I didn't say anything, just followed Ebony into Grandma Lily's house and pretended everything was normal.

Daniel was barely around. He took the opportunity of living with Grandma Lily to get his street hustle on. He was into selling drugs. We weren't the closest siblings due to our separate living arrangements when I was younger. Both Ebony and Daniel seemed to enjoy the free-for-all atmosphere. But to me, it lacked structure and connectedness. Naturally, having never been separated from my mother, I could barely wait to be reunited with her. Staying with Grandma Lily for those two weeks seemed like an eternity. Luckily, however, my dad's visitation weekend fell on that last weekend we were at Grandma Lily's.

My father didn't ask any probing questions during that visit, leading me to believe that Grandma Lily'em didn't tell him what was really going on with Mama. As a matter of fact, before I left to go with my dad, Grandma Lily reminded me of the ole golden rule—What goes on in the house stays in the house. And whether Grandma Lily knew it or not, I'd rather spend the time with my dad, talking about other things instead of the chaos in her house and in my mother's. It was the last thing on my mind, actually.

When my dad brought me back to Grandma Lily's that Sunday afternoon, I learned that we were going back home with Mama the next day. I remember going to sleep happy that night. I even dreamt about being back home with Mama and Tyrone. In the dream, however, everything was good. No more missing things. No more seeing Mama with her hair all over her face. No more hearing knocks and bangs in their bedroom. No more seeing Mama emerge from the bedroom wearing fresh wounds inflicted by Tyrone's hands.

When Mama came to pick us up from Grandma Lily's the next day, Ebony and Daniel weren't too enthused. They were used to living with Grandma Lily. They were even close to that side of the family. Mama's side of the family treated Ebony and Daniel like royalty. It was a different story when it came to me, however. I didn't get selected to run errands with my aunts or uncles like Ebony and Daniel did. Maybe it was because of my incessant whining and crying spells. Who knows the true reason behind it all. All that mattered was that, at the end of the day, a young girl was treated like an outcast and subsequently began to think of herself as less than and not good enough.

I nearly jumped into my mother's arms when Grandma Lily opened the front door, and I saw Mama standing there.

"Hey, baby girl," my mother said, bending down and cupping my face in her hands. "You been good?"

"Nope. That's one crying little girl you have," Aunt Lisa blurted out.

Mama sucked her teeth. "She's just not used to staying anywhere else but home."

"You don't have to tell us that," Aunt Lisa said sarcastically. "She's a whining mess."

"Where's Ebony and Daniel?" Mama asked Grandma Lily, trying to ignore Aunt Lisa's comments.

"In the family room," Grandma Lily said, closing the front door as Mama stepped in. Grandma Lily called out for Ebony and Daniel. Ebony stuck her head out of the family room. "You and Daniel get your stuff. Your mother's here to take you home."

"Gee!" Ebony said, sulking at the news. If you left it up to her and Daniel, they would have preferred living with Grandma Lily over living with Mama. They could get over on Grandma Lily much easier because she was super busy. Busy taking care of her parents. Busy with handling church business. Busy with running a second household where my grandfather lived. Busy with entertaining celebrities. Busy catering special events for the local politicians. Just busy. What that meant for Ebony and Daniel was that they could pretty much do anything they wanted and not have to answer to anyone.

Mama hummed one of her favorite songs as she drove us home that night. She seemed happy.

Tyrone was standing at the top of the steps when we pulled up, waiting for us to come home as if we had just been released from prison.

"Hey, my favorite girl," Tyrone said, patting me on my shoulder as I brushed past him. Ebony mumbled something under her breath, and Daniel walked right past Tyrone without saying a word. Although he tried to play it off, Tyrone was a little taken aback by Ebony and Daniel's behavior. "So y'all just gonna act like I didn't speak to you, huh?" he said, chuckling. But the chuckle didn't sound real. Tyrone's feelings were hurt, and I could see it in his eyes.

"Ebony … Daniel … get your tails back here and say hello or something. Don't you hear Tyrone speaking to you?" Mama said as she walked in the house behind us.

"It's all right, Grace," Tyrone said, not wanting the issue to escalate into a full-blown fight.

"Hi, Tyrone. There. Is that better?" Daniel shouted facetiously before darting into his room and slamming the door behind him. He hated being home, and it was readily apparent.

Mama shook her head. She could barely control Daniel, and if she believed Tyrone had more control than she had on Daniel, she was sorely mistaken. Daniel's animosity toward Tyrone was growing increasingly evident, and it didn't help that Tyrone put his hands on our mama, which made matters even worse. There was no way Daniel was going to ever think of Tyrone as a father figure. Daniel needed his biological father, who unfortunately, wasn't around.

The next day, it was business as usual … in more ways than one. We went to school and Mama and Tyrone went to work. On the way to school that morning, Felicia, one of Ebony's friends, asked why we hadn't been walking to school for the past two weeks. I looked over at Ebony. The golden rule remained in effect at all times … at least for me, it did. For Ebony, it didn't. She voluntarily shared the information.

"We was at our grandma's house."

"Why?" Felicia asked curiously.

"Cause our mama having some problems in the house," Ebony said, eyeing me with a "you better not open your mouth" look.

"Oh … those kinda problems," Felicia said, nodding her head.

"Yeah, those kinda problems," Ebony confirmed.

I sort of think Ebony wanted those people from the State to get involved. Mama had run the whole saga down, saying that if those people from the State got involved, we'd be taken away from her. It was probably a dream come true for Ebony and Daniel, as they would've loved living with Grandma Lily on a permanent basis. Sometimes, I think Ebony told Felicia on purpose. Felicia's mother was a teacher, not at our school, but at an area high school. Being a teacher meant that she was required by law to report all cases of abuse, even suspected cases of abuse. I felt my heartbeat pick up speed. Being taken away from my mother was a scary thought for me. And for the next several days, my heart skipped several beats every time the telephone or doorbell rang. The last thing we needed was having the State get involved … that's what the young mind of a nine-year-old girl thought.

As soon as we hit school grounds, Ebony and Felicia scattered, joining their group of mutual friends. We had to wait in the playground area before they let us in school, which wasn't until eight thirty. I didn't have friends, so I'd wait by the door. This day, however, Mrs. Chambers struck up a conversation with me.

"Why aren't you playing with the other kids, Latwaina?"

"Because," I said, shyly. I wished she hadn't asked the question.

"Because what?" she probed.

"I don't have no friends," I confessed.

"All these kids out there, and you don't have any friends?"

I shook my head. I admitted to Mrs. Chambers something I hadn't admitted, not even to myself. I had no friends. Most kids didn't know that I was Ebony and Daniel's younger sister. We looked nothing alike. They were admired for their best features, and I was teased about my not-so-desirable features— my skinny legs, my dark skin, and awkward body rhythm. I couldn't dance to save my life.

"We're going to get you some friends. You're a nice kid, and you deserve to have friends. Everyone needs at least one friend," Mrs. Chambers consoled. She was right, but I didn't believe her. I knew it would take more than Mrs. Chambers' desire for me to make friends. I didn't know how to free myself from the web of confusion and loneliness that had become my habitat for so long.

We hadn't been back home for a week before chaos between Mama and Tyrone started back up again. The banging against the walls and the thumps on the floor both resumed. It would only be a matter of moments before Mama would emerge from the bedroom, her hair all over her head as if birds were pecking at it and her face decorated with knots and bruises from Tyrone's fists.

"You let that dude hit you again, huh?" Daniel said, having detected a bruise on the side of Mama's face one morning.

All Mama could do was look away. I mean, how could she look at her son and admit that a man she lay with at night beat her?

"When you gonna leave that loser, Mama?" Daniel said as he kicked over a kitchen chair.

"Soon … soon," Mama whispered.

"I'll believe it when I see it," Daniel said as he stormed out of the back door.

I walked over to the freezer and got some ice and put it into a Ziploc baggie, making Mama an icepack for her face. "Here, Mama," I said, handing her the homemade icepack.

"Thank you, honey," she said, retrieving the icepack from my hand and gently placing it on the side of her face.

Luckily, I wouldn't have to make too many more icepacks for Mama, because when she'd had enough of the tumultuous lifestyle she lived when she was with Tyrone, she called it quits. It didn't go over well with Tyrone, who tried to get Mama to stay with him. But his mellow words no longer had the power to seduce Mama … back in his arms … back in their bed … or back into the dangerous streets.

"What are you doing?" Tyrone said as he downed a shot of vodka.

"Packing," Mama said without even looking up at Tyrone.

"I can see that much," Tyrone said, taking it upon himself to inspect some of the clothes in Mama's suitcase, unfolding them and trying to shove them back into place.

"Leave it alone. I got it," Mama said, snatching the items of clothing out of his hands.

"Where you plan on going?"

Mama didn't respond.

"Didn't you hear me, woman?"

"Here what?" Mama said, sucking her teeth.

"Where you plan on going?"

"I plan on going home," Mama said, slapping Tyrone's hand away as he attempted to unfold another item of clothing.

"So, you just gonna leave me here by myself?" Tyrone said, slumping down into the rocking chair in the corner of the room.

"You're a grown man. You'll figure it out just like I have to do," Mama said, closing the suitcase lid, zipping it up, and handing it to Daniel to bring to the car. "Oh, one more thing … the electricity and lights will be off by Friday, so you have a few days to pack your stuff and get out," Mama said as she pulled the handle up on a smaller suitcase leaning against the armoire.

A stunned Tyrone picked up the trashcan on the side of the bed and threw it. There was no need in him fighting Mama because he had already lost. Lost a good woman. Lost a place to live. Lost the stability he'd gotten used to.

"Then go! Leave! No good woman ever leaves a good man!" he yelled, trying to take last minute verbal jabs at Mama. But she paid Tyrone no mind. She grabbed me by the hand, and the two of us walked out of the house and Tyrone's life that night.

It was back to Grandma Lily's house. I could stomach it this time because my mama was there with us. This also meant playing by Grandma Lily's rules again—school. Church. Homework. Church. Church ... and more church.

My grandfather opened the door for us that day. He just so happened to be over my great-grandparents' house. Grandma Lily stayed with her parents because she had to take care of them. And it all seemed to work out, as strange as it was. Actually, I think the physical separation between my grandparents did them more good than harm.

Grandaddy wrapped his arms around Mama, and she almost brought them both to the floor. He knew why she was there. It was in her facial expression, in her disposition. Her clothes didn't fit anymore ... they were too big. Her nails weren't freshly manicured; you could see the dirt underneath her fingernails. Her eyes were dilated from recent drug use and lack of sleep. Drug use was on the verge of robbing her of a great job and the ability to earn a good living. It was also on the verge of causing her to lose her mind .... and her children. Drugs were an invisible enemy that had come to steal, kill, and destroy everything in its path.

Grandma Lily sat on the edge of our bed that night, talking to Mama about her plans ... what she planned on doing about getting clean. Mama told Grandma Lily what she believed Grandma Lily wanted to hear.

"I'm gonna get clean, Mama," my mother said to Grandma Lily.

"How you gonna do that, Grace?" Grandma Lily said, wanting my mama to detail her plans.

"Gonna focus on work and getting back on my feet," Mama said, playing with her trembling hands.

"Grace, do you think it's going to be that easy?"

"I never said it'd be easy. But I gotta do it for my children."

"Do it for yourself, Grace. Baby, do it for yourself," Grandma Lily said.

From that moment on, Grandma Lily observed Mama's words and actions from afar. And it didn't take long for her to realize that the drugs still had Mama. I remember going to bed at night with Mama but waking up in the morning only to discover that Mama had creeped out during the night. Looking back, I can only imagine how my grandmother felt, watching her daughter's life crumble right before her very eyes. Trying to protect the inevitable from occurring was an insurmountable battle, one that we'd all eventually lose in some form or fashion. Mama hid behind her occupation at first, claiming she was at work when, in reality, she had gone on a binge. Eventually, Mama lost her job. The drugs had won again. Grandma Lily confronted Mama once again.

"Now, we both know what's really going on," I heard Grandma Lily say to Mama one morning as they were eating breakfast at the kitchen table. Mama didn't readily respond. "Did you hear what I said?" Grandma Lily said, leaning her head closer to Mama.

"I heard you, Mama," my mother said, dipping a teabag in the ceramic mug.

"You gotta get some help," Grandma Lily said.

"I know," Mama said. But too bad she didn't, because it was only a matter of time before Mama disappeared again … days at a time … weeks at a time, and months at a time. This resulted in Grandma Lily and Aunt Lisa being our primary caretakers.

"Where's your mom?" my dad asked when he picked me up from Grandma Lily's one Saturday afternoon.

I hunched my shoulders. He was my father, and I felt obligated to tell him the truth. But on the other hand, Mama and Grandma Lily's rule was what goes on in the house was supposed to stay in the house.

"You can tell me," my dad assured me.

"I haven't seen Mama," I confessed sorrowfully and almost apologetically.

"What do you mean you haven't seen her?"

"I just haven't … She ain't been home."

My dad shifted the gear back in the park position. "You wait here. Let me go talk to your grandmother," he said. "I'll be right back."

I watched as my father got out of the car, walked up to the house, and rang the doorbell. Ebony answered the door. My father walked in the house and closed the door behind him. I could only imagine what the conversation was like. Grandma Lily had to tell my dad the most painful news—that her daughter, the love of his life, was addicted to drugs.

I could tell the news shook my dad. He tried to play the devastating news off when he got back in the car, but it was too apparent; my dad could barely get a coherent sentence out.

"Ummm … wait. Now … where?"

"Where. Are. We. Going?" I said, trying to help him out.

"Yeah, yeah. Now where are we headed?" he said, trying to focus.

"You said we were going to the store first and then to the circus."

"Oh, yeah, that's right. Thanks, baby girl. Thanks for helping your daddy out. I couldn't think straight for a minute."

"Is it because of Mama?" I asked.

My dad swallowed hard. "Your mother's gonna be all right," my dad said. But for some reason, I believed that he was trying to convince himself more than me. The secret I had been forced to hold for so long was now out. I felt a relief. I didn't like hiding the truth from my dad. It was killing Daniel, Ebony, and me on the inside. It was as though something was stabbing us in our gut, and we couldn't even say, "Ouch." But now that my dad knew, I felt solace in knowing that as far as I was concerned, he would see to it that I was safe, that my needs were going to be met no matter what.

"I miss her," I said, nodding.

"Okay, baby girl. Let's get our day started. We have plans," my dad said, patting me on the leg.

Whether he knew it or not at the time, my dad was my saving grace. I appreciated all that my grandparents, my Aunt Lisa, and our extended family did for my siblings and me, but there was nothing like the love and protection of a mother. And for us, it was missing. We were vulnerable prey and didn't even know it.

CHAPTER 3

Target Practice

Twenty-five-year-old Uncle Nick was Aunt Lisa's brother-in-law. He was young and fun to be around. His youthful energy made him seem as though he was a teenager. On many occasions, he'd buy all the children whatever we wanted or take us wherever we wanted to go. He was that cool uncle … the one the kids would run to when they heard the sound of the ice cream truck driving around the neighborhood. They would yell, "Uncle Niiiiiiickkk … ice cream truck!"

He'd then say, "Come here, y'all."

We'd run up to him and hold our hands out, waiting for him to give each of us five dollars to get whatever we wanted from the ice cream truck. His generosity didn't stop there. If there was a movie that we all wanted to see, all we had to do was ask Uncle Nick. He would give us all enough money to see a show and buy snacks at the movie theater. Every year, he paid for us all to go to the state fair. Everybody in our family and everybody in our neighborhood loved Uncle Nick.

I overheard some of the adults talking about Uncle Nick and his money. Apparently, he won some big lawsuit and was loaded. This caused even the adults to love and adore Uncle Nick, too. He'd often give them money to pay their bills and pay for trips and other forms of entertainment as well. Pretty much anything financially that they asked of him, Uncle Nick saw to it that their needs were met.

Uncle Nick called me his favorite niece. In a child's mind, that title held some weight. With my foundation having been crumbled, I would accept whatever form of prestige that came my way. I felt happy and loved. Moreover, I trusted Uncle Nick.

"Gimme a kiss," he said as he voluntarily handed me money to buy snacks at school. I turned my face, avoiding contact with his lips. "What's wrong?" he asked. I didn't answer. "It's just a kiss … just a little, simple kiss," he said, trying to convince me of the act's innocence. When he didn't get verbal consent, Uncle Nick pressed his chapped lips against mine. "See. It's nothing … just a simple kiss," he said, trying once again to convince me of its innocence.

No one had ever had the conversation with me about inappropriate touching. But I knew in my gut that something about it didn't feel right. It was awkward and left me feeling uneasy. I wiped his slobbering saliva from my lips.

"Latwaina, it's Uncle Nick. You know I'm not gonna hurt you. Uncles can kiss their nieces, especially their faaaa-vorr-atte niece. It's our little secret," he said, pinching my cheek.

I managed to muster a half-smile, and it was all Uncle Nick needed to leave the house that day with a guilt-free conscience. In guess his warped mind, my smile told him that it was okay.

I went to bed that night, thinking about Uncle Nick's crusty lips pressed against mine. An eleven-year-old-girl and a twenty-five-year-old boy-man. You see, like me, Uncle Nick didn't see himself as a grown man … but a younger guy. Why he chose me, I'll never know. But it didn't stop with that kiss, either.

Uncle Nick began to slowly develop an obsession. At nearly every opportunity he had, he'd try to kiss or touch me. He went from a soft pinch or pat on the butt to an all-out slobbering kiss. Then, he would find a reason for us to be alone. But he was very cunning with his obsession. If the house was full of people, particularly other adults who might have been sitting around drinking or talking to each other, he wouldn't kiss or feel me up. He'd also somehow magically appear at the homes of other relatives whenever I was there visiting. And either Uncle Nick was a genius or the adults in my family were too self-absorbed and unsuspecting, because a lot of things happened to me right under their noses … and sometimes even with their unknown participation.

"Latwaina, would you go take this plate of food over there to your Uncle Nick?" Grandma Lily said one Sunday afternoon. Sundays were always big dinner days at Grandma Lily's. She and her sisters were very good cooks and would prepare big meals kend combine them so people from the church and the community could come by and get a plate of food.

My heart stopped beating for a quick moment. I swallowed hard, trying to buy time before reaching for the paper plate Grandma Lily was holding.

"Take that over there to your Uncle Nick. He's probably starving by now."

I took the paper plate, which had been wrapped in aluminum foil. Steam escaped from the open edges of the foil. I walked out of the kitchen slowly, regretting having to carry out the job I'd just been tasked with. Grandma Lily must've told Uncle Nick that I was coming, because I didn't even have to knock on the door. The porch door flung open, and there he stood … Uncle Nick in a pair of boxer shorts.

"Well, look who came bearing gifts," he said, opening the door wider. Come on in," he invited with a sly grin.

"Here. Grandma Lily told me to bring this to you," I said, holding the plate out for him to take.

"Did you put something extra special in here for me?" Uncle Nick said, taking the plate from me and licking his lips simultaneously.

I turned to head back to Grandma Lily's.

"I said, come on in," he repeated, pulling the back of my shirt. "Wait. Where are you going, pretty girl? You don't want to stay here with Uncle Nick while I eat this delicious food your grandmama done cooked?"

"I gotta go," I said, trying to free myself from his hold.

"Now, wait a minute, little girl. You go when I say you can go," he said, pulling the shirt tighter.

I stood still, almost frozen still. He put the plate down on the stack of milk crates in the enclosed porch where we stood. "Come here," he said, pulling me into him. My body stiffened as he pressed his rising manhood against my back. "This is what pretty girls do to men. They make them happy," he said as he reached his hand around and began to rub on my flat chest. I had no boobs.

"I gotta go … I gotta get back to Grandma Lily's. They gone be looking for me," I said, feeling uneasy.

"No, you don't. Nobody's looking for you. They don't care about you. Nobody treats you special like this," he said, now taking his hands from my chest and putting them in his boxer shorts. "Let Uncle Nick show you how special you are," he said, turning me to face him.

When I turned to face him, there it was. His penis was hanging out of his boxer shorts, pointing upwards. "Touch it," he encouraged.

"I don't want to," I said, backing up.

"Come here," he said, grabbing my right hand. "One thing I hate is a cry baby. Don't be a cry baby, Latwaina. Didn't I tell you that you were Uncle Nick's favorite niece?"

I nodded.

"And you know I wouldn't do anything to hurt my favorite niece, don't you?"

I hunched my shoulders.

"You do know that, don't you?" he said, glaring at me.

"I … I guess," I said.

"Now come on and touch it," he said once again, this time, gliding my hands over the tip of his penis, which wasn't as erect anymore.

He pulled my hands tighter, rubbing them around the sides of his penis and moving them up and down and back and forth, until it became erect again.

"See, that's the Latwaina I like. You woke my friend Benji up again," he said, smirking. "Now do it all by yourself," he said, letting go of my hands.

As he instructed, I glided my hands up and down and back and forth on his penis until I saw a creamy liquid start to erupt like a volcano. "Ahh …. baby, that's it. That's it!" he screamed as the white liquid spilled all over my hands. I snatched my hands back. Uncle Nick nearly fell into the stack of milk crates that held his plate of food. He looked like he'd just had a seizure, with his eyes rolling up in the back of his head as he took long, deep breaths.

I couldn't help but shake that gooky white stuff off my hands. It smelled like Grandma Lily's laundry room, like the Clorox bleach she used to wash the white clothes in.

After he gathered himself, Uncle Nick grabbed his plate and told me to follow him. "You have to wash your hands," he said, opening the door to the house. When I didn't move fast enough, he said, "Come on, girl!" as he pushed me into the house. "Come on," he said, leading me over to the kitchen sink. He put his plate of food down on the counter and turned on the kitchen faucet. "Wash your hands," he directed, pouring dish detergent into the palms of my hands.

Vigorously, I rubbed my hands together, trying to get all that white gook off. The strong smell of bleach saturated the air. When I finished, Uncle Nick handed me a crumpled paper towel, and I dried my hands.

"Remember, this is our little secret. You can't tell anybody, or we won't be able to have fun anymore," he said, kissing me on my forehead. "Now, go on back over to your grandmother's house. And remember, don't you tell nobody. If you do, you'll force Uncle Nick to do something bad to you and your family," he said as he led me back to the front door.

As my foot hit the first step, I heard the door slam behind me. Seconds later, I heard the sound of the lock. I kept a steady pace as I headed down the cemented steps outside, even though I wanted to leap down them. I could taste my freedom … freedom from Uncle Nick's hold … his threat … his hot breath … his slithering tongue gliding over my neck … and the white gooky stuff that came out of his penis.

"Did you give Uncle Nick his plate," Aunt Lisa asked in passing.

I nodded. The house was filled with people, some from church, the neighborhood, across town, you name it. I don't think Aunt Lisa, or anybody else, for that matter, even really noticed me. The Latwaina that had walked out of the kitchen door moments earlier was not the same Latwaina that walked back into the kitchen moments later.

That is how it all began.

Just how do little girls become the targets of sexual predators? Are they "fast," wearing makeup and tight clothes, or are they the outcasts that no one pays special attention to? Are they shy little girls who feel they don't fit in with the crowd? Do they feel awkward when their bodies are under-developed or over-developed? They don't necessarily neatly fit into all those categories. In fact, I didn't. I wasn't fast. But I did have low self-esteem, even as a young girl. I didn't seem to fit in, not even with my own siblings. I felt I was the black sheep of the family. Even though I had my mom and dad until things went south, I always felt there was something different about me when it came to Ebony and Daniel. I was treated differently than they were. And when you're young, you don't have a voice to advocate on your behalf. So you end up tolerating the verbal and social abuse. That's what happened to me, and it unfolded in many different scenarios.

Living with Grandma Lily and being so close to our extended family, it became readily apparent. My story resembled a modern-day Cinderella story, except I was a black girl, and the wicked stepmother was actually my extended relatives. This book would be a thousand pages in length if I were to include the traumatic events that stemmed from my childhood.

"Clean the kitchen before you go outside," Aunt Lisa said.

Grandma Lily was out doing missionary work this particular Saturday, and she left Aunt Lisa in charge. Well, sort of. You see, Aunt Lisa lived just next door. She came over often to help Grandma Lily take care of my great grandpa.

I wanted to go outside and play with the kids, but I had been ordered to clean the kitchen after the family had eaten morning breakfast. From the window, I could see all the children playing in the streets and in their yards. My eyes filled with water. I promised myself that day that I'd never do to my children what was being done to me.

I raced to wash all the dishes so I could go outside. But Aunt Lisa had another task for me once I finished the kitchen.

"What about the laundry room? Did you clean the laundry room?"

"No one told me about the laundry room," I snapped back at my aunt.

"Well, it needs to be done," Aunt Lisa said, smirking.

Once I finished the laundry room, Aunt Lisa had a whole new list of things for me to do. My Saturday was beginning to become consumed with domesticated work. That is, until Uncle Nick stopped by. He saved my life that day ... or so I thought.

"Hey, whatcha doing in here?" he said, poking his head inside the entryway leading to the backyard.

"Cleaning," I said, looking up at him.

"Come go with me to the store," he said.

"I can't."

"Yes, you can."

"Auntie's gonna get mad at me," I said, resuming my task.

"Get up from there. I'm gonna have a talk with Lisa. You're going with me," he said, taking the broom out of my hand and tossing it aside.

I don't know what he said to Aunt Lisa, because before I knew it, Uncle Nick and I were backing out of the driveway in his new car.

"Wave at them," Uncle Nick said, his way of trying to get me to make my other cousins jealous.

As he directed, I waved at Ebony, my cousins, and some of the other kids who were out playing in the neighborhood that day.

We drove to the local Dairy Queen spot, and Uncle Nick told me I could order my favorite ice cream. He paid for our orders, and we went back to his car.

"You like my new whip? It's clean, huh?" he said, looking around and inspecting the car's interior as if he hadn't done it previously.

"It's nice," I said between licks of my cherry dipped ice cream cone.

"I paid a pretty penny for it," he said, placing his hand on my thigh.

Without realizing it, I jumped.

"Don't tell me you're scared."

I looked up at Uncle Nick. My eyes gave the response.

"Don't be scared. We share something special," he said, moving his hand from my thigh and now running his fingers through the lose part of my ponytail. "You have pretty hair," he said.

"Thank you," I said, trying to remain calm.

"So, look. You haven't told anybody about us, have you?"

"Us?" I said with a confused look on my face.

"Yeah, us … me and you. You know, like the things we do. The fun things we do."

"Like how I make you feel good?" I asked.

"Well … yeah. But it's not just about me. It's about you too. You make me feel good, and I'll make you feel good. That's how it goes."

I nodded. I had no clue what he was referring to in that moment.

"That's a big girl. I knew I could trust you. You're special," he said, leaning over and planting a kiss on my left temple.

I wasn't even mad at Uncle Nick that day. He came to my rescue and saved me from a torturous day of domesticated duties.

Claiming we had a family emergency, Uncle Nick signed me out of school early on March 30, 1992. Although I did find it strange that Grandma Lily, nor grandpa, my mother, nor my dad were attempting to sign me out. Instead, it was Uncle Nick, a man who really wasn't my uncle at all.

Did the house catch on fire, and they all died? I wondered. My heart raced as one of the assistant teachers walked me to the main office.

"Latwaina, there's a family emergency, and you're being checked out early today," the school secretary, Mrs. Barnett, announced.

Out of my peripheral vision, I could see a person sitting in a chair. I turned to find Uncle Nick. He smiled and stood. "Yeah, gotta take you out early today."

"What happened?" I asked.

Uncle Nick put his index finger up to his lips. "Shh."

I didn't question him any further. Growing up, we were told not to question adults. I followed Uncle Nick out of the school, through the parking lot, and got in his car with him. I didn't have too much to say because my fragile mind was thinking about the millions of horrible things that could have been the reason for me having to leave early. *Did something happen to Mama?*

"Do you want McDonald's?" Uncle Nick asked.

"No," I said, shaking my head. My anxiety had gotten the best of me; my heart was now in my stomach as I rode in the car with Uncle Nick.

We pulled up at Uncle Nick's mother's house. I didn't think anything of it. My school was on the corner of Uncle Nick's street, and Grandma's house was just around the block.

"Come on," he ordered.

Slowly, I opened the passenger car door and exited the vehicle.

"Follow me," he said as he led the way to the back entrance of the house.

I followed him to the basement of the house ... a cold, dark space with no furnishing in it.

"Where's everybody?" I asked, searching for even the dimmest light in the room.

"Shh," Uncle Nick said, grabbing my hand to lead me. When he had led me into a dark corner of the room, he started kissing me, aggressively ... his slobbering saliva traveling down my chin and landing on my neck. "I'm about to f*** you!" he said, pulling on my hair hard.

Uncle Nick forcibly removed my clothes. I could feel his erect penis rub up against me as he tried to lay me down on the floor. A slow, steady stream of tears began to cascade down my cheeks. Whatever he was doing to me didn't feel right. It felt like someone was piercing the sharpest knife through my heart. That's what this type of betrayal feels like.

He covered my mouth as he moved his body up and down … side to side. The deeper he penetrated, the worse the pain became. At this point, I began to scream and yell, which angered him.

"Shut the hell up, little bitch!" he whispered in my ear as he covered my mouth with this right hand. "You like it, don'tcha? You know you want it," he said as he continued to move his body up and down and from side to side … until he let out a loud sound and then collapsed on top of me. I wanted to kick him off me, but I was too paralyzed with shock to even budge.

Finally, when Uncle Nick's body stopped shivering, he put his hands over my mouth once again and said, "And if you tell anybody, I'm going to kill you." I didn't doubt that Uncle Nick would live up to that threat. He was a bully and had a reputation of being a fighter around town.

As I began to put my clothes back on, Uncle Nick gave me the rundown on how things were supposed to go from here on out. "You gonna shut your mouth and don't tell nobody about this, you here? And you ain't gonna tell nobody that I took you outta school early, either. And when you 'round me, you better act like you ain't scared of me. Now, let's go."

Uncle Nick dropped me back off at school and drove off. It was the tail end of the day, and all that was left for me to do was walk home as I'd normally do any other school day. I stood off to the side of the school parking lot and watched the other children happily exit school. Many of them were on their way home to a two-parent household where there was love, affection, and connectedness. Me? I was paralyzed with shock at what had just occurred with Uncle Nick. After some time had elapsed, I managed to muster up enough courage to walk home. And when I finally arrived, there he was, talking with my cousins and acting as if nothing was wrong ... as if he hadn't just raped me. He winked at me, but that's not what stood out the most. I remembered the mean look on his face ... his blank stare as his eyes cased my nakedness ... my innocence. And I also remembered his threat—"I'll kill you." So I did what he told me to do and acted as though nothing had ever happened earlier that day.

CHAPTER 4

The Lion's Den

In the days that followed the incident when he signed me out of school, Uncle Nick began to stalk me. When walking home from school, he'd drive slowly in his car behind me, haunting me like the boogeyman. His piercing stare made me want to pee on myself. One day, he drove up alongside of me and rolled down his window.

"Remember what I said … you better not say anything. I'm watching you!" Then he rolled the window halfway up.

I picked up my pace.

"Do you hear me?!" he shouted.

"Yes," I said, nodding.

"Say it louder," he demanded.

"I won't … I promise. I won't say anything," I said loudly. Sweat pebbles formed on my forehead as I picked up my pace even more. I couldn't wait to get home to Grandma Lily's.

"You better not, 'cause I'll kill you if you do," Uncle Nick said before speeding off down the road, leaving a trail of skid marks behind him. Once his vehicle was out of sight, I ran the rest of the way home. Once inside, I ran straight to the room I once shared with my mama … until she left, that is.

Noticing I wasn't acting normal, Grandma Lily followed me. "What's wrong, Latwaina?"

"Nothing," I lied, trying to catch my breath.

"Well, you came running in this house like a bat outta hell, so I just assumed something was wrong with ya," Grandma Lily said, looking me over from head to toe.

"I'm all right. I just have to use the bathroom real bad," I said, coming up with the lie on the fly.

"All right. Well, come on down for dinner soon. You know tonight is Bible class."

Bible class. I hated going to Bible class. It was boring, and I couldn't really understand what the pastor was talking about anyway. The only way Grandma Lily would let me stay home was if I had a test the next day that I needed to study for. And with the way Uncle Nick had scared the living daylights out of me only moments earlier, I didn't want to take any chances of him popping up and catching me home alone.

I forced myself to gobble down a bowl full of the chili Grandma Lily had made for dinner. I really didn't have an appetite, but I didn't want hunger pangs to pop up during Bible class. After dinner, Ebony and I changed clothes and went to church with Grandma Lily.

We would have gotten home a little earlier if Deacon Wil and Grandma Lily hadn't engaged in a thirty-minute conversation after Bible class. Whatever they were discussing made Grandma Lily cry a little bit. I'd never seen Grandma Lily cry. She was the strong one in the family, no doubt. The matriarch. The joke in the family was that Grandma Lily was made of steel. Not too much could really get to her … at least she didn't let it show. She was about getting things done and done one way—her way. Mama had a lot of Grandma Lily's traits. They looked alike. Mama had those same eyes, starry eyes that seemed like they could see right through you … see your soul. Mama was a lot gentler than Grandma Lily though. I think the church culture and the Black culture combined gave Grandma Lily thick skin. But it was obvious that something Deacon Wil said to Grandma Lily had pricked her little ole heart.

"Why are you crying, Grandma?" Ebony asked, handing Grandma Lily Kleenex from her own purse.

"Oh, it's nothing. I'm actually happy," she said.

"So why are you happy?"

"He just told me some good news," Grandma Lily said, taking the Kleenex from Ebony and wiping her eyes with it.

"Well, why are you crying if he told you good news?" I asked, which was typical of a thirteen-year-old.

"Those are what they call happy tears. Right, Grandma?" Ebony interjected.

"Yes, they are. They are happy tears."

Happy tears. I wondered if the day would ever come when I would be able to cry happy tears. Maybe the day Mama came home clean … clean for good. That would probably be the day I would cry happy tears. But for now, the only thing I could focus on was hiding the very dark secret that Uncle Nick had violated my young body in the worst way imaginable. He had everyone fooled, thinking he was generous and loving, when in fact, he was a monster, throwing piercing darts at me like he was at target practice. And then on top of that, daring me to unmask his true identity.

The following Sunday, Grandma Lily had a big Sunday dinner at the house. We'd had a revival at church earlier in the week, and Grandma invited the guest minister, our pastor and his wife, and a few church members over for dinner. Her dinner parties never stayed small because as soon as word got out that Grandma Lily was hosting a dinner party, people invited themselves over to enjoy the feast.

Since I didn't fit in with the cousins and other kids from church, I just sat in the living room with my grandfather, welcoming guests as they entered the house. I was fine until I heard his voice. He was laughing as he walked up the cement steps outside. My body stiffened as the roaring sound of his laughter grew closer and closer.

"I have to use the bathroom," I said to my grandfather as I dashed out of the front room into the back bedroom. *Calm down. Calm down, Latwaina.* I tried to console myself. My breathing intensified as I paced the small half-bathroom. I counted to one hundred, allowing my breathing to return to normal. I took a quick look in the mirror. You can do this. You can do this, Latwaina. I tried to give myself a quick pep speech before facing my worst nightmare—my rapist … Uncle Nick.

I tried to dart out the back door, but he called out to me from the hallway, where he was standing, pretending to be so amused by the aroma of Grandma's infamous peach cobbler.

"Latwaina, aren't you gonna speak to your favorite uncle?" he said, showcasing his new gold-encased tooth.

"Hi," I said hesitantly.

"Come give me a hug," he said, forcing a fake smile.

Against my will, I walked over to Uncle Nick and held my arms out. He bent down and hugged me, whispering into my ear, "I missed you."

His arms, wrapped around my back, made me cringe. But with everyone around, I knew wrapping his arms around me was the extent of what he could do to me in that moment. When he released his hold, I dashed out of the house. I tried to stay in a pack with the other children. This way, Uncle Nick couldn't catch me alone. But even that didn't curb his mad obsession. He came outside, claiming that he needed to smoke a cigarette. Grandma Lily didn't allow any smoking in the house to begin with, and she definitely wouldn't have allowed it with church people being around.

I pretended to be engaged in conversation with Ebony and some of our older cousins, but Uncle Nick kept his eyes on me, watching my every move like a hawk. He was acting more like a jealous boyfriend than an uncle, and it was beginning to creep me out. I knew sooner or later, he was going to catch me alone and try to do what he'd done before.

Later that night, when Ebony and I were getting ready for bed, she told me that she'd found out why Grandma Lily was crying "happy tears."

"Deacon Wil said Mama is clean."

My eyes lit up. "Clean, like in no more drugs?"

"Yeah. She's clean."

I wanted to believe it badly. But we had been through this saga before … believing Mama was clean when she wasn't. She'd come back to Grandma Lily's for a week or two, and before you knew it, she'd be back on the streets, addicted to drugs once again. Drugs had Mama, and my little heart couldn't take any more heartbreak. "I'll believe it when I see it," I said.

"You'll see. She's coming home soon too," Ebony added.

I took solace in the news. I wanted Mama to be clean so she could come take us to live with her … take me away from the trauma and sexual abuse at the hands of Uncle Nick. I remember praying that night for God to let Mama be clean for good. *I'll give my life to You if you give my mama back to me.* That's the promise I made to God that night.

April 11, 1992. I remember the day like it was yesterday. It was just four days after my fourteenth birthday. I walked to the little convenience store to buy some candy. I listened to music on my Walkman, which was a gift my daddy had given me the previous Christmas. The music drowned out the background noise, and I didn't even hear his car pull up behind me. Before I knew it, Uncle Nick had walked up on me.

"Get in the car!" he ordered as he tugged me by the arm and led me over to the front passenger door and opened it.

"I'm going to the store for my granny," I lied.

"Granny asked you to buy candy?" he said, snatching the bag and peering inside. I was caught in my lie. "Didn't I tell you about lying to me, little girl? Didn't I tell you that lying to me was gonna make it worse for you?"

I nodded in agreement as he pushed me into the car and slammed the passenger door. He got in on the other side, put the gear in drive, and sped off.

"I gotta get back home, Uncle Nick. Grandma Lily gonna be looking for me," I said in a somber tone.

"Ahh … ain't that too bad? You're with good ole Uncle Nick. And don't tell me no more about Grandma Lily or anyone looking for you. No one's gonna be looking for you 'cause no one loves you … but me. No one loves you but me, Latwaina. I'm the only one that pays you any mind around here."

Tears began to stream down my face as Uncle Nick drove to the other side of town.

"Stop that crying like a baby, I said!" Uncle Nick screamed. My crying was driving him crazy.

I tried to gather myself, but when I saw Uncle Nick pull into an alley, I knew what was coming next.

"Get in the backseat," he demanded as he pulled deep into the alley behind a dumpster.

Slowly, I unbuckled my seat belt and attempted to open the car door. It was locked. Uncle Nick chuckled. "You must think I'm a fool, don't you? Climb in the backseat," he ordered as he unbuckled his belt. The jingling sound of the belt rang like a large church bell.

As he ordered, I climbed in the backseat, and he climbed in the backseat afterward. He pulled down his pants and underwear. I tried to look away, but he turned my face toward his penis. "Look at it," he said, squeezing my lips between his hands forcefully.

"Ouch … that hurts," I whimpered.

"Now, touch it," he said, grabbing my right hand and forcing me to stroke his erect penis. He closed his eyes, enjoying the sensation of my hand rubbing the tip of his penis. "Now, take your clothes off," he said, tugging on my shirt.

My body became paralyzed. I knew he was going to hit or slap me, but I couldn't follow his order. He was gonna have to take it again … which is what he did. Without warning, he grabbed my shirt and lifted it above my head. He snatched my training bra off with one pull. "Now lay down," he ordered. His breathing was beginning to sound labored.

As I was ordered, I lay down on my back and he pulled my pants and underwear off and threw them in the front seat of his Cadillac. He put his lips on my breasts—the little stubs I had—and began to suck on them, biting them in between hard suctions.

"That hurts!" I cried out.

"Yell one more time, and I'mma punch you."

Tears rolled down my face as he continued to suck on my nipples, shoving his fingers into my vagina at the same time. "Feels good, don't it?" he said. When I didn't answer, he became even more angry. "Turn your little ass around ... I got something for you now," he said, as he flipped my slinky eight-five-pound body over. Then he lay on top of me and forced my legs open with his. With all his might, Uncle Nick thrust his penis into my anus. Pain shot through my entire body. The pain was so excruciating, I wanted to die on the spot. I would have rather been murdered at the hands of Freddy Krueger than to endure the torture of being raped. I let out the loudest high-pitched scream that I could.

"You don't get it, do you?" he said, thrusting his penis in further. "I told you to shut up," he said, pulling hard on my long ponytail.

I felt fluid began to trickle down my inner thighs as Uncle Nick kept moving up and down and from side to side, making loud moaning and groaning sounds. "Ahhh ... feels so good. This. Feels. So. Good," he would say as he kept moving in a synchronized fashion. "This young pu**y feels good," he kept repeating.

To keep from screaming out loud, I buried my teeth into my forearm. The pain was excruciating for me, but Uncle Nick was enjoying every moment of it. "Now lay on your back," he said.

My body wouldn't move. "I can't. I can't move," I cried.

"Of course, you can," Uncle Nick said, flipping me over. Once he flipped me over, he began penetrating my vagina … thrusting himself inside of me.

Without intentionally doing so, I dug my fingernails into his back so hard that I drew blood. He let out a loud wail. "You bitch," he said, pulling himself out of me and slapping me hard in the face. "Now what did you do that for?!"

"I didn't mean to," I said, trying to apologize.

"Yes, you did, and you're gonna pay for it," he threatened. "Now, turn back over!" he demanded. And once again, he began raping me, penetrating me in my anus.

I must've blacked out, because when I came to myself, I was lying in a pool of blood. The car windows were fogged up, but I could see that it was now dark outside. Uncle Nick was in a straddled position over me, stroking his erect penis and licking his lips intermittently.

I tried to move, but I couldn't. My body was sore all over. "I can't move," I mumbled.

"You gonna get you're a** up and get dressed. I got places to be," he said as he reached into the front seat, grabbed my pants and underwear, and threw them on me. He dressed himself and got out of the car and left the back passenger door open.

My hands trembled as I tried to put my clothes on.

"You know the deal, don't you?" Uncle Nick said as he lit a cigarette. "You close your fat trap. Nothing to no one, or I'm gonna kill you, you hear me?"

I nodded.

"Don't shake your head. Say yes!" he demanded as he blew cigarette smoke in my direction.

"Yes," I said. Blood trickled down my nostrils, into my mouth when I spoke. I was bleeding out of nearly every orifice in my body. I got a quick peek outside. It was dark out. I could hear sirens passing in the distance. How I wished they were coming for me.

After Uncle Nick finished smoking his cigarette, he made me sit in the front seat with him. I could barely move. "There's some tissue in the glove compartment. Get it and wipe your face. I already have to clean that bloody mess out of the back-seat of my car," he said nonchalantly.

I did as Uncle Nick ordered. The last thing I wanted was to cause him to grow any angrier than he already was. Uncle Nick drove me back to our side of town and let me out a few blocks from Mama's house and sped off into the darkness. I stumbled up Pierce Street before collapsing to my knees. The pain was excruciating. I couldn't walk any further. I could hear the sirens getting louder and louder. The sound of helicopter blades swarmed above my head. I began to pray that they were coming for me. I tried to get up, but my strength failed me.

I remember bright lights. My head was spinning in every which direction. I could barely open my eyes. I touched the top of my eyelids, and they were puffy, almost swollen shut. I could hear sirens, faint voices, and shuffling feet in the distance.

"Latwaina!" I could hear Mama's voice calling from afar.

I struggled to get up, nearly collapsing. But this time, I mustered up enough strength and followed the sound of Mama's voice.

"Mama," I wept. I tried to yell, but I didn't have the strength. My soul had been battered and my physical strength stripped.

"Latwaina! Where have you been?!" Mama yelled out to me, having spotted me stumbling toward her.

"Mama … Mama. He hurt me," I mumbled, struggling to make my way up the path.

"Who? Who hurt you?" my mother said, now getter a better look at me as I approached her. Her eyes grew wide as she zeroed in on my badly beaten face.

Bloody, bruised, and savagely raped, I walked home with Mama and Deacon Wil walking behind me. When we reached the bottom of our street, I was able to open my eyes a little wider. There was a crowd of my relatives standing outside. The word was out. I had been called in as a missing person and the police were out looking for me.

I barely had the strength to make it up to the house. I remember seeing the shocked look on people's faces as I hobbled past them, jaws dropping as they looked in horror at my bloodied body. I was brought into the back room at Mama's house. She told the police to give me a minute before they started questioning me. I'm sure that at some point, someone made a call to the family and told them what was truly going on … that I claimed Uncle Nick had raped me and the police were out looking for him. This caused panicked members of Uncle Nick's family to rush over to Mama's house too.

I saw the horrified look on my mother's face as she inspected the bruises all over my body.

"Did he touch you down there?" Mama said, pointing to my private area.

I nodded. And without hesitation, Mama pulled down my pants in front of everyone, blood splattering from everywhere, from my vagina to my anus. Mama's eyes widened as she continued to look me over. Other members of the family started to enter the house, and the looks of horror on their faces were equally disturbing.

"Oh, my goodness! Jesus!" Mama screamed.

"Bend over," one person said.

"Sit down. Lean back. Spread your legs." The show had begun. I was literally a show-and-tell item on display for those who were either brave enough or nosy enough to want to see what happened to me. As if they were the police or the judge and jury, disbelieving family members wanted to see proof that I had been raped. Embarrassingly and shamefully, I had to open my legs and allow people to inspect my torn and bleeding vagina. Then, I was asked to get on my knees so they could spread my butt cheeks open to inspect the trauma inflicted there.

Finally, after some time passed, the police interrupted the show and tell. They said they needed to speak with me … alone. I was interrogated by the Detroit Police for what seemed like an eternity. In that moment, I didn't want anyone, only my mother. But they told me it was protocol that they interview me without anyone in our presence, so they could get an accurate account of what happened. Outside interference, they said, could taint the investigation.

I went through the basics before having to go through the gruesome details about what happened. "What's your name? Are you Latwaina? How old are you? Who did this to you?" I couldn't audibly answer any of their questions. The only thing I remember attempting to do was nod my head when they asked me if I was Latwaina. A female officer by the name of Officer Abrams took out a notepad and began to document my statement.

"Do you know who did this to you?" Tears began to stroll down my face. "Do you?" she repeated.

I nodded.

"Can you tell me who?"

"My uncle … Uncle Nick," I confessed, sobbing.

"Now, I'm going to ask you some tough questions, and I need you to be one-hundred percent honest with me. Do you think you can do that?"

I nodded once again.

"Latwaina … that is your name, correct?"

I nodded.

"I'm gonna need you to speak. Officer Jacobs is recording your statement and I'm documenting it here," she said, holding up her notepad. "We need you to give us as much information as you can. Say yes or no instead of nodding, okay?"

I agreed.

"Now, we need you to tell us exactly what happened to you today.

I recapped the horrifying details of what Uncle Nick had done to me. I must've told the story a thousand times. I guessed they were trying to see if my story was consistent. But it was. My story didn't change one iota.

This trauma seemed as though it lasted for an eternity. A forensics photographer took what seemed like innumerous photos of the injuries all over my body. I lost track of the counting once I got up to number fifty-three.

"We're going to be taking you to the hospital to get treated soon," Officer Abrams promised. But our definition of "soon" couldn't have been more different.

CHAPTER 5

Double Trauma

When Grandma Lily walked into the back room, I broke down. "He did this to me. Uncle Nick did this to me, Granny."

Grandma Lily held me close as she fought back tears. I felt safe, but only for a moment. There was too much activity going on in the house … too much to keep up with. Officers shuffled in and out of the room. Different voices chimed in over their walkie talkies. I could hear the doorbell and the sound of the front door opening and closing. I could have only imagined how many people were in the house.

"He's been picked up," I heard an officer say out loud.

"Got him?" Officer Abrams asked.

"Yes. They picked him up," an unnamed officer confirmed.

"Sweetie, Nick has been arrested. He's been arrested, and he can't do anything to you. Okay?"

"Okay," I said. For a rape victim, arrest means little to nothing when the trauma is fresh. In fact, you don't even wish harm on the perpetrator … you want your own life to end so you don't have to face the shame, the pain, and the embarrassment. You wish you could hold your breath, close your eyes, and wake up on the other side of the incident. Justice is so far down the road that you can't see it, taste it, or smell it. So, although it's part of the process, in that moment, I was dead emotionally. I couldn't relish in the fact that they'd found all the evidence they needed right in the back of Uncle Nick's car when they arrested him—the blood of an innocent fourteen-year-old girl named Latwaina. Me.

As they say, bad news travels fast. It was only a matter of time before Aunt Lisa and her husband, Mike, came to the house. Uncle Mike was Uncle Nick's brother. So, Uncle Nick wasn't really an uncle, we just called him uncle … a title he undoubtedly didn't deserve.

"I can't believe he did that. I just don't believe it," I heard Uncle Mike say. He was standing on the other side of the bedroom door, not allowed in the room. But Grandma Lily told the police it was okay to let Aunt Lisa in. She never made it over to console me. Instead, her eyes cased my naked, bruised body. I guessed she didn't believe her beloved brother-in-law could do such a thing. But it was impossible for me to have inflicted that kind of trauma on myself. She shook her head before attempting to exit the room.

"He did it, Auntie," I blurted out. I wanted her to hear from the horse's mouth that Uncle Nick had raped me.

Aunt Lisa nodded.

Finally, after several more hours, I was transported to the hospital to be treated. Since it was an active investigation and I was a minor, I was admitted under an alias name to protect my identity from family members thought to be capable of exacting revenge as well as news reporters hungry for a salacious news story.

While I was at the hospital, I was interviewed several more times by investigators. My story never changed … with the exception of having to tell them that Uncle Nick had raped me two weeks prior to the most recent rape.

"Did you tell anyone?" the officer asked.

"No."

"Why?"

The answer will always be the same. You don't tell because you've been threatened. And while outsiders can believe the threat to be illogical, the victim, who's been violated and abused, will always believe it, no matter how illogical it might seem. "I'll kill you," is very believable to the victim who has just died psychologically. In fact, it's plausible for any victim to want to die rather than suffer a brutal rape. Trying to collect pieces of your mind, body, and spirit seems like an insurmountable task … one that will take you a lifetime to achieve.

"Because he said he would kill me," I finally uttered.

I thought I was dreaming or the pain killers had me hallucinating. I heard her humming one of her favorite gospel songs—"Walk with Me Lord."

"Hey, honey, it's me," Mama said as she brushed my hair out of my face. Despite the pain I was still in, I tried to give Mama the biggest smile I could. "Don't try to talk. Just rest. Mama's here now. I'm back … for good."

Ebony was right. Mama was clean again. "How did you get here?" I asked.

"Deacon Wil brought me here."

My eyes searched the room for Deacon Wil.

"Don't worry, he's not coming in here. He just dropped me off. He left," Mama said. She "got it." She understood that I was emotionally fragile. Grandma Lily didn't get it, and neither did Aunt Lisa. I was happy that Mama was back. God had answered my prayers. And even though I had a long road ahead of me, I knew that with Mama by my side, I was gonna get through it.

"Daddy? Where's my dad?"

Mama frowned. "Honey, as much as he wants to see you, he just can't. He can't see you like this. He's a wreck. He blames me and himself."

"Why?"

"Well, if we were still together, you'd never have been living with Grandma Lily. It made you an easy target for Nick. And from now on, don't call him Uncle Nick. Uncles don't do this to their nieces."

A single tear escaped its tear duct and cascaded down my right cheek.

"Don't cry, Latwaina. I'm here, and I'm not leaving you."

That was all I needed. I felt my strength being revitalized. I had my mama and my daddy—my rocks, my foundation and support system.

Coached by the pastor and even the counselor of the pastor's wife's at the rehab center, Mama enrolled me into a new school—Nancy M. Boykin Continuing Education Center, which was an all-girl school. Mama said it would be better for me. I had to meet with representatives from the district attorney's office. They prepped me on the status of the investigation and the upcoming trial. According to Nick—my rapist—I'd consented to having sex with him. In the eyes of the law, his statement didn't have wings to fly. A fourteen-year-old cannot give consent to have sex with an adult. Nick was facing up to twenty-five years for the two counts of rape and one count of sodomy. Even though he had kidnapped me, they didn't charge him with kidnapping. Perhaps some technicality prevented them from doing so; I had no clue.

My dad accompanied me and Mama whenever we had to meet with someone at the DA's office. Ebony told me in secret that my father had gone looking for Uncle Nick that night and told Uncle Mike that he'd better pray the cops found Nick before he did. He also threatened Uncle Mike and warned that they'd better not bail Nick out of jail. But even with all the money Nick had, it wasn't enough to satisfy the 1.5-million-dollar bail that was set.

At the direction of the psychologist who evaluated me at the hospital, I needed outpatient counseling. So Mama got me set up to see a therapist once a week. The therapist, Dr. Lindsey, said I was a fighter, that I could get through the trauma. I also had spiritual counseling sessions with the pastor of the church. He told me I was special. That I was going to use my trauma to help heal other girls and women. Truthfully, I couldn't see it at the time. I was dead smack in the middle of trauma and pain that didn't start the day Nick raped me. What made me an easy target for Nick happened long before Nick ever laid eyes on me. Some of it was generational, traveling in the bloodline. Pastor said the buck would stop with me. Latwaina. I had the power to cancel the assignment of the enemy for generations to come. I couldn't fathom it at the time, however.

The first day I stepped foot in Nancy Boykin Continuing Education Center, I knew I was in for another unwelcoming encounter. I was shy by nature, which wasn't the type of personality anyone should have when attending an alternative school. The school was supposed to be for pregnant teens. And although I wasn't pregnant, I had special permission to attend the school. Someone had to let the school and its administration know why I needed to enroll in the school. For one, the rape had traumatized me. I didn't want to go back to familiar grounds. In fact, the first rape happened when Uncle Nick had signed me out of school early, which was something the school administration paid for dearly.

I was being thrown into another lion's den … at least it felt like that in the beginning.

"Why you here? You don't look pregnant," a girl said in between popping her chewing gum.

"I'm not pregnant," I said softly.

"Then whatchu here for?" she said, stepping back and staring me down from head to toe.

"'Cause it's a better school for me," I said, which was what I had been coached to say. The all-girls school was in high demand, as the teen pregnancy rate in Detroit Metro was at an all-time high. To prevent an uproar by those on the waiting list, I had been coached by the administration to keep my name under the radar by quoting that statement.

The first person who befriended me was a girl named Keisha. Visibly pregnant, she approached me in the cafeteria one afternoon.

"The food here isn't the greatest," she said as she helped herself to a hefty spoonful of mashed potatoes.

"Tell me about it," I said, passing on the mashed potatoes and opting for a baked potato instead. The cafeteria food couldn't stand up against Grandma Lily's cooking.

Keisha followed me over to a table at the far end of the cafeteria. We hadn't been seated for ten minutes before she gave me the 4-1-1 on everyone and everything.

"So, that girl over there ... her name is Brandy. I hate her. We have the same baby daddy."

"Oh really?" I said with raised curiosity.

"Yeah, Brad."

"I guess y'all don't get along."

"I can't stand her, and she can't stand me."

"Well ... which one of y'all are with Brad?"

"Me. Brandy wants Brad back, but he doesn't want her."

I nodded and allowed Keisha to tell me the rest of the scoop about the place. But for once, I felt like I was beginning to form a genuine friendship. I no longer felt invisible when I was in a room full of people. This was why school felt more like a safe haven to me than homelife did.

There was no questioning whether the rape divided the family. Without a doubt, it did. Half of the family couldn't wrap their heads around the fact that it happened, and the other half was embarrassed by the publicity and exposure it caused. The counselors and therapists believed that putting me in a new school was one of the ways my family could try to protect me from the public. But little did they know, I needed emotional protection from my own family.

I was no longer allowed to come to certain family functions. I was a distraction, my therapist said. By keeping me from the family functions, family members didn't have to be reminded of the fact that they'd failed me … that our family was not perfect … we had a predator running rampant … and we didn't know how to deal with our truth. I was forced to reckon with the fact that not only was I different; I was treated differently by my family. I often wondered if Ebony would have been treated the same if she was raped instead of me. Fortunately, and unfortunately, I would never know. But as much as I envied the way they lovingly treated Ebony; I didn't wish my reality on her. It was a painful way to live. Every morning, I had to look myself in the mirror and remind myself that I deserved to be loved. Whether I received it from my family or not … I still deserved to be loved. That's what my therapist also told me. It was a mantra I was told to repeat. "Repeat it until you believe it," Dr. Linsey said.

CHAPTER 6

Changing Places ... Trading Spaces

"Where's your sister?" my mother asked.

"She's on her way," I said. Ebony was never in any rush to come home from school. We were attending different schools, but Ebony's routine never changed. She always stopped by the neighborhood candy store and hung out with her friends for a little while before coming home. Coming home meant chores, church, and homework, none of which we enjoyed.

Mama didn't bother asking about Daniel. Apparently, she'd heard that he was running the streets, and she knew there was very little she could do to ring him back in. He needed his father in his life.

I watched as Mama danced around Grandma Lily's kitchen as she helped her prepare dinner that day.

"What's going on?" I asked. "Why are you so happy?"

"Your mama's got her own place now," Grandma Lily said.

"What?!" I exclaimed.

Mama had done several stints in rehab, but this last time seemed to have worked. Grandma Lily had enlisted the help of the reverend from church, and I could see a big difference. Mama was glowing.

"Honey, I was going to tell you, but first I wanted the house to be set up just right for you to move in. I want you to have a perfect bedroom, with your favorite colors, a duvet, and matching curtains. I want you to love it there."

"Mama I'm going to love being anywhere you are. Can I please go with you tonight?" I asked with excitement in my voice.

"Of course," Mama said, eyeing Grandma in her peripheral vision. No matter what, Mama still wanted to please Grandma Lily. She knew her lifestyle had Grandma Lily on her knees for years.

After dinner, I packed up my clothes, as much as I could, and Deacon Wil picked us up and drove us over to the new place.

"Go ahead, open the door," Mama said, encouraging me to open the door to the new place she had just rented.

Fresh paint filled my nostrils when I pushed the steel door open. Mama gave us a tour of the house.

"You guys don't have to share a room anymore," Mama said, showcasing our bedrooms.

"I'm gonna finish out the school year with Grandma Lily," Ebony said as she inspected the furniture and closet space in the room Mama had dedicated to her.

Mama frowned. "You sure?"

"Yeah. I don't want to leave my friends," Ebony said.

Although Mama was disappointed by Ebony wanting to stay with Grandma Lily, it worked out perfectly because my grandpa became ill, and Mama moved him in with us at the new place. He took the room that was supposed to be Ebony's.

Every night before going to bed, I took a long, hot bath. Things were beginning to change, and I could feel it. Mama made it part of her routine to put me to bed every night. Before turning out my light, she gave me a long, tight hug. In that moment, all I could think about was the trauma I had endured. But the safety of being in Mama's arms made it seem as though the rape was far removed from me. I could no longer smell Nick's strong cologne in my nostrils, even when he was nowhere in sight. I could no longer see his piercing stare that made my insides tremble when I closed my eyes. All of it was gone, almost instantaneously.

When I came home from school the next day, Mama had more good news to share with me.

"Guess what?"

"What?" I replied.

"I want you to guess," Mama said, smiling from ear to ear.

"Umm … you and Daddy getting back together?"

"Noooo," Mama said, giggling. That's over. Me and your dad are good friends, but we are not good mates," my mother confessed. "Plus, he's with Rose now. Don't you like her?"

"She's okay," I said. I had nothing against Rose. But if I had a choice in the matter, my parents would have given the relationship another shot. "But why weren't you and Daddy good mates?" I probed.

"Hmm," Mama said before pausing. "How can I say this?" She paused again.

"Just say it," I encouraged.

"Your dad is a great father. He's a lot older than me, and our personalities couldn't be more different. I don't think your dad's love could have survived my addiction, and I'm honest enough to admit it," Mama said. This was the first time she shared this type of information with me. Mama was never this transparent in the past. Rehab had changed her for sure. But Mama also gave credit to God, saying that without God and the prayers of Grandma Lily and the saints, she would have never been able to complete the rehab program.

"Then what?" I said, giving up any chance of guessing correctly.

"I got a new job!"

"Really?" I said, trying to sound happy for her. A new job meant long hours because she was a nurse.

Mama could sense in my voice that I was disappointed, even though I was trying to pretend I was happy for her. "But guess what?"

"Mama, you know I'm not good at these guessing games," I said, shifting my weight to one side of my body.

"Okay, okay … You ready for it?"

"Yes, Mama," I said, huffing.

"I'll be working for the church. No more long hours. I can bring you to school and pick you up too."

"For the church?" I questioned.

"Yes, as a staff nurse. I'll be Deacon Wil's assigned nurse," she said gleefully.

Then it dawned on me. Deacon Wil's name had been mentioned one too many times. He was the one who told Grandma Lily about Mama's release from the rehab program. He and Mama had to have a thing.

I decided to let her response stand, at least for the time being. Truth be told, I didn't want to hear about Mama and Deacon Wil. I had enough going on in my mind with the rape and the upcoming trial. If you asked me, I think Mama needed to take a break from men. She didn't have a good track record with them, and in all likelihood, Deacon Wil was probably just a rebound guy. But I didn't want to judge Mama, so I lied and pretended I was happy for her.

I was trying to live a normal life as much as reasonably possible. With my grandpa living with us, I tried to quiet the haunting thoughts about the rape by staying busy and helping my mama take care of him. Although his dementia was beginning to take a toll on us, contributing to his care gave me a feeling of purpose.

Mama had Grandad on a good routine. She talked to him, fed him, gave him his meds, and had him go to bed by eight o'clock in the evening. Then, like clockwork, Deacon Wil would come over.

Like Grandma Lily said, Deacon Wil *was* sweet on Mama. But his nightly visits also proved something else—he was nice and probably wasn't just a rebound guy. Mama seemed to really like him. He spent a lot of time talking with us about important things in life, like education and having a relationship with God. He never once made me feel uncomfortable, and he never once even attempted to ask me anything about the rape, although I was sure he knew about what happened to me.

Come to find out, Mama needed Deacon Wil more than ever after my granddad's condition began to deteriorate. He was in and out of the hospital, and Deacon Wil was right there by Mama's side, taking her back and forth to the hospital to visit Grandaddy. I purposely stayed away from the hospital; it gave me flashbacks of the rape. I fought hard to keep my sanity, even though I had to rehash the incident, either as part of a therapy session or after having to meet with someone from the district attorney's office in preparation for the upcoming trial.

Nick was still in jail where he belonged. And because I wasn't going around the family, I wasn't privy to what was going on *in* the family. Mama did her best to shield and protect me, but it was obvious there was a rift in our family. After overhearing Mama and Grandma Lily talking one day, I learned that Aunt Lisa and Uncle Mike were having major problems in their marriage. It didn't take a genius to guess that it had everything to do with Nick raping me. But as my therapist told me, "It wasn't my cross to bear." It sounded good in theory, but living out its practicality was going to take some time.

Even though I liked my new school, I couldn't wait until the end of the school year came. I always looked forward to spending the summers with my dad. But this summer, I looked forward to going to my dad's more than ever before. I was looking forward to the change in environment. I walked around on eggshells in my house, never sure when I'd walk up on a conversation I wasn't supposed to hear, even though the conversation was about me. I also looked forward to not being told I couldn't go over Grandma Lily's because of x,y, or z reason.

There was never a dull moment when I went to stay with my dad. He took me everywhere with him, even to work. I was never ostracized by my paternal side of the family. As a matter of fact, they adored me … made no comparisons. I was Latwaina. I wasn't a "stupid, retarded bitch," as I had been called by my other relatives.

The rape forced me to grow up. To learn a few hard facts about life, like "It's not what they call you; it's what you respond to," and "Your sanity is worth fighting for." So while it may have been true that Nick stole my body, he did not steal my mind. I might have suffered some damage, but my faculties were still intact, and I purposed in my heart that I would fight, not just for my sanity, but I'd fight for the sanity of my descendants for generations to come.

All packed up and ready to spend the summer with my dad, I dashed down the front steps and ran to his car. He stayed in the house talking to my mama for a few minutes. I could only imagine that they were talking about what was going on with the case. Whatever it was, it upset my mother because she slammed the door after my father walked out of the house … without even waving goodbye to me.

"Is Mama mad?" I asked when my dad got in the car.

"Baby, don't worry about your mama. Me and your mama don't always agree on things. But that's between me and her. You don't have to worry about that. When it comes to you, we both have the same goal, okay?" he said, forcing a smile.

"Okay," I said, half-believing him.

"What do you want to do today?" my dad asked as he turned onto the main road from our street.

"Go to the movies?" I responded in a question-slash-statement fashion.

"Yeah, we can do that. We can go to the movies and then go grab something to eat."

After we left the movies, my daddy took me to his favorite restaurant, Ponderosa. As we ate our meals, I could tell he was struggling with his vocabulary to find ways to ask me how I was feeling.

"So … so … how have you been feeling after … after. Well … you know what I'm trying to say, right?"

"Yeah," I said, nodding.

"You know this trial thing will be coming up. How do you feel about that?"

"I don't know," I said, twirling my fork around the spaghetti noodles.

"All eyes are gonna be on you, baby girl. But you're a fighter like your dad. You don't give up or give in. That's how they win. We don't let the bad guys win … ever. We take them out if we have to," my dad said, patting me on the head.

For a few minutes, neither of us said anything. I devoured the spaghetti, not because it was good but because it kept me from speaking. Finally, my dad broke the verbal silence. "Baby girl, I'm so sorry. I'm sorry Daddy wasn't there to protect you.

I promise you, though, I'll never let anything like that happen to you again. Never."

I nodded once again. I knew he meant it. I remembered Ebony telling me about how he went looking for Nick. I hesitated before mustering up the nerve to ask him about it. "So did you try to find Unc … I mean, Nick?"

"You damn right, baby girl. I went looking for that son of a you know what. I wanted to kill him," he said, fighting back tears.

"But then, you'd be in jail too, Daddy."

"I know. I know. But I'll go to jail to protect you. Remember that."

And from that day on, that declaration of reassurance hovered over me like a cloud. Just hearing those words from my daddy gave me a greater sense of protection. I won't say that I had built up enough confidence to face Nick, but I had just enough to do the right thing, so Nick could never do to anyone else what he had done to me.

When I came back home at the end of the summer, a different Latwaina walked through the doors of my mother's house. Fathers have a way of arming their children with confidence that can't come from anyone else. And my dad had done it to me that summer. I had come to terms with the fact that my life with my mother wasn't ideal in any shape or form. The maternal side of my family was considered family based on genealogy alone.

By the time Thanksgiving came around, things were heating up with the trial, and it had a negative impact on the family.

"Well, you know Aunt Lisa is hosting Thanksgiving this year, and Uncle Mike ..."

"Doesn't want me there," I said, finishing Mama's sentence for her.

My mother lowered her head. "Yeah ... he doesn't want you there." She paused. "But I'll bring you some food home," my mother said, trying to sound enthusiastic about it.

I nodded. I felt as though Nick had raped me all over again. Tears began to roll down my cheeks. I was helpless, and for some reason, my mother seemed helpless too. Her battle with drugs caused her to lose her own power. Our family held it over her head, and for some reason, she spent a lot of time begging for forgiveness and acceptance by relinquishing her power to them. She didn't stand up for herself, so she definitely was not going to stand up for me. So I learned that if no one wanted to celebrate with me, I could still celebrate by myself.

That year, I made my own Thanksgiving meal and celebrated the holiday by myself, setting the precedent for what would be customary for years to come.

CHAPTER 7

David Versus Goliath

"The truth. Tell the truth about what happened that day. That's all that matters," Attorney Haskins said. Attorney Haskins was from the DA's office. She was, as they said, on my side. She swept a long strand of her blonde hair out of her face. She was part of the team that would be prosecuting Nick on the rape charges. They decided not to charge him for kidnapping me from school. And they told me not to bring it up. Just tell them what happened at the house.

"Remember, we're only focusing on what happened in that basement and in the car. You tell the truth about those two things, and Nick Washington goes to jail for a long, long time," Attorney Bradford, a tall, lanky white man added.

"Now, we're going to ask you if you see your uncle—"

"That's not her uncle," my dad said, interrupting the male attorney.

"Excuse me. For the sake of trial, we need her to refer to him as she did when these assaults occurred. I understand how painful it might be, but this is how it must be. This helps strengthen the case against Mr. Washington."

"But I have a problem with you calling him by his formal name and these titles. Uncles don't rape their nieces."

"I hear what you're saying, but I've been a prosecutor for going on twenty years, and I'm sorry to tell you that not only do uncles rape their nieces, but fathers rape their daughters and mothers rape their sons. I've seen it all. I know it's hard for you, but you have to put your emotions on hold temporarily. The end goal is to make sure Mr. Washington goes away for a long time. And the only way we can ensure this is to make sure your daughter's testimony is strong and powerful."

"And who's going to pick up the pieces after my daughter is forced to relive those rapes over and over again? Are you going to be there in the middle of the night after she's had a nightmare about the attack again?" my father said with growing frustration.

"Do you think it's better that we work with your daughter alone? I mean, I know it's tough for you to hear these questions and answers. I get it. But we have to do what we have to do," Attorney Haskins interjected.

My mother grabbed my dad by the hand, and I could see the tension in his face relax. "Okay," he said, nodding, his way of telling me to proceed.

We rehearsed the questions over and over, until my mouth felt like I'd eaten a box full of cotton balls. They seemed confident in their case and satisfied with the way I answered their tough questions. At least that's what they said to me.

I didn't sleep well that night. I remember waking up in the middle of the night, sweating profusely. I sat up and turned on my lamp light. My clock read 3:43 AM. Mama said we'd get up and get ready around seven o'clock. So I knew the clock was ticking. I reached into my nightstand drawer and pulled out the journal Dr. Lindsey had given me. And then I began to write … writing out my feelings like Dr. Lindsey said.

In a few hours, I will face Nick. I'm scared.

I stared at the words on the page. Then I remembered the story about David and Goliath, the story I learned in Sunday School. The giant seems undefeatable at first. But you must believe you can beat him, even if you have to sling a rock. In my case, the rock was the truth. My words. My testimony. That's what I was armed with. The truth.

Mama said her nerves were too bad to drive, so Daddy drove us to court that day.

Deacon Wil didn't go to court with us. I tried to focus on the scenery outside as we rode to court. I counted eleven stoplights and four stop signs. I saw two Cadillacs that looked like Nick's car, except they were different colors, one red and the other one white.

"Well, we're here," Mama said as my dad let us out in front of the court building.

I looked up at the large brick building. I couldn't have ever imagined that this many people went to court on any given day. As he always did, my dad got out of the car and opened the door for me.

"I'm going to park the car, but I'll meet you and your mama inside. You go on … you got this," he said as he cupped his hands around the sides of my face and planted a soft kiss on my forehead.

David and Goliath. David and Goliath, I repeated as Mama and I walked toward the front entrance of the court.

After we went through the metal detectors, we stood off to the side to wait for my dad to park the car. I found myself wondering why people were there. What was their story? If I saw a little girl, I wondered whether she had been raped. But you can't see rape on a person's face. Rape is buried somewhere deep in the soul. It feels as though the wound is so deep that it can't be touched. Because of this, the wound remains un-healed. The infliction stays raw. The wrong word can make the wound bleed or cause it to ooze with infection, poisoning other parts of the body.

We were met by a younger black woman and led to a pri-vate room where Attorney Haskins was waiting for us.

"Good morning, Latwaina," she said as she took a sip of coffee.

"Good morning," I answered.

"I need to talk to your parents for a moment. There's some pastries and juice over there. You can help yourself to some," she said, pointing to a table in the far corner of the room.

I knew that meant whatever she was about to tell my parents was something I wasn't supposed to hear. But I nodded anyway, pretending to accept the invitation, nonetheless. But if truth be told, food was the farthest thing from my mind in that moment. My stomach was in knots. *David versus Goliath. David versus Goliath*, I repeated with each step I took. When I reached the table, I turned back to look at my parents and Attorney Haskins, who were all huddled up. My dad, realizing I had been staring at them, looked over at me and winked, giving me the thumbs up sign simultaneously. I threw the sign back up at him.

Attorney Haskins motioned for me to come back over to them when they'd finished their little conference.

"Mom and Dad are going to sit down in court. You'll stay back here until it's time for you to testify. Miss Yolanda, the court clerk, will be in here with you," Attorney Haskins said, pointing to the young black woman who had initially escorted us to the waiting room.

I nodded, watching the three of them—Mama, Daddy, and Attorney Haskins—exit the waiting room. When the large brown door closed behind them, pebbles of sweat began to form on my forehead. The sound of the closing door produced a soft echo.

Miss Yolanda made small talk with me while we waited. She asked me about my family, my school, whether I had any pets. She certainly helped take the edge off, because for a moment, I had forgotten about why I was there in the first place.

Then, the big brown door opened, and a short, stocky sheriff motioned for me.

"They're ready for you," Miss Yolanda said. "You can do this," she said as we shuffled over to the door.

I don't remember walking the halls that led to the court. What I do remember is the sheriff opening the doors of the courtroom. "Keep your eyes on the judge," she reminded me as we entered the courtroom and proceeded to the front.

The faces of those in the room were like blurry objects to me. I kept my eyes on the grey-haired judge as I had been instructed. I can't be sure he meant to crack a half-smile or not, but he did. And when he smiled, the thumping in my chest lessened.

"Raise your right hand and repeat after me," another court official said as we approached what I remembered them telling me was the witness stand.

I raised my hand as was instructed.

"Do you solemnly swear to tell the truth, the whole truth, and nothing but the truth, so help you God?"

"I do," I said, as I had been coached.

"You may have a seat," the court official said, helping me to the stand.

I sat down in the witness seat and tried to remember what Attorney Haskins had coached me on. "Look at me," she said. Keep your eyes on who's talking to you. Don't look for your mother or your father. They'll be there rooting for you. Keep your focus on the truth." And then I remembered what Dr. Lindsey said. "Tell the truth. That's your rock. You must take Goliath down." I was ready for the questions.

"Can you tell me your name?"

"Latwaina."

"What's your full name?"

"Latwaina Tyler."

"How old are you, Latwaina?"

"Fourteen."

"How old were you on April eleventh, nineteen ninety-two?"

"I was fourteen," I said, keeping my eyes on the prosecutor, the tall, lanky man, again.

"How old were you on March thirtieth, nineteen ninety-two?"

"I was thirteen," I said, looking up at him.

"Do you remember what happened to you on March 30, 1992?"

"Yes, sir."

"Can you tell us about that day?"

I swallowed hard.

"Take your time, Latwaina. Take your time," the prosecutor added.

As I was told, I went into details about how my day started, filling them in on the routine of waking up, getting ready, and going to school. Then, he followed up with another set of questions.

"Was there anything different about this day than any normal day?"

Little did he know, nothing about my life was really normal. But I had been coached well, so I just followed the script. "Uncle Nick signed me out of school."

"Have you ever been signed out of school early?"

"No," I replied.

"Who signed you out of school?"

"My Uncle Nick."

"Uncle Nick?"

"Yes," I confirmed.

"Why did Uncle Nick sign you out of school?"

"He said we had a family emergency."

"A family emergency, huh?"

"Yes, sir," I replied.

"Would you tell the court what happened after Uncle Nick signed you out of school early on March thirtieth, nineteen ninety-two?"

"He drove me to his mother's house."

"Was there an emergency?"

"No."

"Tell the court what happened."

"Uncle Nick started feeling on me."

"When you say feeling on me, what do you exactly mean? Can you be specific?"

"He rubbed his hands on my private parts … like my nipples, and then he touched my vagina and put his fingers up in me." Once I said how Nick had put his fingers in me, loud gasps rang out in the courtroom. I remember looking around at what seemed like a room of blurry faces. Remembering I was told not to look at them, I tried my best to keep my focus on the person asking me the questions as I had been directed.

"What else did he do?"

I fought back tears. "Then …" I paused.

"Take your time."

I took a deep breath before resuming. "Then he made me lie down on the floor and he got on top of me."

"What did he do then?"

"He put his wee-wee … I mean, his penis." I was told to use the word penis instead of the word wee-wee. "Then he put his penis in my vagina and started moving around … up and down and from side to side."

"Do you remember saying anything?"

"He told me to say things."

"What things?"

"Yes … and give it to me." I heard the gasp coming from the crowd again.

"Did you say anything else?"

"I told him to stop. I begged him to stop," I sobbed as the tears began to cascade down my cheeks.

"Did he?"

"No," I said, continuing to sob.

I answered the remaining prosecutorial questions, including providing details and responses related to the rape in the car. Then, the final question was asked of me. "Do you see the man who raped you in this courtroom?"

"Yes," I answered in a tone just above a whisper.

"Can you point to him?"

And for the first time, my eyes moved from the prosecutor and into the crowd of people who were seated, facing me. My eyes scanned the room quickly. I got a quick glance at Grandma Lily, Mama, Daddy, and Aunt Lisa. Sitting next to Aunt Lisa was Uncle Mike, who sat with his arms folded.

"Remember … don't look for your parents." I remembered those words and immediately zeroed in on Nick, who was seated between his two attorneys … the attorneys who would ask me questions next. Nick was wearing a bright orange suit, making a statement of some sort, I guessed. His hair had grown out; he now sported a curly Afro, a slew of lumps on the sides of his face, and two black eyes. He seemed to have gotten beaten up pretty badly in jail once the other prisoners learned what he was in there for. He was looking down, concentrating on a piece of paper he was writing on. Taking notes? I doubt it. Nick didn't seem to be the studious type. He was just scribbling on a piece of paper. But then he looked up, and our

eyes met. I forced myself to remember what Dr. Lindsey had said to me. I was David and he was Goliath. I lifted my right hand and pointed my index finger at Nick.

Once again, the crowd gasped.

"Your Honor, can we take a break?"

We took a brief break, and they escorted me back to the same waiting room where I had waited earlier. Attorney Haskins stopped by once again and praised me for my testimony.

"You did fantastic, Latwaina! I'm very proud of you," she said, patting me on the back. "Now you just have one last hurdle to get over, and that's the questioning from the defense attorneys. Remember what I told you. Listen carefully to each question. Think about your response before you start speaking. Last but not least … don't be afraid."

Going back into the courtroom to face the defense attorneys was less intimidating than when I was giving my testimony to the prosecution. For some reason, I felt empowered. Emboldened. Maybe it was just for the moment, which happened to be a critical moment in time. But all that mattered was that I was prepared. I was ready to take the giant down. I was ready to be free from the fear, the intimidation, the threats, the stalking, and being ostracized. I was fighting against more than just the sexual assault against my body; I was fighting for my freedom.

I answered the defense attorney's questions just as I'd answered the prosecutor's questions, which was with honesty. A huge sigh of relief came over me when they announced, "You may step down now." It was over. I had done what I came to do, and that was confront the monster who had savagely raped me twice.

Then … it was over. A huge weight had been lifted from my shoulders, it seemed. We were told that we should be expecting the verdict within a few days. First, they had to give closing arguments and then the jury would decide whether Nick could go home or stay in jail. In other words, the jury had to decide whether they believed me or lying Nick, who tried to say a thirteen-year-old girl consented to having sex with him, which wasn't legal by any stretch of the imagination.

In the days that followed, Mama was on edge. In hindsight, I think it was because she knew what was coming down the pipeline if Nick got convicted. I don't think any of us could have ever prepared for either outcome. Daddy said there was going to be hell to pay if Nick didn't get convicted. The family was in shambles, to be honest. So, you can guess that things went further downhill the day Mama got the call that a verdict had been reached. She and Deacon Wil dropped Granddaddy and me off at Grandma Lily's house, and she and Deacon Wil went to the courthouse. Granddaddy's dementia was too much for me to deal with by myself. So Grandma Lily told Mama she would watch Grandaddy while Mama went to court.

I kept my eyes on the clock on the wall in Grandma Lily's living room. My heart dropped into my stomach when I heard car doors opening and closing.

"They're back," I said as I wiped the dripping sweat from the sides of my face.

CHAPTER 8

Bits And Pieces

What if I just swallowed this whole bottle of pills and just end it all? No more tears. No more pain. No more accusations. No more anything. Just be gone away from the turmoil I'm living on a day-to-day basis.

My hands gripped the bottle and shook it. The pills rattled against the sides of the bottle. My life was literally in my hands. I could pop open the top and swallow every last pill in the plastic bottle. I closed my eyes, imagining what would happen in the event my mother were to find my lifeless body on the bathroom floor. I also envisioned the paramedics coming to our house to try to resuscitate me, giving me CPR and mouth-to-mouth resuscitation. *Would they be able to save my life, or would it be too late?* Was I ready to end my life? If so, that meant Nick, Uncle Mike, Aunt Lisa, and the rest of the naysayers would have won. But I was a fighter. I clenched the bottle harder and tighter. This wouldn't be the day I'd let them win.

I raised my hand that held the bottle in the air and inhaled. Then I released the bottle and it hit the floor … hard. The top flew off, allowing the contents of the bottle to splatter onto the ceramic-tiled bathroom floor. They didn't win … at least not this time.

I went to bed that evening, thinking about the day ahead of me. For the most part, I didn't mind going to an all-girl school. But I still didn't really fit in, and because of my personality—reclusive and shy—I didn't make friends quickly. My self-esteem was at an all-time low, which affected my confidence when it came to participating in class. Things came to a head one afternoon when I lashed out at a girl named Brittany, a snooty, know-it-all girl who shared my science class with me. She went for the gusto when Mr. Day, my science teacher, asked me to answer a question about chemical bonding.

"So Latwaina, what answer did you get for question two?" Mr. Day said, stroking his chin.

"Um, question two … on what page?" I replied nervously.

"Question number two on the chemical bonding worksheet, hun."

"Maybe somebody should read it for her since she barely speaks," Brittany remarked, smirking under her breath.

"Sure, why don't you go ahead and help her out," Mr. Day encouraged.

In very proper English, Brittany read the equation. "Using the electron diagram, determine what kind of bond has formed between the carbon atom and the two oxygen atoms."

"Okay, your turn Latwaina. What's the answer?" Mr. Day asked, looking at me and then at Brittany.

"Meeetallic, coveeeleeent, ionic, or mole-cu-ler," I stammered reading the multiple-choice options.

"Yes, but you have to pick *one*," Mr. Day replied impatiently.

"I'm not sure which one to choose," I drearily said. I felt the pebbles form on my forehead. Suddenly, I was nauseous. I wanted to pass out.

"It's like she's not even here, guys," Brittany blurted out. The entire class erupted in laughter.

"Because I. Don't. Want. To. Be. Here!" I yelled. I could feel all the pressure I had been holding beginning to erupt like a volcano, ready to take out anything and everything in my path.

Those were probably the most words my teacher and classmates had ever heard me speak. "I don't want to be in this class. I don't even want to be in this world anymore!" I yelled, accompanied by tears of anger, hurt, and frustration.

Mr. Day walked over to me and attempted to hug me. I positioned my back to him. I didn't want him to touch me. With my back facing the class, I saw an open window, and I made a leap for it. Was I going to jump to my fate or my freedom? I didn't have that long to determine which one it was going to be … I just remember leaping.

You can imagine that with that move, other people got involved. My mother was called down to the school and was informed about what happened. I was already sitting in the school counselor's office when she and my cousin Tiffany arrived. As if it was in slow motion, the door opened and in walked my mother, in an almost strutting fashion, with her eyes fixed on me. I don't remember what the counselor initially said to my mother, because by now, it all seemed like I was having an out-of-body experience.

"Are you okay?" my mother said, stroking my hair, which was pulled back into a raggedy ponytail by this time.

"I'm—" I attempted to answer.

"Miss Tyler, she's not okay," Mrs. Dunbar, the school counselor said, cutting me off. "Why don't we have a conversation. All of us," Mrs. Dunbar continued.

My mother took a deep breath and took a seat at the round table across from where I was sitting.

Mrs. Dunbar took a deep breath before she spoke. Finally, she went for it. "Miss Tyler, as you know, the majority of the girls in this school are here because they are pregnant or are already mothers. We accommodate this special group of students by the programs, services, and academics that we offer. Latwaina is an exception. She is here because of a different set of circumstances. And it's becoming more apparent with each passing day."

"So ... what are you suggesting?" my mother said, cutting to the chase.

"I'm suggesting she gets the help she needs."

"And what do you say that is?" my mother snapped. "I mean, she's been going back and forth to counselors ever since the rape. What more do you think I need to do, because I'm about to lose my mind too!" my mother said matter-of-factly.

And there. She had said it. She'd finally acknowledged my trauma by saying the word "rape." Tears began to stream down my cheeks.

"I think she needs to see a counselor at a behavioral health institution," Mrs. Dunbar said, sitting down at the table with us.

"Like a mental hospital?" my mother said with raised eyebrows.

"An institution. We don't use the words mental hospital anymore. There's a negative connotation to the term. We call it behavioral health, and likewise, a behavioral health institution," Mrs. Dunbar said, trying to make light of it.

"Well, in my community, we call it the mental hospital or the psych ward!" my mother said in comeback fashion.

I jumped up from my seat and nearly flipped over the table where we were seated. Unsuccessful, I turned around and lifted the chair I'd been sitting on in the air. "If you think about trying to make me go see some shrink, I swear, I will throw this chair across the room, and I don't care what it damages. I'm not crazy! I'm a victim!" I yelled. "No, I ain't going to no crazy house. No!" I added.

"Latwaina, you really need to calm down," Mrs. Dunbar warned. "You can go voluntarily, or I can send a medical referral indicating that you're a harm to yourself and others, and you'll be made to go involuntarily. That means by force."

"Grace, maybe it's the best thing for her," Cousin Tiffany said, combing her hair with her fingers.

That's when it dawned on me. The possibility of being put in a straight jacket and hauled off to an in-patient mental facility was real. I calmed down immediately.

When we got home later that day, I went straight to my bed to lie down. I could hear my mama and Cousin Tiffany talking about me. Cousin Tiffany was still trying to convince my mother to check me into a mental facility. But Mama said

I had been through enough, and she just couldn't do that to me. *Thank God,* I thought.

I knew that if I didn't show improvement in school, both behaviorally and in my academics, the referral from Mrs. Dunbar was going to become a reality. But just how do you make changes in your life when trauma and abuse haunt your very existence? When you seem to not be able to escape it all because it's there twenty-four seven. Torturing your every breathing moment. You become paranoid. And any degree of ostracization makes it that much worse. So you mask it all. The hurt. The pain. The castigation. The resentment. The blackmail. The lies as well as the truth.

You mask it until you have to confront it, like I did the day I ran into April, a cousin of Nick and Uncle Mike.

I went to the little convenience store in my neighborhood to grab some snacks, and that's when I spotted her getting out of a reddish-orange Mustang. I smiled as I picked up my pace to catch up to her.

"Hi, April," I said, tapping her on the shoulder. She swung around so fast that it caught me off guard, causing me to take a step back.

She sucked her teeth as if she was disgusted by the very sight of me. "You. Don't ever touch me!" she snarled.

I imagine that the smile disappeared from my face instantly. "I ... I was. I mean, I was just saying hi," I said, hesitantly.

"Nick should have killed you when he had the opportunity. Then, then he wouldn't be locked up like this!" she said in a tone that seemed to penetrate my skin.

I lost my appetite for the snacks I'd come to the convenience store to buy. The rejection seemed to come from everyone. I knew that the only way I could get away from the rejection was to go live with my dad. It would probably hurt my mother, but no one could have been hurting any worse than I was hurting … and I was sure of that.

Mama had already said that Rose, my dad's new girlfriend, wouldn't want me crashing in on her and my dad's thing. But I wasn't sure I believed that. Rose was nice, and she hadn't showed me any signs that she didn't like me or didn't like me around. So, I kept the possibility of living with my dad as an option.

Mrs. Dunbar and Cousin Tiffany were able to convince Mama to sign me up for group counseling. I was scheduled for my first session after school one Tuesday afternoon. Mama and Cousin Tiffany, who was my mother's first cousin, dropped me off at the first meeting.

The walls of the small room were painted a dull shade of peach. Neutral is what they called it. Bright colors might invoke anxiety, they said. And dark colors could make people feel sad. A few pictures accessorized the room. One was a picture of a woman dancing. Another picture was of a beautiful rose garden. One last picture was of a rainstorm.

"Ahh … you must be Latwaina," the counselor, a heavy-set black woman, said. I nodded. "Take a seat wherever you like," she invited.

I sat next to a young woman wearing heavy makeup. When I looked closer, I could tell that she was trying to disguise a black eye. She held her hand out. I held my hand out to shake hers. After a firm handshake, she held on to my hand, squeezing it. "You're in the right place," she said, nodding. "We're all in this together." She paused. "My name is Maya, by the way," she continued. This time, offering a smile.

"Latwaina. I'm Latwaina," I said in a voice just above a whisper.

She and I talked to each other in between other group members sharing their stories. For the most part, I remained quiet and just listened to everyone else's stories during the first meeting. When it was Maya's turn to speak, she vowed to do a little spring cleaning in her life. I guessed that's what they called getting rid of unwanted things in your life and "cleaning your life up," so to speak.

We exchanged phone numbers and a friendship formed almost immediately. We would spend a lot of time on the phone just providing emotional support to one another. Even though Maya was older than me, we had a lot in common. We shared quite a bit with one another. In my mind, however, I struggled with just how much to share. My past wasn't just traumatic, it was complicated too. My parents weren't married; they weren't even together; I'd lived with my mother and my grandmother; my mother was an ex-addict; I'd been raped and ostracized by my family because of it. How do you tell someone that everything around you reminds you of pain?

"I know I should get all the negative people out of my house. The people who are there for the wrong reasons. I know I need to focus on my kids. I just feel like I'll be lonely without another adult to talk to. I wish I had a roommate," Maya said during one of our phone conversations.

I pepped up after hearing Maya say that. Exciting and happy ideas began to run through my mind. *Maybe I can get a part-time job and be Maya's roommate*, I thought.

During the next group counseling meeting, Maya walked in on crutches.

"What happened to you?" the counselor, Ms. Cole, asked quizzically.

"Ahh ... I broke my foot."

As many times as we'd spoken over the phone, Maya hadn't mentioned breaking her foot. She was clearly in pain, evidenced by the "ooh and ahh" noises she made every time she moved. It was obvious to everyone that she was in an abusive relationship.

Obviously concerned about Maya, Ms. Cole began to speak to her in code language. But we weren't dumb. Everyone knew what Ms. Cole was implying,

"That dirt in your home seems to be getting more and more dangerous, Maya. When are you going to spring clean ... once and for all?"

"I want to, Ms. Cole. But honestly, I'm afraid to live alone. I feel like I'd be safer if I had a roommate," Maya said, holding back tears.

That's when I decided to go for it. After the meeting, I told Maya I would move in with her. That night, we went to my house, and I packed a few of my belongings. I told Mama we were just gonna try it out, and she didn't really object. Besides, she was spending most nights at Deacon Wil's house. The only thing she cautioned was, "Two women in one household ain't gonna make it."

I moved in with Maya, a stranger I had known for only two weeks. Only fifteen years old, I didn't think of all the odds and ends or the practicality of the situation. I was just in desperate search for peace ... in body, mind, and spirit.

Maya's boyfriend, Kenny, lived with her. It didn't take long for me to realize that he was the "spring cleaning" that both Ms. Cole and Maya were referring to during the counseling sessions.

"This is Latwaina. She's gonna be staying with us for a while," Maya said as she introduced me to her man.

"Hi, Latwaina," he said, looking me up and down. "Hey … I'm having a little get together here at the house tonight. I'm sure you'll have fun," he said, this time showcasing a set of poorly kept teeth.

"Okay," I responded.

Before long, people started piling up in Maya's house. I stayed in one of the extra rooms she had. I didn't plan on joining the party because I had school the next morning. But going to sleep was next to impossible. The sound of loud rap songs and the stench from marijuana seeping under the door kept me up. I heard a knock on the door at some point.

"Come in," I invited.

Maya was standing on the other side of the door. "Come on out for a minute. You can come back in here, but just come on out and have a little fun," Maya invited, almost beggingly.

Hesitantly, I got up, threw on a pair of Yoga pants and a shirt. I fixed my hair and put a light layer of lip gloss on my lips, just something to look presentable.

"Come here, Latwaina," her boyfriend Kenny called out to me, motioning with his hand. "I have something for you," he said as I approached the sofa where he sat. He handed me a glass of red juice.

"I don't drink," I confessed.

"Just take a sip. You'll like it."

I knew he would try to persuade me into drinking the concoction, so I took the glass from his hand and took a sip. It tasted weird.

"Oh, you gon' get to feelin' good in a minute. Just wait," he said, winking.

Before I knew it. The concoction kicked in. I was up, dancing like the rest of the partygoers. Suddenly, I felt dizzy. I needed to go lie down. My eyes scanned the room for Maya, but I couldn't locate her. I stumbled across the front room, leaning against as much of the wall as I could. Finally, I spotted Maya, but I couldn't get her attention. She and Kenny were arguing. And that's when I saw it for myself. Kenny *was* abusive. He punched Maya dead smack in the mouth. I wasn't sure whether it was the alcohol or just his nature.

I changed course and tried to find my way back to the bedroom that I was staying in. That's when I met Maya's sister, Kyndall.

"You need help?"

"Yeah, I'm dizzy. I want to go lie down in my room," I said.

"Oh, you must be the new roommate," she said.

"Yes."

"I'm Kyndall, Maya's sister."

I tried to muster a half-smile. Whatever I'd taken a sip of had my lips feeling as though they were paralyzed. I wasn't sure they even moved at all.

Kyndall walked me back to the bedroom and helped me get in bed. "I'm finna go play a few rounds of Spades, but you'll be good in here. I'll turn out the light, so no one comes in."

"Thank you," I said. Her words echoed and the light was making the dizziness even worse. *I wish I could just go to sleep and it be gone*, I thought as I slid between the comforter and the flat bedsheet.

Tears pricked the corner of my eyes and my chest tightened. I didn't know how long I had been holding my breath, but it felt like an eternity. My throat was dry, and I wanted to scream, but I couldn't. I knew I wouldn't be able to produce an audible sound, let alone an actual word. And even if I did, no one would hear me over the music and loud talking on the other side of the bedroom door. The party was jumping, as they say. Music … talking … and laughter. And my little ole cry for help couldn't compete with any of that.

He maintained a firm grip around my neck. His thumb and forefinger outstretched, pushing into the base of my neck with just enough pressure to make me afraid to move. I didn't even want to think about where his other hand was or what it was doing. His leg was wrapped over me, pinning me to the bed, like I was a part of some type of World Wrestling fighting match. And if I was, there was no doubt that I was certainly on the losing end.

I couldn't focus on any one thing. All I felt was terror. Terror and his hot breath against the back of my neck. Lying on his side, he had my back pressed firmly against the front of his chest. I tried to breathe, but the air was caught in my lungs, unable to be released due to his tight grasp on my throat. His other hand was lost under the blanket, exploring the sacred parts of my body. I could feel his erection pressing against my backside, and every time he pushed it against me, I felt sick. I felt dirty. Helpless. I wanted to scream. To fight. But my body wouldn't respond to those inner demands. *Another Nick moment*, I thought.

Everything was happening so fast, but it also seemed to be moving in slow motion … in frames. I didn't know how long it had been since I'd awakened to him sliding into the bed with me. Was it the bed moving that woke me or the pressure of his fingertips pushing into my neck? I couldn't be sure which one. Didn't know how it had happened or how many silent tears had fallen down my cheeks since the bodily intrusion began. I was too afraid to make a sound. I could have sworn I heard the same sirens and saw the same lights from the police cars and the flashes of light from the helicopter that hovered over me the night Nick raped me in his car. In my mind, I was screaming at myself to do something to make him stop. Bite him. Kick him. Heck, even spit on him. Something. Anything. But my lips never moved. Couldn't utter a sound. And while there was total chaos going on in my mind, on the outside, everything seemed quiet … except for the creepy sounds he made in between his loud breaths, the sound of his zipper being pulled down, and the rustling of clothing as he pulled and tugged at it. The music that was playing was no longer playing. I could hear the muffled sounds of people still talking in the front room.

When it was over, he rolled off me, off the bed, slipped his clothes back on, and slipped out of the room, joining the remaining partygoers. The room was pitch black, except for the little light that entered the room from the bottom of the door. I couldn't move. My mind began to race with fleeting thoughts. Dirty. Again. Tainted. Dirty. I wanted to take a bath. Wash the dirt, leftover semen, the strong scent of his Obsession cologne, and the disgust off my body. Don't ask me how I mustered up enough strength to run my bathwater and get in the tub, but I did. I scrubbed my body with the dark blue washcloth Maya had given me. No amount of water, soap, body wash, or scrub seemed to make me clean. After a full forty-five-minute bath, I still felt dirty.

Lying in bed after my bath, I tried to steady my breathing. I felt as though I was suffocating. I tried to calm myself because I didn't want to cause a stir in the now quiet house … bring attention to myself. The party was over, and the house was now quiet. It took a few minutes to even out my breathing, and I realized my body was still, almost rigid like a body stiff with rigor mortis. When I was finally able to maintain some control over my own body, I urged my muscles to relax just enough to curl up into fetal position.

Wiping a tear from the corner of my eye, I slowly brought my hand to my neck. I needed to know that his hand wasn't still there because I could still feel the tight grip. I had to touch various parts of my body just to know that I wasn't still in his grasp. I told myself to calm down. That it was over.

CHAPTER 9

A Chance at Love

"He has a twin brother," Keisha said, rubbing her expanding belly.

I cracked a half-smile.

"So?"

"So what?" I said.

"Do you wanna meet him?"

"I guess," I said, feeling almost pressured. I wasn't sure I was ready for this relationship stuff. But seeing that I was in an all-girls school for pregnant teens, it wasn't like I could escape looking at large bellies or the incessant conversations about "baby daddy" this or "baby daddy" that. "Sure," I confirmed.

"His name is Chad. Remember, he's the twin to my baby daddy, Brad. They're both fine too."

"You have any pictures of him?"

"Not on me. But I have some at home. I'll bring some in tomorrow," she said, finishing the last of her ice pop.

"Are you ready to be a mother?" I asked, changing the subject.

"It's a little scary," Keisha admitted as she sat down next to me on the cafeteria bench.

"What's scary about it?" I asked inquisitively.

"Everything. Like, I'm going to be someone's mother. *A mother.* Can you believe that? Somebody will call me Mommy. I'm going to be responsible for someone else's well-being. I mean, it blows my mind, honestly," Keisha said, tearing up.

"Feels sort of funny being the student here that's not pregnant or has already had a baby," I responded. I couldn't relate. I wasn't pregnant, and I didn't have a boyfriend. The strangest thing is that I felt somewhat jealous. Jealous that Keisha was going to experience someone loving her unconditionally … something that was foreign to me.

"Think you and Brad will get married one day?" I asked.

"Hmmph … I don't know. Everybody says those Jackson boys are lady lovers, and they won't ever settle down," Keisha said, chuckling.

I smiled again.

"But I don't pay them no mind. Brad and I will always be family no matter what."

That night, I lay in bed thinking about Chad. Keisha seemed sure we were a good match. She said he was fine. Like Omari Hardwick fine. She called me earlier that evening and told me that Brad and Chad were going to pick us up from school the next day. I was so excited that I laid my clothes out for school the next morning. Everything. Down to my accessories—socks, tennis shoes, necklace, and earrings.

The next day, the afternoon bell couldn't ring fast enough. We'd made arrangements to meet "the twins" in the student parking lot after school. Keisha and I met on the westside exit, which led out to the student parking lot.

"Are you nervous?" Keisha said with a wide grin.

"A little," I responded. I could feel pebbles of sweat popping out on my forehead.

"Don't be nervous. He's cool. He'll like you," Keisha tried to reassure me.

When we walked out of the exit door, Keisha spotted Brad and Chad's car almost immediately. The smoke gray Honda Accord slowly turned the bend and stopped in front.

"That's them!" Keisha said with excitement in her voice. "Come on," she said as she wobbled her way down the walkway.

I took a deep breath as I followed her. The front passenger door opened as we approached the car. A high-yellow, light-skinned young man with jet black curly hair emerged. He had the widest smile, revealing the whitest set of teeth.

"This is Brad's twin brother, Chad," Keisha said, smiling.

"Hi, cutie," he said, holding out his hand to shake mine.

"Hi," I said, eagerly extending my hand.

"Keisha, you weren't lying. She is pretty," he said, opening the back door for me to get in, after which he followed. Keisha got in the passenger seat alongside the person I assumed was Brad, and we were off.

"You guys hungry?" Brad asked.

"You know I'm always starving; I'm preggo, remember?" Keisha joked, stroking the back of Brad's head.

"Where do you want to go?" Brad asked.

"Anywhere but McDonald's. I can't eat their food anymore," Keisha said.

Keisha's taste buds had changed due to the pregnancy, obviously. I wasn't picky about where to eat, so I let the three of them decide on the restaurant. And when all was said and done, we ended up going to a local eatery by the name of Detroit One Coney Island.

Chad acted as though we were already going out. He sat right next to me at the table. Keisha was all smiles, most likely praising her matchmaking skills on the down low.

"Can I get you guys anything to drink?" the frail older waitress asked, flipping her crumpled order pad.

"We want to order," Brad responded.

"What do you want? I got you," Chad said, looking at me.

"Burger and fries, and I want my burger done medium well," I replied.

"Drink? What would you like to drink?"

"Coke. I'll take a Coke but not with a lot of ice."

After the nice little old waitress had taken all our orders, Chad turned to me. "So, tell me about yourself," he said, revealing his pearly whites once again.

"Umm ... well, I'm Latwaina—"

"I know that already," Chad said, chuckling.

I giggled. "Well, Tyler is my last name. I'm fifteen years old."

"What about your family? Any sisters or brothers?"

Family. There was that word again. Family. Did I *really* even have a family, when I wasn't even allowed over to celebrate holidays? Did I really have a family, when they were ashamed of me because of the trauma that had been afflicted upon me? Did I have a family, when they seemed comfortable hiding my pain just to hide the family's ugly secrets? No, the closest thing I had to a family was my relationship with my dad. Of course, since my dad adored me, my family on his side had no other choice but to accept me as well. But outside of this dynamic, I really didn't have a family … well, at least not yet.

"So do you?" Chad asked?

"Oh, yeah, sorry," I said, realizing it was taking me too long to answer the question. "I have my parents, of course. But my mom and dad are not together. I have a sister named Ebony and a brother named Daniel."

"Cool. Well, I have a twin, as you already know. And I also have an older sister named Kalifa. Got my mama, and that's it."

"Cool," I said.

"You didn't ask me about my dad."

"I assumed that since you didn't mention him, you didn't consider him to be that important in your life."

Chad let out a loud boisterous laugh. "I like you. You're funny," Chad said, placing his left hand on my right thigh.

I could feel the heat in my cheeks intensify. So, he said he liked me. Well, I think I liked him too. Chad seemed nice. Not only did he offer to pay for my meal, but he also said he would pick me up from school for the rest of the week. That would make any girl feel special.

Chad and I were in our own little world, talking as we waited for our food to arrive. Keisha and Brad sat across from us all huddled up like lovebirds. That is until a loud voice from the other side of the diner interrupted.

"Brad, why you do me like this?! That's all right, 'cause I'mma put you on child support, and take all your money!" the girl screamed as she was being held back by two other girls, who were most likely friends of hers.

Keisha attempted to get up but was pulled back down by Brad. "I got this," he said, getting up.

"That ain't my baby!" he yelled back as he walked toward the girl making the commotion.

"You liar! It's your baby, and you know it's your baby. But you just tryna protect your little girlfriend over there!"

"You damn right, I'm tryna protect her!" Brad yelled back.

"Go get your brother," I said to Chad. I could see a bigger commotion coming on, even if no one else saw it.

Chad shook his head. "I told him she was trouble."

"Go get him before something goes down," I begged.

After giving it a few more seconds of thought, Chad got up and went to get Brad before the situation got physical. And luckily, the girl's friends were able to pull her away by pushing her out of the diner. When Brad came back to the table, Keisha was wiping tears from her eyes.

"Really, Brad? Another one? You got another girl pregnant?"

"She's lying!" Brad argued. "She's a liar! She just wants me. Doesn't want me to be with you."

Well, as you can imagine, this double date didn't happen exactly as planned. We ended up leaving the diner, but not before Chad and I exchanged phone numbers. He was digging me, and I was digging him. Late night phone calls turned into early morning conversations. After school dates soon turned into early evening dates. Chad and I were inseparable.

It wouldn't be long before Chad wanted what all young boys want from their girlfriends. Sex.

There I was … at yet another crossroad.

CHAPTER 10

Love Lessons

Just about every young girl has heard the declaration, "If you love me, then you'll let me." And I was no different. Chad wanted to have sex, and since I was his so-called bonafide girlfriend, I acquiesced.

Because of the sexual trauma inflicted upon me by Nick, I never really thought about how sex would be once I met someone that I genuinely liked. But to my surprise, in my young mind, I believed I was ready … ready to give my body to someone I really liked. Consensual sex.

He slid his right hand up the back of my shirt and un-snapped my bra. I took a deep breath. Then he pulled the bra down and lifted my shirt, caressing my erect nipples with his free hand. To be a teenager, Chad was quite experienced. As though he was leading me in a dance routine, Chad "escorted" me over to his bed and gently laid me down on my back. I could see the bulge in his pants like I saw the bulge in Nick's pants. I closed my eyes. I knew Chad wasn't Nick, but the flashback almost made me vomit. But then, I opened my eyes and saw Chad's naked body standing over me. He was breathing hard, eager to have sex.

"Take off your pants," he said as he began to stroke his penis in front of me.

"Help me," I said, unbuttoning the top part of my jeans.

Leaning over, Chad unzipped my jeans and pulled them off. For a split second, I felt awkward. There I was, lying on my back, completely naked. I had to talk to myself. *He's your boyfriend, Latwaina. It's different this time. This is what girlfriends and boyfriends do. And if you don't let him, someone else will.*

Chad slid my legs apart and climbed on top of me. He began to suck on my neck ... hard, intentionally planting a hickey to "claim me," as he said.

"I've been waiting to make love to you," he said.

"Me too," I lied. I think I could have waited a little longer to introduce sex into our relationship. But I knew that Chad was a good-looking guy, and there was a line of other girls who would have eagerly given him sex if I didn't.

I remember thinking to myself ... *So, this is what making love is supposed to feel like.* And interestingly enough, I don't remember hurting this time. In fact, it was nothing like the traumatic experience I'd had with Nick. This time, it was consensual, and it even felt good. Sex was a turning point in my relationship with Chad as well as in my life. I was coming into myself, as they say.

That night, I remember staring into the mirror before I took another shower. Even though I had showered earlier that day after Chad and I had sex, I had to keep up with my same routine at home. I showered three times a day, including at night. Looking at myself in the mirror, I smiled. I hadn't enjoyed a genuine laugh or smile in a long time. I reminisced on the events that occurred earlier that day. Butterflies danced in my belly. I was in love.

"So … did you?"

"Did I what?" I said to Keisha. I knew what she was inquiring about. But I was never the kiss-and-tell kind of person, so I wasn't going to volunteer any information about what had transpired between Chad and me.

"You don't have to admit it. I already know y'all did it. Chad told Brad."

"Told Brad what?" I said, trying to act oblivious.

"That y'all did it," Keisha said with a wide grin on her face. "So, did y'all?" Keisha said, popping her gum between words.

I nodded.

"So … how was it?"

"It was good … I guess," I said.

"But you know he's just like his twin brother, right?"

"What do you mean?" I said inquisitively.

"He's a cheater," Keisha said nonchalantly.

"We spend too much time together," I said, denying the accusation.

"That don't mean nothing," Keisha said, continuing to crackle and pop the chewing gum, which was becoming rather annoying by this time.

"I guess I'll cross that bridge when I come to it," I said defensively. After all, that was what all the women in my life did … defend their men. I guess I learned to do the same.

That evening, however, I decided to ask Chad about the accusation, but it didn't go so well.

"Look, I like your girl Keisha and all. She's my twin's girl, but she don't know how to mind her business. She'll wreck your relationship if you let her. Be careful around her," Chad said, coming to his own defense.

"Keisha didn't say anything," I lied. The last thing I wanted was for Keisha and me to have a falling out over "the twins," as they were often called.

"Keisha runs her mouth just like the rest of those chicken heads out there. But they're just jealous. Jealous of you. Jealous of me being with you. Just plain ole jealous. They'll do anything to ruin our relationship. So, if you want us to make it, you're gonna have to stop listening and believing everything you hear," Chad said matter-of-factly.

I didn't say anything. I knew time would tell. Besides, I liked Chad. He was a constant in my life, and I wanted to hold onto anything that was constant and not traumatic. Hanging out at his grandma's house seemed like going to hang out at my own relatives' houses, which was something I was prohibited from doing.

"So why does everyone call you Mom?" I finally mustered the courage to ask. Mom was what everyone called Chad and Brad's grandmother, including her own children.

"I don't feel old. I hate the name 'Granny,' and I think the name 'Grandmother' sounds too formal. 'Mom' makes me feel young. Plus, I'm raising these boys of mine over here, and I feel much more like a mother than a grandmother to them."

"Oh, I see," I said, reaching for the small plate she was handing me.

Mom sat down at the table across from me. She'd offered me a serving of pepper steak and rice she'd just made. She wasn't the smiley type, but she was friendly. Chad had run down to the corner store to pick up a bottle of Jamaican pine-apple pop, which was her favorite drink. So she and I made small talk until Chad came back to the house.

I helped her wash the dishes after we ate, and then we all hung out in the living room until it was time for me to go home.

"Thank you for dinner," I said, giving Mom a hug.

She held her arms out to give me a warm farewell hug. But neither Chad nor I were prepared for what came out of Mom's mouth next. "Somebody's got a bun in the oven," she casually remarked.

"Go 'head, Mom," Chad said, trying to make light of her remark.

"What does that mean?" I whispered to Chad.

"Means I'm gonna have me a great-grandbaby," Mom said, having overheard me ask Chad the question.

I managed a fake smile. *Baby?* I thought as I followed Chad out of the house to the car. Once in the car, I asked Chad, "Do you think I'm pregnant?"

"Well, I told you to come on and let's make a pretty baby," Chad said. He seemed the least bit worried about me being pregnant. I hadn't even really missed a period. But I began to count the dates as we rode to my house.

"I haven't missed a period," I said.

"Well, Mom got this spidey sense. She always knows when a woman is pregnant. She knew my mama was pregnant, and she knew it was twins before my mama and the doctors knew," Chad said, taking his eyes off the road and glancing over at me.

"What are we gonna do?"

"We gonna have this pretty baby and be together," he said. "I'm not gonna leave you," he promised.

I never imagined that I'd be pregnant at sixteen. But who does? I guess I'd have to do what every other person who found themselves in the same predicament did—deal with it.

I don't think I got more than a couple hours of sleep that night. All I could think about was the church and being judged. Becoming a mother and having to grow up much faster than I imagined and having to deal with all the unforeseen experiences that came with the territory. I envisioned Chad and me getting married, having more children, and living our lives happily ever after. For some reason, however, I knew deep down inside that it was just a figment of my wild imagination. A hope. A wish. A fairytale.

Getting dressed for school the next morning, I looked at my naked body in the full-length mirror. I rubbed my hands over my flat stomach. I couldn't fathom that a living being was possibly growing inside. It seemed almost impossible. I felt the same. I didn't feel this thing called morning sickness that many women described. But what did I know? I was just a silly sixteen-year-old.

When I caught up to Keisha at school, it was the first thing I said to her. "I think I'm pregnant," I said.

"Did you miss your period?"

"No," I said emphatically.

Keisha chuckled. "Then you're not pregnant."

"No, I think I'm pregnant," I repeated.

"You have to miss a period."

"Well, Mom seems to think I'm pregnant."

"She told you you're pregnant?"

"Yes."

"Whoa … then you just might be," Keisha said, acquiescing. Apparently, she knew about Mom's unusual gift to detect pregnancy, even before the expecting mother knows.

"Well, what are you gonna do?" Keisha asked.

I hunched my shoulders. "I don't know." I didn't have a plan.

"Does Chad know?"

"Yeah, he was there when she said it."

"Well, then our children are gonna be cousins," Keisha said in a congratulatory tone. "You're gonna need to go to a doctor and get checked out."

"I know," I said. My head was beginning to spin. "Maybe—"

"Excuse me," an unnamed girl said as she approached Keisha and me and cut Keisha off mid-sentence.

"She's talking to you, Latwaina," Keisha said, pointing to me.

"Are you messing around with Chad?"

"Who, me?" I said, shocked by the question. "Why?" I said defensively.

"Because I wanna know."

"It ain't none of your business," Keisha said, butting in.

"Well, I'm pregnant by Chad, so *it is* my business!" the girl said, lifting her shirt to reveal a pudgy stomach.

"Well, seems like you have a problem, 'cause my girl, Latwaina, is Chad's girlfriend. His main girl. You might be pregnant with his baby … and that's *if* you're really pregnant by him.

"This is Chad's baby!" the girl screamed, pointing to her stomach.

"Look, I don't know who you are. I ain't never really seen you around here nor with Chad. Seems like you have a personal problem if you're pregnant by a dude that already got a girl. And he ain't leaving my girl, right here. You're just a jump off," Keisha said, grabbing me by the hand and pulling me away from the confrontation.

I swallowed hard as I followed Keisha. I couldn't help but think about the possibility of Chad having another girl pregnant. I couldn't wait to steal the chance to page him.

Keisha and I went straight to the girls' bathroom. She seemed unbothered by what had just transpired. Me? My heart stopped beating … figuratively, that is.

I burst into tears as soon as the bathroom door closed behind us.

"He's cheating on me," I sobbed.

"Stop crying, Latwaina," Keisha said, trying to console me. "You're his girlfriend. You're the girl he likes the most. You're his main girl. You gotta act like it. How do you think I've been able to deal with chicks coming up in my face, telling me that Brad is their baby daddy?"

"But he's been lying to me about not seeing other girls."

"All guys lie," Keisha said nonchalantly. Now, do you wanna go through this pregnancy by yourself or with the father of your child?" Keisha said, handing me handwipes to dry my eyes.

I pretended as though I bought into Keisha's mentality and the pseudo reality that she'd just proposed. The truth of the matter was that I couldn't stop the tears from flowing. I went to my language arts class, pretending the tears were representative of me not feeling well.

"Do you want to go to the nurse's office?" Mrs. Davis said, noticing the incessant tear wiping.

"No, I'll be okay," I lied. After class, I paged Chad. The code 9-1-1 meant that I wanted to leave school early. Within thirty minutes, Chad was pulling into the student parking lot where I was waiting. I made sure to walk to the back, so I wouldn't stand out to any of the security officers who often paroled the school grounds.

With a tear-stained face, I got into the passenger side of Chad's vehicle.

"What's wrong with you?" Chad said with an almost terrified look on his face.

My brain couldn't find the words to utter from my stammering lips.

"What's wrong, Latwaina? You're scaring me? What the heck is going on!?"

"A girl … a girl walked up to me today and said she's pregnant by you," I said between sobs.

"You're kidding, right?" Chad said, slamming on the breaks.

"No," I said, shaking my head.

"What does she look like?"

I forced myself to remember what the girl looked like, because in all actuality, I was focused on what came out of her mouth, not what she looked like. But then I remembered one faint detail about her face—the large mole under her right eye. "She had a mole under her eye," I said.

"Nadia. That's Nadia. Don't even worry about her. She sleeps around with everybody. For all I know, any dude in Michigan can be the father of that baby. It ain't mine," he said, letting his feet off the breaks and screeching out of the parking lot.

"Slow down, Chad! You're gonna kill us!" I yelled.

"Here," Chad said, pulling a handful of Dunkin Donut napkins from the middle console in the car.

I wiped my eyes again. This time, the flow of tears began to wane. In my heart of hearts, I didn't believe Chad. But for some reason, his lie was soothing. His so-called allegiance to me was like a drug, and I was an addict … an addict to Chad's lies, his half-commitment, and the fairytale life that we were living. In fact, it even got worse. The cheating was just as bad outside of school. Instead of girls walking up to me to tell me they were pregnant by Chad, I began to receive phone calls from girls telling me they had sex with Chad, they were pregnant by him, or they were his girlfriends. But even though I knew Chad was doing me wrong, I stayed with him. I convinced myself that I was staying with him for my unborn child. But I soon learned that I was only fooling myself. You can only run from reality but for so long. Sooner or later, reality catches up with you and forces you to reckon with it. That's exactly what happened to me.

I want to get him back … never see him again. Leave him high and dry. He doesn't deserve me or the pretty baby he made with me. These were my thoughts. I wanted to get Chad back for his betrayal. I wanted him to hurt like I was hurting. Feel betrayed like I felt.

"Are you gonna answer the question today or tomorrow?" Mr. Day said sarcastically. He'd been waiting for me to answer a question about humidity and vapor. But my mind was far away from science. I had more troubling things on my mind. Something was happening to me for sure. I believed I was pregnant by this time. Although I wasn't changing physically; I was morphing into a different person emotionally. And this person was dangerous.

I could hear students in the back of the class snicker at Mr. Taylor's sarcastic remark.

I picked up my thick science book and hurled it across the room. The clashing sound of the book hitting the wall produced a loud noise. "I don't know, and I don't care!" I shouted as I stood up and kicked the legs of my desk. I felt the rage erupting on the inside. All of it. I could see Nick's face. Chad's smiling but lying face. The police officers' faces as they hovered over my bruised and battered body. My family members' faces, staring at my private parts, inspecting the trauma Nick had inflicted upon it. Aunt Lisa's face, red with anger after Uncle Mike and Aunt Lisa had a falling out. Mama's face after Tyrone had beat on her … her face after she'd had a hefty dose of crack. Grandma Lily's face after she told me to "stay away for a while." It had been trapped inside of me and turned into a volcano now beginning to erupt, the hot lava oozing out.

I remember the look of astonishment on Mr. Taylor's face. He'd obviously never seen the "quiet girl" in such an uproar. I vaguely remember being led out of the classroom by two school counselors and walked to the nurse's office. Mrs. Favors was our school nurse at the all-girls school. She was empathetic and warm, always. And this day was no different.

"It's gonna be okay, Latwaina. You're just having a moment. It's normal. We all have them," she consoled. She paused. Then she continued. "Here," she said, handing me a small plastic cup. "I need a urine sample."

"I don't have to use the bathroom," I said, wiping my eyes with my bare hands.

"I'm gonna need you to force yourself to pee. Give me something in the cup."

I went into the bathroom and provided the urine sample as requested. I had already dealt with the possibility of being pregnant, so I was the least bit worried. After I handed Mrs. Favors the urine-filled plastic cup, she walked into a separate part of the office where I couldn't see exactly what she was doing. But after a few minutes, she returned and asked me to lie down on the bed.

After pressing on my stomach for a few moments, she nodded at the assistant nurse who stood close by.

"Latwaina, you're pregnant," she said. "Have you missed your period?"

"No," I said, shaking my head.

"Are you sure?" she asked quizzically.

"Yes," I said in a soft tone.

"Hmmm … Well, you're about three months pregnant. You're gonna need to get prenatal care right away, especially since you haven't missed your menstrual cycle at all. That's not normal," she said, shaking her head. She was stumped. But I wasn't. Nothing about my life up until that point had been normal. So, I guessed that a normal pregnancy would have been out of the norm for me anyway. No missed period. No morning sickness. No weight gain. No weird food cravings. No funny sleep patterns.

"Well, we're gonna make sure that you get the medical care you need so you can give birth to a beautiful, healthy baby," Mrs. Favors said. "I'm going to give you the information for Dr. Moore. He's a fantastic OB/GYN. He'll take good care of you and your baby," she added.

"Thank you," I said as I got off the small bed in the nurse's office. Mrs. Favors' words were comforting, but it still felt as though my world was crashing in on me.

Mrs. Favors pulled a card from one of the drawers and handed it to me.

"Thank you," I said, glancing down at the card.

"I'll be right back," Mrs. Favors said, excusing herself and walking out into the hallway.

I could hear muffled voices. And when Mrs. Favors walked back into her office, three men in uniform accompanied her, rolling a stretcher.

"These fine young men are going to take you to the hospital to get checked out."

"Checked out?" I said, looking at the card and then back at Mrs. Favors.

"Yes, we think it's best that you go get checked out at the hospital."

I was too emotionally drained to put up a fight. I knew I wasn't sick enough to need to be seen at the hospital, but I was too naïve to know what was *truly* going on. Without putting up a fight, I allowed the paramedics to help me onto the stretcher, roll me out of the school, and take me to Henry Ford Hospital.

People wearing white coats. Lots of them. They came and went. They poked and prodded on me. No one told me exactly what was going on. And by this time, my mother had been notified. She and Deacon Wil had come to the hospital.

"What's going on?" I finally mustered up the courage to ask.

Finally, a male doctor wearing the nametag Dr. Stew McDonald came in the room and stood in front of Mama and Deacon Wil. "Well, we've ran a battery of tests on you, and for the most part, they've all come back normal."

"Well, what do you mean, 'for the most part'?" Mama interjected, placing her hands on her hips.

The doctor paused before he responded. "Well, Mrs. Tyler, you're going to be a grandmother. Your daughter is about six months pregnant."

Six months?! I didn't have time to examine the expression on my mama's face, because I was dumbfounded. If I was six months pregnant like the doctor said I was, it meant that in just three short months, I was going to be a mother. This reality hit home in a different way.

CHAPTER 11

A Love Worth Living For

If not for myself, I knew I had to live for my unborn child. No matter what happened between Chad and me, I knew I was on the hook physically, emotionally, and financially. That's why Deacon Wil made the comment, "It's a mama's baby but a daddy's … maybe."

Chad came with me to my first outpatient doctor's appointment. They told me I'd be given an ultrasound. I could hardly sleep the night before. The thought of being able to get a glimpse of my baby had me beyond excited. Mama came with me to the appointment too.

A short, chubby, older nurse waving a chart in the air called my name. "Tyler … La-wain-nah?" she said, with full knowledge that she had botched up the pronunciation of my name. I stood, nonetheless. She wasn't the first person to totally mess up the pronunciation of my name. Chad and Mama stood too and followed me and the nurse to the back.

"How do you pronounce your name?" she asked, making small talk as we walked to Room 9.

"It's Latwaina … La-wan-nah. The 't' is silent," I said, smiling.

"Your chart says you're pregnant, but is that correct?" she said quizzically. "I mean, you don't look pregnant at all, let alone six months," she said, shaking her head.

"I looked the same way when I was pregnant with my son, Daniel," Mama said. She just had to mention her favorite child—Daniel.

"Maybe it runs in the genes. My mother always called it 'good genes,'" the nurse said, smiling as she opened the door to the exam room.

"I'm your nurse, Janet. I'll be taking your vitals and helping you get prepped before you see the doctor. You'll need to remove everything and put this on," she said, eyeing Chad. "Who's he?" she asked.

"I'm the father," Chad said boastfully. He was proud of his accomplishment of having gotten someone pregnant … several of us pregnant, according to the claim made by other girls. But I tried to keep my focus on me and my baby so I wouldn't end up having another emotional crisis … one that could possibly land me in a psych ward this time.

The doctor walked in. "I'm Doctor Preston," he said, extending his hand and peering over the top of his rimless spectacles. He was tall, dark, and handsome. His salt-and-pepper hair complemented his complexion nicely.

"Latwaina Tyler," I finally said, extending my hand.

"Chad Jackson," Chad said, firmly shaking Dr. Preston's hand.

"And I'm Latwaina's mother, Grace," Mama said, extending her hand.

"So now, let's see what we have going on with that little one in your stomach," Dr. Preston said as he slid on a pair of rubber gloves.

He pulled the curtain, separating us from Mama and Chad while he examined me. When he finished, he paused and just stared at me.

"Is something wrong?" I asked, getting a little concerned.

"Doesn't appear to be. Seems like your body is adjusting to the pregnancy well. Baby seems fine, but I'd like to perform the ultrasound as was scheduled.

I liked Dr. Preston almost immediately. He reminded me of my dad—caring, compassionate, and nonjudgmental. And it was just what I needed at this point in my life. When he adjusted the display correctly, I could see a tannish-brown figure moving around on the screen.

"Is that my baby?" I asked with wonder.

"Yes. That's your baby," Dr. Preston said, bringing the image into clearer focus.

"Is it a boy or girl?" Chad blurted out.

Dr. Preston looked up at me as if he were waiting for me to give him permission to answer Chad's question. I don't think he liked Chad. But I didn't want to focus on Chad and who did or didn't like him. I focused my attention back on the ultrasound screen to look at my baby. My own child.

Finally, I nodded, giving Dr. Preston the nonverbal go ahead.

"Well, let's see what we have here," he said, meticulously moving the device that looked like a computer mouse over my stomach. Then, a warm smile appeared on his face. "Congratulations. In three more months, you'll have a beautiful, bouncing baby girl.

A girl! I was having a girl. A little Latwaina. A precious, sweet angel of my own. I couldn't stop smiling. I even saw a wide smile spread across Mama's face. She seemed happy too. I guess we knew that we had to do what we had to do, and all would be well. And I decided right then and there that my daughter would be my reason to live. The thought of committing suicide would become a thing of the past. I had my daughter to live for.

It would only take a few more visits to discover just why Dr. Preston wasn't particularly fond of Chad. Dr. Preston shared his practice with another OB/GYN, and the nurse practitioners also saw patients. If the patients weren't high risk or didn't need an in-depth cervical examination, they were seen by a nurse practitioner. But when Dr. Preston entered my exam room with a concerned look on his face, my intuition let me know he didn't have good news.

"State law requires that we run a battery of tests on pregnant women and girls. Your test for chlamydia came back positive."

I swallowed hard, nearly choking on my saliva. "So … I have an STD?" I asked, even though I already knew the answer.

"Yes, it's an STD. And thank goodness it's something that is curable. I'm going to be very frank with you. You're not the only girl that's come to this practice claiming that same young man you brought here a few weeks ago is also the father of their unborn child. If you don't leave that young man alone, you're going to ultimately catch something that you can't get rid of … something that could possibly take your life. It's dangerous out there. You're too smart of a young lady to let that happen to yourself. That young man is spreading himself all over town. Your life is too precious to go to waste over sex."

Tears welled up in my eyes. Everything I knew in my heart of hearts about Chad was true. He was a serial cheater. None of the girls had lied about him getting them pregnant. The only liar was Chad. And as I sat there half-naked on that exam table, I made a vow to myself … that I was going to adhere to Dr. Preston's advice. I knew there was a possibility that I'd have to do some explaining to my daughter somewhere down the line, but my proposed course of action was truly a no brainer.

I confronted Chad almost immediately, paging him first with the 9-1-1 code. But just as I knew, Chad didn't fess up. He wasn't man enough to fess up. Instead, he started with his lies when I told him about the STD. But I was just as strong and adamant about leaving Chad alone, even though he threatened to walk out on me … on us—our baby and me.

"Well, if we can't be a family, then I don't want to be around," Chad said, pouting like the immature young man he was.

"We can't be a family because you keep cheating on me," I said, giving him the real, raw scoop.

"Whatever, Latwaina. But like I said. If we can't be a family, I'm out."

I was crushed, no doubt, but I had my daughter to live for, and all bets were off when it came to living for my daughter and being the best mother I could possibly be. As unfortunate as it was, I was used to being abandoned. My family had done it to me, so Chad was just one in the number as far as I was concerned.

Life went on. And in just three short months after finding out I was pregnant, I had my daughter, Anna. Since my birthday had recently passed, I was now a seventeen-year-old parent. After being discharged from the hospital, I brought Anna home to my mother's house, which soon became the house that she, Deacon Wil, and I all shared. This living arrangement was something that became problematic for me.

"You know that two queens can't live in the same castle," Mama said when we clashed one evening over me asking Deacon Wil for ten dollars.

"What do you need ten dollars for?"

"I want to buy something from the store," I said, defensively. Mama was getting welfare for Ebony, Anna, and me. And she rarely wanted to give me any money. I was walking around virtually broke, depending on her, Deacon Wil, my dad, and Rose to put a few dollars in my pockets. Since Chad had made his infamous vow on leaving us if he couldn't be with me, I couldn't get lint from him. Mama throwing her weight around made me furious.

"What? The baby got milk, food, clothes, a roof over her head, and you got everything you need as well."

"Never mind. Never mind!" I shouted across the room to Deacon Wil, who was caught in the middle. If Mama hadn't been in the house when I asked for the money, he would have given it to me without blinking an eye. Mama liked being in control. She loved when people had to beg her for things. The game was growing quite boring, and I'd had enough of it. I called my dad.

"Can you come get me and Anna?"

"It's almost nine o'clock, baby. Can you guys wait until tomorrow?"

"No, I gotta get out of here."

"What's going on over there?"

"Mama tripping like she always does. I gotta get outta here for a few days."

"All right, I'll come, but I'mma have to talk to your mama to see what's going on between you two."

I told you what's going on. Mama be trippin," I said as I stuffed a few things in a duffle bag, packed up Anna's diaper bag, including her food and formula, and prepared to leave the house for a few days.

I stayed in my room when the doorbell rang, since I knew my dad wanted to speak with my mom before hauling Anna and me off with him. I could faintly hear my mother denying the claim I'd made earlier that night.

"Who are you gonna believe, Sam? An adult or a kid who can't get her way? That's one thing I don't like about you. You always take her side!"

"Grace. Stop it. This ain't about taking sides. This is about how asking for ten dollars has caused me to come out of my house at nine o'clock at night."

"Give her the money then, Sam!" Mama screamed. "And take her spoiled butt with you!"

"I plan to," my dad said, which angered Mama even more.

"And don't bring her back."

"That's fine with me. But just know that if she stays with me, I'm stopping the child support."

"You can't do that, Sam!" Mama yelled. And that's when I emerged from my bedroom with the packed bags and Anna in tow.

"The car doors are open," my dad said. It was his way of letting me know that he wasn't finished talking with Mama.

I walked past Mama without looking at her. If looks could have killed, I would have died that night. I walked out of the house that night feeling empowered—I had beaten my mother at the game of domination.

I played this little game for a while. Whenever I didn't get my way in my mother's household, I ran to my dad's house. And whenever there was a rule there that I didn't want to follow, I ran back to my mother's house. This back and forth went on for quite some time. Trying to juggle motherhood as a single person was difficult, even though Mama and Deacon Wil tried to help me as best as they could as well as my dad and his girlfriend, Rose. I liked Rose and took to her as though she was really my stepmom. Although her and my dad were not married, Rose was a mature woman that sensed my insecurities and tried to fill in as a mother in ways that my biological mother did not. I trusted Rose.

Although I initially thought going back and forth between Mama's house and Daddy's house was good for my sanity, in hindsight, it wasn't. Without a doubt, my emotional and physical instability had a major effect on my sanity, and it affected my grades in school as well. I was falling behind. I hated school. I felt I wasn't as smart as the other kids, and I wanted to drop out. By the time I reached my eighteenth birthday, my mama didn't force me to go to school anymore. I dropped out. Even though I couldn't articulate my plan, I had one. I knew that I loved my daughter so much that I couldn't fail her. She had given me a reason to live, and I made a promise to her and myself that I wouldn't fail either one of us. My daughter had done her part—entered my life. That's all she was required to do. I can remember waking up to her kisses and warm embraces in the morning. She had filled the hole in my heart, and it was unmatched by anyone, except the love of Christ. It was time to woman up and do what I needed to do to take care of Anna and myself physically, emotionally, and financially. I had no other option.

Two Years Later

I worked a lot, trying to take care of Anna's needs. I was hired at Henry Ford Hospital. That's where I met my son's father, Eric. Eric and I had an unusual relationship. It ended almost as quickly as it started. All would have been well if I didn't miss my period. Unlike my pregnancy with Anna, where I didn't miss a period, I missed my period this go around, which was a clear indication something wasn't quite right. I didn't hesitate to go to the doctor's office for a pregnancy test, and that was when I learned that, indeed, I was pregnant. And this pregnancy changed the game.

No doubt, I thought about what it meant being a single mother of two. What it meant both to society and to the church. But the thought of having an abortion was out of the question. When Michael was born, I fell in love all over again. A son to call my own. My experience with Chad taught me that a baby doesn't get a man and neither does it keep him. That said, Eric and I came to the realization that we were just going to be co-parents. There were no sparks in our relationship. But one thing we both had for one another was mutual respect. As the mother of his child, Eric treated me with love and respect, and as the father of my child, I treated Eric with the utmost respect. Together, we co-parented, putting the needs of our son, Michael, before ours and any feelings of indifference.

CHAPTER 12

Gone Too Soon

Things were looking up in my life, and I was finally ready to move out on my own, just me and my children. I approached Sister Deborah one Sunday after church, inquiring about renting a house or property of some sort. What Sister Deborah said to me in the parking lot that Sunday changed my life forever.

"Why would you want to rent when you can buy your own house? You do have a job, don't you?"

"Yes," I answered, albeit hesitantly.

"Well, like I said … if you can rent, then you can buy.

"But I don't know how to buy a house," I responded.

"I will show you," Sister Deborah said, smiling.

Sister Deborah took me by the hand and successfully led me through the homebuying process. I was just twenty-one years old, but I was undertaking an endeavor that single, young people rarely undertake.

I worked as hard as I could, trying to keep up with paying my bills on time so my credit wouldn't suffer. I also needed to save up money for my down payment and closing costs. Nothing about the homebuying process was seamless. Buying a home is a monumental endeavor that should not be taken lightly.

I shared the good news with my family about being in the process of buying a home, but if I expected them to be excited for me, I was a fool. They thought I was getting into something too deep.

"Are you sure you're ready for this?" my mother asked.

"Yes," I said. By this time, I needed to prove to myself that I could accomplish the task.

I was convinced that Michael was going to pursue journalism as a career because he had a peculiar desire of wanting to watch the news. As if he had an internal clock, he'd come into the living room to watch the news. And like any other normal day, on New Year's afternoon, I turned the channel to the news channel for him.

I was preoccupied, reading some emails on my laptop, but I could faintly hear the news reporter reporting the story of a tragic car accident that had occurred in the early hours of New Year's morning. *That poor man barely made it into the new year*, I remember thinking as I watched the white sheet they placed over his lifeless body become increasingly drenched in the victim's blood. I knew I didn't know the man, but I felt an eerie feeling in the pit of my stomach as I watched the broad-cast of the tragic story.

Before the broadcast could end, my cell phone rang. It was Aaron, Rose's son. I called Aaron my bonus brother. I was closer to him than I was my own brother.

"Latwaina …"

He didn't have to say anything further. I could hear it in his voice. Knots formed in the bottom of my belly. I fought back the tears. "Is it my daddy?" I finally mustered the courage to ask.

Aaron didn't readily answer.

"Is it my daddy?" I repeated.

"Yes. He was killed in a car accident."

I looked back up at the television. The body beneath the blood-drenched sheet was my daddy! "Nooo!" I screamed. I slid off the sofa onto the floor. The television was so loud that it drowned out my voice. Mama and Deacon Wil didn't hear me. But when I had composed myself somewhat, I managed to stumble into their room. I could barely knock on the door.

"Come in," Mama said, having heard the faint knock.

When I opened their bedroom door, I just collapsed onto the floor. Mama and Deacon Wil both jumped up and ran over to me.

"What's the matter?!"

I could barely utter a word. "My … my …"

"Something the matter with one of the kids?" Mama asked as she bent over, reaching her arms out.

"My daddy. My daddy!" I screamed. "My daddy is dead. My daddy is dead!" I yelled out. Deacon Wil lifted me up, and he and Mama helped me over to the bench at the foot of their bed.

"What happened?" Mama asked.

"He's dead … he's just dead. Car accident. He got killed in a car accident," I said, sobbing uncontrollably.

I don't think I got an ounce of sleep that night. I tossed and turned, thinking about how the trajectory of my life might change. My greatest hero had succumbed to a tragedy. No one had my best interest at heart like my dad did.

In the days that followed, I had to mentally prepare myself to say goodbye to my dad. But I felt zombie-ish, if that's even a word. I felt as though I was just getting through the day without a great sense of purpose. Without my children to help me remain somewhat occupied, I would have probably sunk into a deep depression. The loss was one thing, but feeling disconnected from my family on my dad's side was altogether another.

As the cab pulled up to the church, I took a deep breath. I could see the top of the hearse a few cars ahead … a reminder that a funeral service was getting ready to take place and not just some regular church service.

A tall, slender older gentleman approached the cab and opened the door for me. "Are you with the family?" he asked.

"Yes, I'm his daughter," I said, prepared to exit the cab.

The older gentleman helped me out of the cab and escorted me into the vestibule of the church where the family waited.

"You made it," Rose said as she approached me.

"Yeah," I said, realizing the reality of Rose's statement. Because she and my dad had never married, she was robbed out of the right to handle my father's burial arrangements.

Instead, his next of kin, my older brother, Darius, and older sister, Chantel, handled the arrangements.

"Did you get a program?" Rose asked as she held hers up and sucked her teeth.

"No," I said, looking around for one.

"Here," she said, handing me her program.

I took the program and flipped through its pages. When I finished, I looked up at Rose and managed a half-smile.

"You don't have to pretend," Rose said, sucking her teeth once again.

The bow finally broke ... due to the mistreatment I'd received from Mama, Nick, Grandma Lily, Aunt Lisa, Uncle Mike, and my now, those on my dad's side of the family. Yes, my name was mentioned in the obituary, but I had no input on funeral arrangements for my dad. And while they were all wearing blue and white, my dad's favorite colors, I was dressed in black, not because I didn't own any clothes of those colors but because no one volunteered to share they'd be color coordinating for the funeral. Tears began to flow down my cheeks incessantly.

"I'm so sorry," Rose apologized. I assumed she was apologizing on behalf of my brother and sister, mainly.

"It's okay," I lied. I wanted to collapse. The pressure of it all gave me an instant headache. "I'm so sorry they did this to you," Rose said, reaching for a Kleenex to give to me.

Before I couldn't say anything else, the funeral director ordered us all to line up so the processional could begin. And that's when it really dawned on me. I was there to say goodbye to my dad ... forever.

Seeing my father's body lowered into the ground was the most difficult thing I had to endure in my life. I felt empty, almost deserted ... as though a piece of my heart had been cut out and removed from my chest cavity. But I have to say that God allowed me to discover an awesome healing process. Whenever I missed my daddy, I would do the joyful things that he loved doing while he was still living. One of the songs he'd often sing was, "Precious Lord Take My Hand" while he was gardening or taking long walks. To feel close to him again, I picked up his hobbies and habits. When taking long walks to clear my mind, I'd sing his favorite song. I also started cooking his favorite meals, which included corned beef, collard greens with hot peppers, pig feet, and hog head cheese, which he made from scratch. I even started planting flowers as a hobby, which was something else my dad loved to do.

Soon after Daddy's burial, I received the keys to my new, three-bedroom home on my twenty-first birthday. It was the best birthday present ever! And the Lord's blessings didn't stop there. The previous owner had left all three beds in excellent condition in the house, along with comforters and pillows. All I had to do was move in and buy a stove, refrigerator, washer, and dryer.

Rose and I stayed close even after my daddy died. She continued to play a significant role in my life. By this time, I started calling her Mama Rose. As a housewarming gift, Mama Rose bought me a full dining room set. She made sure she stayed in my children's lives. And if I ever needed anything, I knew who I could call.

The hole in my heart due to my dad's passing left me longing for the love of a man once again. A wounded soul is a danger to itself. And unfortunately, I would learn this lesson the hard way.

CHAPTER 13

Money Still Can't Buy Love

They say that God gives you double for your trouble, and I am a living witness to the sentiment. Picking up the pieces and trying to move past the loss of my dad required keeping busy. I applied for a teacher's aide position at Anna and Michael's elementary school. And to earn extra money, I ran a daycare in my home. The dual income allowed me to take care of my children, myself, and our home without utilizing social services. When things became hectic, Rose, whom I considered my bonus mom, would help me out by babysitting Anna and Michael for me. As you can imagine, because of what happened to me in my youth, I was an overprotective parent. There weren't too many people who I trusted with the lives of my children. Outside of their fathers and select people on their dad's side of the family, few people saw my children outside of my presence.

Because of the fun daycare atmosphere in our home, many of the neighborhood children gathered at my house. Although I wasn't permitted at family functions at other relatives' homes, I didn't forbid my extended family from visiting mine. As a matter of fact, I made it a mission to create a warm and inviting atmosphere in my home. I wanted anyone who walked through my front doors to feel welcome and loved, of course.

"There's an opening at my school," my friend Candace said to me, handing me a flyer.

"Oh, really?" I said, taking the flyer from her and scanning it over.

"It's for the afternoon program, if you don't mind working late in the afternoon. I know you have the kids and all, but it's a good way to earn extra money."

I didn't have to think long and hard about the opportunity. I was gung ho for anything promoting my independence, especially financial independence. Once I accepted the job, I went in head first. Because of the experience I had running my own daycare, it made the work at the afterschool program easy. If someone asked me to complete a task, I did it fast and efficiently. I was proud of the work I was doing, especially since I was working with children, something that was a hidden passion until I started my in-home daycare.

A lady by the name of Maxine Channing was the executive director of the afterschool program. Her raspy voice could be heard a mile away as it traveled through the halls and corridors of the building. I thought we were pretty cool, until she began making snide remarks about my accomplishments.

"I don't care how many accolades you get around here, my job is already filled," she said one Friday afternoon after our quarterly meeting had ended.

"Excuse me?" I said with raised eyebrows. I wanted to be certain I heard her correctly.

"You heard me. I ain't going nowhere, so you can stop doing what you're doing to get noticed around here," she said as she flung her oversized purse over her shoulder.

"I think you have things twisted, Maxine. I'm not after your job. I do things with excellence because that's who I am," I said, looking her directly in the eye.

"Hmmph," she remarked before strutting off.

As I drove home that day, I rehearsed the events that had unfolded just moments earlier. *I don't have to deal with this*, I thought. If my past didn't teach me anything else, it did teach me what not being appreciated looked and felt like. That evening, I typed up my resignation letter.

A couple of weeks later, I returned to the afterschool program to pick up my check. I headed straight to the check cashing center, which was next to a truck loading and unloading area. Somehow, and unfortunately, a few boxes fell off one of the trucks and landed on me, causing me to fall and sustain injuries to my head and back. It was this fall at the Joe Rock Check Cashing store that set off a chain of events that would invite both friends and foes into my life.

I won a lawsuit for a sizeable sum of money. I had been paying my tithes and offerings in church all along the way, so it was quite natural for me to pay my tithes on the proceeds from the lawsuit as well. Thus, when I'd healed up well enough to return to church, I did. Paying thousands of dollars in tithes was equivalent to the opening bell ringing at the New York Stock Exchange.

"Let me help you," he said, holding the door open for me.

"Thank you," I said, releasing the door handling.

"You're pretty new around here, aren't you?" he said, smiling and revealing his pearly set of white teeth.

"No, I'm not new. I was injured and just started coming back to church a few weeks ago," I said, pointing to my neck brace.

"Oh, I see," he said, walking alongside me as I made my way through the vestibule area.

I smiled. He was good looking.

"What's your name?"

"Latwaina," I said, smiling.

"La … who?"

"Latwaina. It's pronounced, La – wanna."

"Oh, that's a nice name. It's a beautiful name, actually. You know … a beautiful name for a beautiful gal."

I blushed.

"I'm Jamel, by the way," he said, holding out his hand.

"Hi, Jamel," I said.

"You got a man?" he asked as he looked around cautiously.

"Who wants to know?" I said, flirting back, because he was obviously getting his flirt on with me right in the church vestibule.

"Me. I want to know."

"Why?"

"'Cause maybe I might be interested."

"Interested in what?"

"Taking you out." I blushed again. This Jamel guy was going hard for me. "Can I have your number?" he continued.

Before I could reach in my purse and grab a piece of paper and a pen, he had reached in his jacket pocket and took a pen and piece of paper out.

"Here. Write your number down," he said, handing me the pen and paper.

"You gonna call?" I said, handing him the pen and paper back after I'd written my number down.

"Heck yeah … I mean, of course," he said, winking.

"So you're just gonna curse all up in the church, huh?" I said, teasing him.

"I didn't curse … well, not really," he said, as he opened the glass-stained door that led to the sanctuary.

Jamel helped me to my seat. "I'mma call you," he said, winking before he walked away.

I couldn't get into the service that Sunday. My mind was consumed with the good-looking brother named Jamel. There was something alluring about him.

After service, we bumped into one another again.

"Well, well, well … Either one of us is stalking the other or it's just fate." We both chuckled.

"I can assure you that I'm not stalking you," I said.

"Then it's fate."

"I can get with that," I said.

"Wanna go grab something to eat?" he offered.

"Hmmm … I'm still healing up. I don't go out all that much. I'm much more comfortable hanging out at home. I usually cook on Sundays, anyway. Why don't you come over and have dinner at my place?" I suggested.

"I … I can't. I can't have you cooking dinner, not when you just said you're still trying to heal."

"Honestly, Jamel, while I'm in the middle of being fully restored, it's more comfortable for me to be at home most of the time," I said, reiterating my stance of not wanting to go out to eat.

"Okay. Yes. That makes sense. How about I'll grab us something from the soul food takeout joint and bring it by?" Jamel offered.

"That sounds perfect," I replied.

I gave Jamel my address, and we went our separate ways, planning to meet up about an hour or so later.

Over our meals, we both asked the typical questions people ask when they're getting to know one another: "How old are you?" "When is your birthday?" "How many siblings do you have?" "Where were you born?" "What's your favorite food?" "What are your hobbies?" etcetera, etcetera … until silence crept in.

"What's on your mind?" I asked.

"Nothing … just thinking," Jamel said, looking me over.

"A penny for your thoughts," I said, trying to persuade him to reveal his thoughts.

"Seems like you have quite a few pennies. Your place is beautiful. Is this your house?"

"Yes. It's my house," I said proudly.

"You're quite young to be a homeowner."

"I was blessed to meet a realtor who told me to dream bigger than renting an apartment. She took me by the hand and showed me the steps to being a homeowner."

"Yeah, but this place is immaculately decorated," Jamel said, adoring the interior design.

"Well, I also came into some money when I got injured. So I was able to redecorate my entire home," I confessed. Although my house was decorated nicely before I came into the lawsuit proceeds, the new décor was a little richer in style.

"I bet it's difficult to drive wearing that neck brace," Jamel said.

"Yeah," I said, nodding.

"Well, I don't mind running errands for you, like if you need me to go shopping or something. You and your kids shouldn't have to worry about anything. If you need anything, just let me know," he said.

"Thank you; that's so nice of you," I said. I felt I had struck gold.

"Of course. That's what good church folks are supposed to be for. Plus, I would love to see that beautiful smile of yours more often."

A warm smile plastered across my face. The fact that he was well respected in the church and said he loved the Lord was a bonus.

Jamel did exactly what he offered to do. Before long, he was running errands for me. Of course, this caused us to spend quite a bit of time together. Our plutonic relationship quickly evolved into a hot, steamy sexual relationship. Jamel was what I called "over experienced." His bedroom game was beyond on point. But he wasn't just over experienced when it came to his sexual performance, he was over experienced when it came to running head game—mind games, that is.

"Hey," he said as he walked in the front door, barely making eye contact.

"Hey, babe," I said, happy to see him. Jamel sat down on the sofa. He wasn't his normal giddy self. "So," I inquired. "What's wrong?"

"Ahh … nothing," he said, fidgeting with his fingers.

"You can tell me anything. What's wrong?" I said, sitting down on the sofa next to him.

"My check was short this week. But I don't want to bother you with it."

"Do you need money to cover a bill or anything?" I said, unconsciously volunteering to come to his aid.

"Yeah, for my electric bill."

"How much do you need?"

"A couple of hundred," he said, lowering his head.

"Well, I don't keep that kind of cash in my house. I can get it out the bank and give it to you."

"I gotta bring it to them as soon as they open."

Knowing there was no way I could get the kids to school and the money to him by eight o'clock the next morning, which was the time the power company opened, I went into my bedroom and took my debit card out of my wallet. Against all conventional wisdom, I gave Jamel my debit card.

"Thanks, babe. I swear, I'm gonna pay you this money back as soon as I get my next check," Jamel promised.

"Don't worry about it. You've been helping me out with running errands. I got you."

I was overly generous with the money I received from the lawsuit. Jamel wasn't the only one that I gave money to, so I didn't flinch one bit at giving him my debit card. But unfortunately for me, this set a precedent in the relationship between Jamel and me, if a relationship is what you want to call it. In the weeks and months that followed, Jamel had my debit card in his possession more than I had it in mine. On the outside looking in, I was the poster girl for stupidity. But on the inside looking in, I wanted love, and I was willing to pay for it at any cost.

I finally saw Jamel for who and what he really was when I saw him pull up to the church parking lot in a brand new 2006 Monte Carlo. The faint shadow of what seemed to be another person sitting beside him in the front passenger seat sent my heart into tachycardia. I stopped in my tracks and waited for him to park. The driver side door opened, and Jamel emerged and walked over to the other side of the door and opened it. Out popped long legs in heels. I squinted my eyes to get a clearer view but could not make out the face of the woman, not until they began to walk toward the front of the church. As they got closer, not only did I recognize the face, but I also knew the name. It was Melissa. Melissa Newton, the granddaughter of one of the lead mothers in the church. I walked over to the center of the walkway, making sure they'd have to pass me to get in the church. After making eye contact with me, Jamel smirked as he squeezed Melissa's hand. When they were within earshot, I confronted Jamel.

"Is there something funny?" I said, referring to the smirk he still had on his face.

"What are you talking about?" he said, trying to act oblivious.

"Why are you smirking?" I accused.

"Who's smirking?"

"You and this scraggily looking chick you have beside you," I said, pointing at Melissa, who, by this time, could sense what was happening.

"Ain't nobody scraggily over here," she said, fanning her hand at me.

Melissa was no prize as far as facial features were concerned. But one thing she had was an amazing body—the perfect waistline, bust size, hips, and long legs. You know, the perfect body type seen in pageants. Yeah, that was Melissa.

I tried to take my focus off her and direct it back toward Jamel. Afterall, Jamel was the one who had conned me out of my money. Looking back at Jamel, I confronted him again. "So, is that what you really did with all the money you so called needed to borrow … buy yourself a car?"

"I have a job, Latwaina," Jamel said, trying to walk around me.

"Obviously, you don't because you ask to borrow money from me like it's going out of style," I said, getting in his face.

"Latwainna, please don't do this here. I don't want to have to embarrass you. Now, me and my girl tryna get in the church. Can you leave us alone!" Jamel said in a stern voice. He was both angry and embarrassed at the same time.

I moved out of their way, getting the sense that it could get physical at any moment. I stood back and watched Jamel escort Melissa into the church, watching her hips sashay down the walkway and her long legs climb the five steps leading to the church vestibule.

"Don't cry, baby," a voice from behind consoled.

I closed my eyes, trying to fight back the tears. Searching for love had once again landed me in a vulnerable position, wounded and probably broke.

"He's no good. He's my baby boy, but he ain't no good. You need to leave him alone. You're too good for him," the soft voice uttered. It was Sister Shelby, Jamel's mother.

"He lied to me," I said, nearly folding into her arms.

"That's all right. He's gonna pay for his dirty deeds. But you get yourself together out here. Don't you ever let no man see you lose your cool over him … especially one that doesn't deserve you in the first place."

In theory, Sister Shelby was one hundred percent correct. But in reality, my heart was bruised and bleeding, and her words did nothing to soothe my heartache. I forced a smile.

"Here," she said, handing me tissue she'd grabbed from the pocket of her bible cover.

"Thank you," I said, wiping the tears that began cascading down my cheeks.

Sister Shelby waited until I finished. "Come on, baby. Let's go on in here and praise the Lord," she said, grabbing me by my hand.

I was anxious during the entire church service. Jamel. Melissa. My money. The car. My debit card. The excuses. And down to the lovemaking. It was the lovemaking that always made me fold. Our lovemaking was explosive. I think I was more in love with Jamel's bedroom game than anything else. Don't get me wrong, he was extremely good looking, but his true personality was trash. He had me fooled when he pretended to care about me and my children. I couldn't believe how cold he was toward me that day. But like Sister Shelby said, I deserved better. Somehow, I was going to have to make peace with myself about the poor judgment I had and move on … but not before getting down to the bottom of it.

The next morning, I jumped out of bed, brushed my teeth, took a quick five-minute shower, threw on a pair of denim shorts and a t-shirt, splashed on a little Lancome's Beautiful perfume, and headed out. I was enroute to the bank to check my bank account. You could almost guarantee long lines and long wait times on Mondays. But to my surprise, I didn't have to wait as long as I had anticipated.

"Ms. Tyler," the bank lobby rep said, looking in my direction.

I held up my hand.

"Mrs. Oliver is ready to see you. She's in the third office, the one with the pink balloons on the door," the petite rep said, pointing to the office door.

I stood and walked over to the representative's office as directed. A very pregnant woman sat behind her office desk, leaning back in her chair. "How can I help you?"

"I want to check my account," I said as I took a seat on the opposite side of the desk.

"Sure. What is it you want to check?" she said, leaning forward.

"How much I have in it."

"You mean your balance?"

"Yes. My balance."

"I can help you with that. Do you have any ID on you?"

"Yes, I do," I said, fiddling through my purse to locate my wallet. When I found it, I took out my driver's license and ATM card and handed them to the representative.

"Thank you," she said, taking them from me.

I tried to focus my attention on the clock on the wall as I listened to the click-clacking sound of her nails tapping the computer keyboard. Suddenly, the click-clacking noise stopped. I turned my head toward her. She was staring at the computer monitor, her eyes not blinking. Then the click-clacking resumed … then paused. Once again, the rep focused her attention on the screen. Finally, she looked at me. "Ms. Tyler, is there any particular reason you wanted to check your balance?"

"I just want to know how much money I have in it," I lied.

"According to what I see here, you have twelve dollars and eighty-two cents," she said, turning the monitor around for me to see.

I leaned over and my eyes ballooned. I nearly fell completely out of the chair when I saw the balance. Just as she'd indicated, I only had twelve dollars and eight-two cents in my account. "Something's wrong," I said as I wiped the sweat from my forehead.

"Are you saying you haven't made all of these withdrawals?" she said, pointing at the transactions on the screen.

"No," I said emphatically. "I've barely bought anything for myself. I had over eighty thousand dollars in my account! How can I only have twelve dollars in it now?!" I said, standing. "Can somebody take money out of my account?"

"No … not if they come into a branch. They need identification before we will let anyone withdraw money. Now, with an ATM card, it's a different story. Have you ever given your

ATM card to anyone?" the rep said, turning the monitor back to face her.

I wanted to lie. But I was too shocked to even think straight. I nodded, confessing my mistake in judgment.

"I'm afraid you might not be able to get your money back. When you sign up for an account with us, you agree not to give out your ATM or PIN. In order for anyone to withdraw money using the ATM card, they have to know your PIN," she said, shaking her head. I bet she was calling me all sorts of dummies in her head. To her, I probably was dumb; to me, I was just naïve.

"I've been suffering from bad head and back injuries, so I gave my boyfriend my card when I needed him to run errands for me."

The bank rep cleared her voice. "There's hundreds of dollars taken out of this account … some on the same day and others, only days apart. There's no amount of errands or bills that requires this many withdrawals. I think I know what happened. Ms. Tyler, let me give you some good advice; when it comes to *your* money, don't trust anyone. It's clear you've been taken advantage of here. Now, what about these in-person withdrawals?"

"What about them?"

"Did you make all of them?" she said, turning the monitor back around.

"No, ma'am," I said after skimming the transactions on the computer screen.

"Are you sure?"

"Yes, ma'am, I'm sure. I barely come in the bank. I haven't really bought anything beside a little furniture for my house and bikes for my children."

She shook her head in disbelief. "Ms. Tyler, I don't think we can do anything about these withdrawals. They appear to be withdrawn by you. We have a strict policy in the bank. Customers must show legal identification in order to make withdrawals."

"I swear I didn't make all these withdrawals. Isn't there anything we can do to get my money back?"

"I really don't think so. The fact that you've waited so long … more than ninety days, makes it appear as though everything looked all right on your end. We send statements out every thirty days. You have been getting them, haven't you?"

I just nodded. I knew I wasn't going to get anywhere with the representative. All she saw was a naïve, black girl sitting in front of her, trying to get her money back after she'd been milked dry by a manipulating liar that she called her boyfriend. She'd obviously seen the scenario before. As I sat there watching her type away on her keyboard, obviously making notes about our conversation, that's when it dawned on me. Brother Jason from the church worked at the bank. He knew the family well, and I wouldn't have put it past him to allow my family members to withdraw money out of my account. Heck, they probably even gave him a cut!

Finally, when she was done clicking away on the keyboard, she looked over at me. "Is there anything else I can help you with?"

"No," I said stoically.

Handing me back my driver's license and ATM card, she said, "Well, I'm sorry about what happened to you. But the best advice I can give you is to guard your heart and your money too."

"Thank you," I said, standing.

"If there's anything else you can think of, give us a call," she said, handing me her business card with an accompanying "poor little girl" look on her face. No doubt, I looked like one of those silly girls to her … foolishly in love with a fool.

I drove home in complete silence. No radio. No audible talking to myself. From eighty-thousand dollars to twelve dollars and eight-two cents. I was broke … again. I felt empty. I learned that Jamel wasn't the only one that stole my money. Mrs. Oliver was probably right. Someone in my family knew someone at that bank, and together, they colluded to rob me blind. It was just me and my kids again. I vowed not to ever make that mistake again … at least not consciously.

CHAPTER 14

From Bad to Worse

Empty. That's how I felt when I walked out of the bank that day. Empty. I thought about the loss all the way home. But I had to admit there were signs all along. I had been played, as they say. But doing anything physically harmful to Jamel would never bring my thousands of dollars back, although it might have given me some sense of satisfaction. Truth be told, I don't believe Jamel was the only one that stole money from me. But what did it matter now? My money was gone, and all I had to show for it was new furniture, a few clothes, and bikes for my children.

I tossed and turned all night long. I sat up and flipped my pillow on the opposite side; the wetness of the pillowcase on my cheek was growing cold. I began rehearsing all the lying lines Jamel gave me. Short on his check. Short on his electric bill. Short on his rent. Short on everything. And I fell for it all … hook, line, and sinker. I knew I would never see the money again, but I wasn't going to remain silent. I made up my mind that I was going to confront Jamel.

The next day, I pretended as if nothing had ever happened between us. That it was no biggie that I saw him driving a brand-new car that he'd bought with the money he stole from me. I inhaled deeply before I pressed the final digit of his phone number. He didn't pick up. I called back. It rang six times before he finally picked up.

"Yeah," he said nonchalantly.

"Yeah?" I said inquisitively.

"Yeah … what do you want?"

"I wanna talk; that's what I want."

"About what?"

"You know what about," I charged.

"No, I don't," he said in a stern tone.

"Well, I'm just gonna cut to the chase."

"Please do," he sarcastically retorted.

"I went to the bank today, and—"

"And?" he said, cutting me off.

"Can I finish my sentence?"

"Look, I already know where you're going. So let *me* just cut to the chase. What you and I had was good while it lasted. It was what it was, but it's over now. I've moved on."

"Me and you and you moving on has nothing to do with the fact that my account is on E, when there was eighty-thousand dollars in there three months ago."

"So, what you saying? I got you for some dough?"

"Come on, Jamel. Be for real. How are you driving a brand-new car?"

"I work."

"Barely. You don't make that kind of money! A brand-new car?"

"You gave me your card, didn't you? You said I could get money when I needed it, didn't you?"

"Yeah, I did. But I never thought you'd rob me blind!" I shouted.

"Look, like I said, I didn't take you for money. You knew what time it was. I helped you out when you were down. Just think of it as repayment. I scratched your back, and you scratched mine. Now, we're even."

"We ain't even. I went to the bank today, and they're starting an investigation!" I lied. The bank rep had already advised that I had little to no recourse because I had given Jamel my ATM card and my PIN. But I wanted to call his bluff … see him sweat a little.

"They can't do anything. I'll just tell them you gave me your card and PIN," Jamel said, chuckling.

"That's what you think," I said, wiping the tears that began to slowly glide down my cheeks.

"Look, Latwaina, like I said, I'm kinda busy right now, hanging with my girl. It was good while it lasted, including the sex. But I've moved on. The only thing you can do for me now is go get me some more money, okay? Check me when you do," Jamel said before hanging the phone up in my face.

It was a hard lesson for me. But I had to lift my head, pick my heart up off the ground, and keep pressing. Thankfully, however, favor was resting on my heels, even in the mist of the hurt and pain from being financially exploited.

That fall, after hearing how well I'd been doing as a teacher's assistant, the principal of Anna's middle school, Ms. Joy, approached me with a proposition I couldn't refuse.

"Hey, Ms. Tyler, one last thing. I've heard about how well you were over at the elementary school."

"Did you?" I said, surprised by the comment.

"Absolutely. Bad news is not the only thing that travels fast. Every once in a while, good news travels fast too," she said, smiling.

"You're right about that," I said, trying to muster up some excitement in my voice. I was still down about the money but trying to push past it.

"Well, we have an open position here at the school, and if you want it, you can have it."

"What's the position title?"

"Office assistant. You'd be my personal assistant."

My heart leaped. I needed the job. I had to replace some of that money and get back on my feet.

"Are you interested?" she continued.

"Absolutely," I said.

"I'll have Nancy, the HR person, reach out to you and give you all the particulars. But just to give you a heads up, the salary should be somewhere in the ballpark of thirty-two thousand dollars."

I wanted to run around the block. Thirty-two thousand was a significant increase and a much needed one at that. I didn't have anyone else to depend on. Daddy was deceased, and my family was shattered into a million pieces. All my children and I really had was each other.

Because of my consistent hard work, I was able to buy myself a brand new, fresh-off-the-line 2008 Toyota Corolla. I was now bringing in enough money and saved up a small nest egg, which allowed me to stop doing daycare in my home. Besides, most of the children I cared for had become too old for babysitters. They were young adolescents and teens.

I was excelling in life. If you would have had to give me a grade, I would say it was A+. According to my self-inventory, I was doing well. House? Check. Car? Check. Beautiful, well-behaved children? Check. Decent income? Check. Food in the refrigerator? Check. *I'm not doing too bad*, I thought.

Before long, I had forgotten all about being taken for tens of thousands of dollars by Jamel and whomever else. In my mind, I had received double for the trouble I endured. But I have to admit, as I prospered, my ego got out of hand. I developed an "I got this, God," disposition. And it wouldn't be too long before God, once again, reminded me that I wasn't Superwoman, Supermomma, or Superdaddy. I was Latwaina—His child. I had to learn that there is absolute truth in Proverbs 16:18—"Pride goes before destruction, and a haughty spirit before a fall."

Your life can change, for better or worse, in the twinkling of an eye. Just when things were going well and I was flying high, I received a call that most employees dread.

"Hello," I said in an excited tone, having recognized the phone number on the caller ID.

"Hi, Latwaina. This is Ms. Joy."

"Yes," I said, expecting her to share some generic information related to a change in her day's routine, which happened often.

"Hey, how are you?"

"I'm doing well," I replied.

"Well, umm … I … ahh … I don't really know how to say this."

"Say what?" I asked, rubbing my right hand against my high.

"Well, there's been some changes to the school budget I need to discuss with you."

"What kind of changes?" I asked.

"Let me be frank with you, Latwaina. The school district cut a third of our budget. We will be combining classes and laying off staff. This has nothing to do with performance, as I just said; it's all financial."

I didn't readily respond.

"Are you there?"

"Yes, I'm here."

"Did you understand what I just shared with you?"

"I did. So how does this affect me? Am I being laid off?"

"Please know that I love having you as my office assistant, but the budget just doesn't allow for it. I've thought it through, and what I *can* do is place you in the cafeteria as a lunch aid. We have two school lunches, so that should give you about three hours a day."

"So that's about fifteen hours a week," I responded, as if to let her know I could do the math, and it wasn't adding up … not as far as my needs were concerned.

"Yes. Unfortunately, you will lose over half of your hours. And …" She paused before continuing. "The pay rate is minimum wage, so your pay rate will be cut by half as well. I'm so sorry to have to deliver this news to you, Latwaina," Ms. Joy said, offering her regrets

I could hear the sincerity in her voice, but it did my plight no good.

I calculated the new salary in my head. Minimum wage was seven dollars and twenty-five cents an hour. At fifteen hours, it equaled almost one-hundred and nine dollars per week, before taxes. I knew me and my children couldn't live off that salary. There was no sense in trying to beg or plead with Ms. Joy; she'd already told me what she could do for me. Sadly, it wasn't enough.

"Let me know what you decide. I know the salary isn't much, but it's something."

When I didn't respond, she continued. "Just let me know what you decide."

"I will," I said.

The clicking sound of the call ending sounded like a thunderous storm in the sky.

"What am I going to do?" I said aloud. I knew that losing my principal source of income could have a domino effect.

By this time, I had been a homeowner for nearly twelve years. My home with my children was my pride and joy. I couldn't imagine where we'd live if I lost the house. But something on the inside kept nudging me ... that voice saying, "Let it go."

My house? No, not my house, God. I worked too hard to get it. And the harder I tried to hold on to it, the more difficult it became to do so. There was just no calculating the very near future. With more bills than money coming in the house, it didn't take long for the delinquency letters to start rolling in. Past due notices piled up on the dining room table, which was where I'd toss them out of frustration, knowing I couldn't pay them. This included the mortgage as well.

Without knowing that I had options, such as calling the bank and requesting a forbearance or a modification, I couldn't act on any of them. Eventually, the sheriff delivered the final notice to vacate. I had less than forty-eight hours to move all our belongings out of the house. But where? Where was I going to get the money to move? Where was I going to move to? If I moved into someone's house, where would I put my furniture? And most importantly, who was I going to call?

I packed what I could of our belongings and put them in my car. As a final resort, I called my mother and explained the situation. The silence on the other end was deafening. Finally, I asked again. "So … can I?"

"Umm … I don't think that's a good idea. It's quiet over here. I don't think I want all y'all over here. It's just me and Deacon Wil, and I like it like this."

I don't remember hanging up the phone. I felt a pressure building up in my chest. I closed my eyes and took several deep breaths. Then I made another dreaded call to plea for help.

"Hello," he answered in a hurried tone.

"Hey, Daniel, it's me. I need to ask you a question."

Daniel hesitated. It wasn't the norm that I'd call him out of the clear blue sky. He probably sensed the desperation in my crackling voice.

"I think I need a place to stay for a little bit."

"Need a place to stay?"

"Yeah. Me and the kids."

"Why?" he said, sighing.

"I lost my job a little while back, and I can't afford to stay here anymore," I said.

"So, you losing the house?"

"Umm humm," I admitted. And admitting it to myself in that moment nearly brought me to my knees.

"I don't have that kind of room in my place, Latwaina. Why don't you let the kids stay with their dads and you stay in your car until you can get back on your feet?"

I couldn't believe what he was proposing. I shook my head. I was truly on my own. "Never mind. I don't want to separate my children, and neither do I want to be separated from my children. They need me."

"What about Mama? Did you ask Mama?"

"She said no."

"Well, I really don't know what else to tell you," he said, allowing an awkward moment of silence to creep in.

I held the phone. I had nothing else to say. A layer of my heart peeled away. I promised myself I would never seek my family's help again. If I didn't know it before this day, I surely knew it now—I was alone and on my own in this cold, dark world. Besides God and my children, I had no one.

I knew I had to end the call. Daniel's mind was made up, and so was my mother's. Finally, I said, "It's okay" as I mentally tried to prepare myself for the harsh reality that I would most likely be living in my car … my children and me. In that moment, I couldn't help but think about the money. If only I had saved some of my money from the lawsuit, my children and I wouldn't have been on the brink of homelessness. Even though some would say it was water under the bridge, I thought about it at that moment because it certainly would have eliminated the predicament that I found myself facing.

CHAPTER 15

A Blessing Or A Curse

Call it luck or a blessing, whatever it was … its timing seemed perfect. I joined an online dating site, something that would allow me to vent my frustrations, hook up for a quick lunch or dinner, and sometimes, go out with someone just to forget about the dire situation I was in.

In the world of online dating, everyone had a pseudo name, including me. Mine was "Faith." And when you assume a semi-pseudo persona, for some reason, you can be a little more vulnerable … a little more direct … and even a little more risqué. But in a weird sort of way, the fake you reveals more about the real you than you truly realize. One of my online friends happened to be a man named "Charles." Of course, I knew Charles wasn't his real name, just as Faith wasn't mine. But Charles sent me a "like" one day, and an interesting exchange took place not long thereafter.

"What do you do for a living?" he asked.

"Well, right now, I work at a school as a lunch aid."

"You like it?"

"Nah, not really. But it's the only thing I have for the moment. I was laid off from my full-time job."

"Ahh … that's unfortunate. Bet it's a little rough for you, huh?"

"Yeah, very rough."

"But I bet a beautiful woman like you have lots of people that can help you out."

I wished his assumption was correct; but it was light years away from my reality. There I was, nearly homeless and almost hopeless … but on a dating app just to maintain my sanity. "I'm not really close with my family," I embarrassingly said.

"Why not?"

"Just things that happened in the family that I don't really want to go into right now," I replied. The last thing I wanted to do was tell this stranger all my personal business.

"You have a place to stay, obviously," Charles said, digging for information.

Knowing my situation was dire and the possibility of being evicted in the near future was looming, I decided to be a little transparent with Charles. "For right now …" I confessed.

"What do you mean, 'for right now,'?"

"I'm not making enough to afford my mortgage. I need to move, but I don't have anywhere to go."

"Not even your parents?"

"My dad is deceased, and my mom … well, she just can't," I sorrowfully and ashamedly admitted, feeling as though I'd just undressed in front of this stranger named "Charles."

"Well, you're talking to the right person. My wife and I own"

"Your wife? You're married?"

"Yes … I thought I told you?" Charles said with no shame in his game.

"No, you didn't."

"Well, yeah, I'm married."

"So why are you on a dating site?"

"To meet new people like yourself. Have a little fun. No harm."

"Does your wife know?"

"My wife knows I have lady friends," he said, chuckling.

"But does she know you're on a dating site?"

"She doesn't care."

"I don't know if I believe that," I said, trying to get him to go into details.

"Look, we have an arrangement. We're together for financial reasons."

"Like?" I said, probing.

"We have tons of real estate together. We're in the process of moving from where we are now to a different house. So, I can actually help you, if you let me."

"Help me?"

"Yes. Look, I know your predicament. You won't have to give me a security deposit right now."

"How much will my rent be?"

"Well, we normally charge seven-hundred and fifty a month."

"Whew! That's too steep for me. I don't think I can swing that."

"Look, don't worry about it. We can work out something on the rent," he assured. "But first you have to look at the place, fill out an application … that kind of stuff," he continued.

"That's fine," I said, agreeing.

"How does tomorrow sound?"

"I can't do it tomorrow. I have to run some errands with my mother."

"Your *mother*?"

"Yeah, my mother," I said, sensing where he was going with his line of questioning.

"You mean the mother that won't open her doors for you and her—" Charles stopped mid-sentence. I supposed he didn't want to dig into the mud, if you know what I mean. "Oh, never mind. Well, how about Thursday?"

"I can meet on Thursday."

"Okay. Well, let me give you the address."

"Okay, let me grab something to write on," I said, reaching over to grab a pen out of my nightstand drawer.

I wrote down his address and agreed to meet him that Thursday at one o'clock in the afternoon.

An unexpected blessing or a looming curse? I wondered after the call ended.

Now that Mama was sober, she was gainfully employed again. She didn't work in the hospitals anymore, just worked with agencies that provided in-home care for people who were disabled and needed extra help with carrying out their daily routines. Sometimes, she'd ask me to go along with her, so I could watch the patients or clients while she handled important business matters. She'd peel me off a few dollars, so I almost always agreed to tag along for the little extra money. So, after I'd gotten Anna and Michael off to school that morning, I got myself ready and waited for my mother to pick me up.

As she'd normally do, she tooted the horn to let me know she'd pulled into the driveway. I turned off the television and headed out to the car.

"Hey, Ms. Cassie," I said, greeting my mother's client. "How are you?" I said, sparking up a little conversation.

"Not too bad … not too bad. My good ole days outweigh my bad. So, like the songwriter says, 'I won't complain,'" Ms. Cassie said, smiling.

Ms. Cassie wasn't really disabled; her late husband, Mr. Theodore, was a disabled veteran. Mr. Theodore was my mother's primary patient. However, since his passing, my mother's primary responsibilities shifted from Mr. Theodore to his surviving spouse, Ms. Cassie.

"That's nice to hear," I said, easing my way into the front passenger seat. "Where are we going first?" I said, looking over at my mom.

"Bank. Gotta take her to the bank," she said, putting the car's gear in reverse.

The bank, of all places. It was truly the last place I wanted to visit, especially after the ordeal I'd recently experienced. But I forced a half-smile anyway.

Once we arrived at the bank, I sat down on the small loveseat in the bank's lobby while Mama helped Ms. Cassie with her transaction. I watched other patrons carry out their transactions as well. An older man with a cane counting his money down to the penny before approaching a teller. A younger woman inquiring about overdraft charges assessed to her account. A middle-aged couple wanting to order traveler's cheques for their upcoming honeymoon. Another widow, like Ms. Cassie, there to notify the bank of her husband's passing. And finally, the security guard entering and exiting the bank lobby, guarding his post.

By the time Mama and Ms. Cassie had finally finished their transaction, I had nearly fallen asleep on the comfortable mini-sofa.

"We're ready," my mother said, tapping me on my shoulder.

"Okay," I said, letting out a wide yawn. "Where are we going now?"

"Ms. Cassie needs to go to the post office."

"All right," I said as I stood. "Ms. Cassie, do you need any help?" I said, reaching for her free hand.

"No, sweetie. I'm quite all right," she said, tucking her purse under her arm.

I followed Mama and Ms. Cassie as we exited the bank, only to be stopped by the tall security guard as I attempted to walk past him.

"Excuse me, ma'am."

"Yes?" I said, stopping in my tracks.

"I'm gonna make this real quick. Do you have a man?"

I blushed as I fanned my mother and Ms. Cassie on. "A what?" I asked, prompting him to repeat the question.

"A man?"

"Maybe," I flirted.

"Is that a yes or a no?"

"It's just what I said ... maybe. Depends on who wants to know and for what reason."

"Well, I want to know. I think you're beautiful, and I want to get to know you. You don't find anything wrong with that, do you?"

"No," I said, giggling. I was turning into the little girl on the school playground.

"Then can I have your number?" he asked matter-of-factly.

"Do you have something to write on?"

"Sure," he said, reaching into his shirt pocket to retrieve a pen and a piece of paper.

I wrote down my phone number on the miniature notepad and handed it back to him.

"My name is Jeff, by the way."

"Latwaina," I said, smiling.

"I'll give you a call later," he said, showcasing his gold-encased front teeth. Laced teeth were the thing back in the day. Some people wore it for fashion and others sported the look to disguise chipped or cracked teeth.

"Okay. I gotta go," I said, rushing off to the car, as Mama had just beeped the horn.

Before I could even get in the car good, she made a comment. "Picking another one up, I see."

I didn't respond. I wasn't a married woman, so there was nothing wrong with me giving out my number. And Mama was the last one to talk about my choice in men. If I remembered clearly, Tyrone was no prize. But this Jeff guy wasn't someone I would have normally been attracted to; yet there was something about him that attracted me to him.

I could barely finish dinner when my phone rang. "It's him," I said, not recognizing the number on the caller ID.

"Him, who?" Anna said, stacking the plates on top of one another as she cleared the table.

"Oh, never mind. Just somebody I met today," I said, looking at Anna through my peripheral vision. My children were just as protective of me as I was of them. "He's just a nice guy I met today," I said, throwing the dish towel over my shoulder, a habit I'd picked up from Grandma Lily. "And Michael, you make sure you help your sister with the kitchen," I said as I headed for my bedroom to have some privacy. Finally, I answered the call. "Hello."

"May I speak with Lawanda?" he said, pronouncing my name incorrectly.

"It's Latwaina, not Lawanda. I'm speaking."

"Oh, my bad. Please forgive me."

"No problem," I said as I closed my bedroom door.

"It's Jeff … Jeff from the bank today."

"I know who it is," I said. I'd already recognized his velvety voice.

"Can you talk?"

"Yes, I can," I said, plopping down on the side of my bed.

We went through the preliminary questions about how each of our days went. And before long, our conversation became more interesting.

"What do you like to do in your spare time?" Jeff asked.

"Go to the show."

"What type of movies do you like?"

"All kinds," I said, not wanting to get into the different type of genres that interested me.

"I like movies too."

"What kind?" I said, regurgitating his line of questioning.

"All kinds," he said, regurgitating my response.

"So, tell me … why are you single?"

"That's a question you should be asking all my exes," I said, chuckling.

"They must be fools. You seem like a nice young lady. You need a good man in your life."

"You know any?" I flirted.

"You're talking to one."

"Oh, am I?"

"Yes, you are. I'm a good man, one with a lot to offer."

"Oh, really?"

"Yes, really. And I like to spoil my women."

"Oh, do you?"

"Absolutely. I can already see myself giving you whatever you want."

"Hmm … you might not be able to afford what I like," I joked.

"I'll do my best. How about that?"

"I'll take that," I said.

"What are you doing Saturday night?"

"I don't think I have any plans. Why?"

"I'd like to take you to dinner. What do you like to eat?"

"Steak and pasta," I said, which were my favorite cuisines.

"Perfect. Got the perfect place in mind to take you to dinner. Is seven a good time? I know you have to get the kids a sitter and all."

"Yes, I need a sitter," I said, mentally searching my brain for a sitter.

"Don't worry. I'll give you the money for the sitter."

"You don't have to," I said, although I was elated by his volunteerism.

"Didn't I tell you I'd spoil you?"

"Yeah, you said that."

"Did you think I was lying?"

"No. I just haven't had a stranger be so willing to help me."

"That's because you've never dated a real man."

"Oh, really?"

"Yes, really. Look, stop by the bank tomorrow. I wanna give you something."

"What?"

"Just come by the bank. I wanna give you the money for the sitter and a few extra dollars to get yourself ready for Saturday. You like braids?"

"Yes, I love braids," I said.

"Good. My sister has her own shop. I'mma call her up and let her know I'm sending you over there. They'll give you whatever you want. It's on me."

"Jeff, let me stop you. You really don't have to do this for me."

"I know, but I want to. Why are you so opposed to me giving you money?"

"Because I don't want you to expect anything from me," I admitted. "Of course, I could use the money. But it's just that anytime a man offers a woman money, it's usually tied to some type of sexual favor."

Jeff laughed loudly. "Tied to a sexual favor? Do you think I have time for games? I'm a grown man who handles his business. I ain't got time for games. If anything, men who play games are the clowns who ask women for money, not the other way around."

Jeff was right, I guessed. My past experiences had me overly skeptical and paranoid. I mean, what did I have to lose by accepting his generosity? He could have been the disguised blessing that I'd been praying to God for. And then again, he could have also been the trap the devil was setting me up to fall into. But like Jeff said, what did I have to lose? It was just a date ... a first date, where we'd get to know each other a little better. I wasn't obligated to see him again if I wasn't feeling him. And neither was he obligated to see me again if he wasn't feeling me.

"Okay, okay, maybe that came out wrong. I just vowed to start my next relationship off the right way."

"Lawanda, there is no right way. We men see something we like, and we go after it. It's that simple. Just go out with me Saturday, and let's have a good time. No strings attached."

"Okay. No strings attached," I agreed. I didn't bother correcting him; he'd mispronounced my name once again.

"But I still want you to come by the bank and get the money. I want you to feel special."

I fell backwards on my bed. Jeff was blowing my mind. He seemed too good to be true. And we all know the saying ... "If it sounds too good to be true, it usually is."

CHAPTER 16

Leopards Never Change Their Spots

"**C**harles" was standing next to the flower bed in the front yard when I pulled into the driveway. Situated in a quiet suburban neighborhood, the modest brick home was nestled between two other brick homes, one with a For Sale sign in the yard and the other one with Beware of Dog signage in the windows. Charles waved and began to head toward my car. After putting the gear in park and turning off the car's engine, I threw the car keys in my purse. Before I could reach for the door handle, the door flung open.

"You look just like your picture—beautiful," Charles said, holding the door open.

"Thank you," I replied, stepping out of the car.

"So did you have any trouble finding the house?"

"Not too much. I got a little turned around, but then I figured out where I was going."

"Cool," he said, looking me up and down. "So, umm … let's go see your new home," he continued.

I followed Charles up the outside steps and into the house, landing in the living room first. "This, as you can see, is the living room," he said, showcasing the room's country-styled décor. It wasn't particularly my style, but neither was homelessness.

"Nice," I said, allowing a smile to sweep across my face.

"Well, come on, let me show you the rest of the house," he said, pointing down the hallway toward another part of the house.

I followed Charles as he showed me the entire house, including the backyard. Essentially, I was just following protocol. I was in no predicament to turn the offer down.

"So, what do you think?" Charles said, opening the front door to lead me back outside.

"I like it. When do you think I can move in?"

"Well, right now. My wife and I are still living in it until we close on our new home. It's still being built. But it should be ready in a couple of months. I know your situation, but if you can wait just a couple of weeks, you can move on in."

"Okay," I said, taking mental note of how I was going to coordinate the move. "And what about the rent?"

"Like I said, you've been up front about your situation. I can work with you until you get on your feet. How does four-hundred fifty sound? Think you can swing that?'

"Yep," I said, nodding.

"Then, we have an agreement. And this special agreement is between you and me. Don't tell anyone else about it, not even Delores."

"Who's Delores?

"My wife. Her name is Delores."

"Well, where is she? I would like to meet her," I said, my way of letting him know I'm not *that chick.*

"Who knows? Probably somewhere spending my hard-earned money. Ain't that what you women do?"

"I wish," I said. I wasn't lucky enough to have full access of some man's money. My life thus far seemed as though that kind of luck just wasn't in the cards for me.

Charles and I chatted it up for a few more minutes before I told him I had another errand to run.

"Well, I gotta go. I have another appointment," I said. I promised Jeff I'd stop by the bank before three. It was on the opposite side of town, and I needed to be headed back in that direction.

"All right. I'll get the paperwork together, and we can meet again so you can sign it, okay?"

"Sure," I said as I got in my car and cranked up the engine.

"Are you going to be online later?" Charles said, holding the car door open.

"Yes," I said. I liked the dating site. I had fun on it, meeting all sorts of other people.

"See you online then," Charles said, winking and closing the car door at the same time.

I smiled on the outside, but on the inside, I cringed. Charles wasn't the least bit attractive. He sported a large bald patch on the top of his head and a pot belly. He wasn't the best dresser either, wearing wide-legged denim overalls. But despite how I felt about his physical appearance, I needed Charles. Me and my children. Homelessness was not an option.

I pulled out of the driveway slowly, being careful not to run over the large decorative rocks that lined the edges of the asphalt driveway. I made sure to blow my horn as I pulled off, enroute to the bank to meet Jeff.

Jeff was standing post outside the bank when I pulled into the bank's parking lot. He smiled when he spotted me and pointed for me to park in the space for the disabled in front of him.

"I don't want to get a ticket," I yelled out as I rolled down my window.

"You won't. I'm standing right here. And you don't even have to get out of the car."

"Okay now … if I get a ticket, you're gonna pay for it," I teased as I pulled into the parking space.

"I don't mind. That's no biggie," he said, walking up to the car. "You look good, you know," he complimented.

"Thank you," I said, putting the gear into park.

"How's your day?" he said, leaning against the side of the car.

"It's been fine. I had to go look at a place I'm supposed to be moving into soon."

"So?"

"So what?"

"Did you like it?"

"It was okay. Not really my style. But I can work with it. Just need to change up the way it's decorated, mostly."

"Do you have movers?"

"Not yet," I admitted.

"Well, my boy Clayton has his own moving company. If you need someone to move you, he can do it."

"I was thinking about having some friends help me move," I lied. I had no one to help me move.

"No, not Cousin Ray-Ray and Cousin Leroy. I'm talking about professional movers. You don't want people damaging your nice things."

"That's true," I said, glancing up at Jeff.

"I'll get you hooked up. Don't worry about that. You did the hard part, and that was finding a place. I got connections."

I nodded. Jeff was too nice. What had he seen in me? Was he an angel sent by God? When I didn't have anyone else to turn to, he brought Jeff into my life, someone who was willing to help me.

"Look, as much as I want to stand right here and stare into your beautiful eyes, I can't. Gotta get back on my post. But here's a few dollars to get your hair braided and your nails and feet done. A little pampering, you know?" Jeff said, holding a stack of neatly folded bills.

My eyes nearly popped out of their sockets. I wanted the money, no doubt. I definitely needed the money. But I didn't want Jeff to think I was one of those thirsty chicken heads from the 'hood. Besides, who's to say he wasn't testing me? So I played the integrity game with him. "I can't take this kind of money from you," I said, trying to push his hand away.

"Take the money, Lawanda," he said, trying to force open my hand.

"It's Latwaina, not Lawanda." I laughed.

"Girl, just take the money," he said, throwing the bills into the car. "Take the money. I've already made you a hair appointment at my sister's salon for tomorrow morning. You can go get your nails and feet done afterward. And I gave you money for the babysitter too. You did get a sitter, didn't you?"

"Yeah, yeah, I got a sitter," I lied. I was going to either have to beg Ebony or call Rose. Between the two of them and the offer of money, I knew it wouldn't be a problem finding a sitter for Anna and Michael.

"Well, go on. I'll call you when I get off. I gotta get back to work," Jeff said, stepping back and away from the car.

Jeff stood on the edge of the sidewalk, watching as I picked up the dollar bills, refolded them, and stuck them into the cup holder next to me. When I'd finished, I rolled the window up and put the car in reverse, smiling as I backed up and pulled out of the bank parking lot. I glanced down at the bills once again. *Am I dreaming?* I thought.

Rose agreed to watch Anna and Michael, and I dropped them off at her house early the next morning. And as agreed, Jeff picked me up and drove me to his sister's salon so I could get my hair braided.

"Morning," I said as I got in his car, a 2008 BMW 328 Series.

Good morning, beautiful," Jeff greeted.

"Nice car," I said, inspecting the car's interior.

"Thanks. My all-time favorite make and model."

"It smells brand new," I said, tilting my head backward and inhaling deeply.

"That's because it is. Just picked this baby up last week. This is the result of being a hustler and working hard," he said, congratulating himself for the accomplishment. "I like nice things. You'll see. And if you stick with me, you'll get to enjoy some of the finer things in life too. You see, I don't just do security at the bank. I own a studio downtown withy my business partner, Mac."

"Mac? That's his name?" I said, quizzically.

"That's what we call him. His last name is MacDonald. We call him Mac for short."

"Oh, I said. So you own a music studio?"

"Co-own, I co-own a music studio," Jeff said, correcting me.

"Wow," I said, impressed by the revelation.

"I'll take you down there one day. Some big names drop by from time to time."

"Oh really? Like who?"

"Stevie Wonder's been there. The Clark Sisters have used our studio before too."

"The Clark Sisters?" I said with astonishment.

"Yep. A few times," he bragged.

I got the sense that Jeff wasn't as humble as he pretended to be because he spent the remainder of the drive to the salon talking about himself. Jeff has done this. Jeff has done that. Jeff's been here. Jeff's been there. Jeff knows this person. Jeff knows that person. Jeff has this. Jeff has that. If it wasn't for the pampering day that he had planned for me, I would have acted as though my cycle came on suddenly and had him take me home. But I got a break when we arrived at the salon.

Big gold letters that read "Stephanie's Hair Creations" were painted on the windows of the salon, which was located in a small shopping plaza on Detroit's westside. A tall, thin woman smoking a cigarette stood in front. She smiled and waved as we pulled into a parking space in front of the salon.

"Hey, little sis," Jeff greeted the tall woman, who I assumed was Stephanie. Her hazel eyes protruded some, but they were stunning, nonetheless.

"Hey, big bro," she said, puckering her dark lips to give Jeff a kiss on the cheek.

"This is Lawanda … the girl I told you about," Jeff said, nudging me in front of him. I didn't bother to correct the name pronunciation. It would have exerted more energy than it was worth. He wasn't going to get it no time soon, and that was okay … for now.

"Hi, I'm Stephanie," she said, holding her free hand out.

"Hi, I'm Latwaina," I said, putting special emphasis on the pronunciation of my name. Stephanie caught the gesture and smiled.

"So, you want braids, huh?" she said, dropping the butt of the cigarette and pressing down on it with her left foot.

"Yeah, micro braids," I said.

"Cool. Well, I got you," she said, visually inspecting my hair.

"Well, come on in. I have you down. I'm personally going to work on your hair with another hair braider. That way, you won't be in here all day," she said, opening the door and leading us in the salon.

I was surprised Jeff didn't turn around to leave but instead, followed us into the salon. "You're staying?" I asked.

"Yeah, I'm paying, so I'm staying," he said sarcastically.

After five and a half hours, my hair was finally done.

"It looks fine," Jeff said, taking the mirror out of Stephanie's hand as she held it out for me.

"Jeff, let her look at her hair for herself," Stephanie said, snatching the mirror out of Jeff's hands and giving it back to me.

"She got the money to pay you," Jeff said, storming off.

"What's up with him?" I asked once Jeff was out of sight.

"Ahh, nothing. That's just my impatient, gotta-have-it-his-way brother, Jeff," Stephanie joked, trying to make light of her brother's bipolar behavior. "He don't mean no harm; he just has some strange ways."

I paid Stephanie, giving her a handsome tip as directed by Jeff before he left the salon. "Where's Jeff?" I asked, looking around.

"He went to the car," Stephanie said as she placed the bills in the register drawer.

"Thank you, Stephanie. I love my hair," I said, peering into the mirror on the checkout counter.

"You're welcome. Anytime."

"Thank you once again," I said, gently rubbing Jeff's right hand as he maneuvered the gears of his stick shift. "I really enjoyed myself. I haven't enjoyed myself this much in a long time," I added.

"So, you really enjoyed yourself, huh?" Jeff said, blushing. Yeah, he was blushing.

"Yes. The entire day was fabulous," I said, pouring the compliments on him. And he was soaking them all up.

"Cool. Cool."

I did enjoy myself that day, but not as much as I led Jeff to believe. I needed him at this point in my life. The conversation drew quiet once again as it had over dinner earlier that night.

"Penny for your thoughts?" Jeff said, looking at me and then at the road.

"Nothing," I said, forcing a fake smile.

"No, seriously. What's on your mind?" he said, looking over at me once again.

"How come you've never told me your age? I told you mine."

"Does it matter how old I am?"

"No … but—"

"Don't worry about age. It's just a number, remember? You've heard that saying before, haven't you?" he said, cutting me off.

"I'm just saying. I mean, it ain't no big deal."

"Then we both agree; since it's not a big deal, it doesn't need to be discussed, okay?"

I nodded but didn't respond. And just like that, the leopard's spots were beginning to shine through.

The same day, Delores and Charles, who I now knew was really Robert, moved out of their house, and I moved in. Per our "special agreement," I would have the carpets shampooed and the walls painted at my own expense if I wanted them done. And just like Jeff promised, Clayton Moving Company moved me in.

We were good and tired by the end of the day. Jeff volunteered to order Chinese food for us to eat. Robert-slash-Charles left the utilities on, including the cable, giving me a couple of days to have them switched over in my name. We watched movies on the sofa until we both fell asleep. But some time in the wee hours of the morning, I was awakened by the touch of Jeff's hand rubbing up my thighs and his hot breath breathing down my neck. "I want you," he whispered in my ear. "I want to make love to you."

My body grew stiff. I knew this was coming, but I wasn't prepared for it. I wasn't physically attracted to Jeff. I could tolerate him in small doses, whenever his bipolarism wasn't seeping through, which wasn't often. "I'm on my cycle," I lied. It was the default excuse many women use when they don't want to have sex.

"I don't care," he said, now pulling on my pajama shorts. "I want you. I want you now," he said, positioning his body up against me.

I could feel his manhood against my buttocks. I felt obligated. After all he'd done for me over the past few weeks. I gave into his advances … And. It. Was. The. Worst. Sex. I'd. Ever. Had. For his height and weight, his "manhood" sure didn't match in terms of size. Talk about Pee-Wee Herman!

When he finished, he rolled off me and slid onto the floor. I closed my eyes tight. I wanted to erase the experience from my memory. I got up, took a shower, and slept on my bedroom floor, since I didn't have the chance to put clean sheets on the mattress.

I woke up to the sound of banging coming from the front area of the house the next morning. When I went to explore the source, I found Jeff hanging my pictures on the wall in the living room.

"Like it?" he said, stepping back from the picture he'd just hung up.

I forced a smile. I wished I liked him more than I did. I wished he was better looking. I wished he wasn't bipolar. I wished his penis was bigger. I wished he was better in bed. I wished. I wished. Then again, who was I? I had my faults too. I knew Jeff wasn't going anywhere anytime soon. We had a strange chemistry, one that kept us together even though we probably needed to be apart. He needed me, and I needed him. We needed each other in our own twisted ways. But the fact remained, we were both stuck with each other, at least for the time being.

CHAPTER 17

Situationship

The smell of bleach saturated my nostrils as I sat up and pulled the sheets back. I could hear the sounds of Jeff fidgeting around in the adjourning bathroom. After getting out of bed, I made my way over to the entryway of the bathroom.

"Good morning," I greeted, startling Jeff.

"Oh, hey, baby. Never mind me; I'm a little O.C.D, so I wanted to clean up the bathroom good before we took another shower in here," he said, throwing a dry rag over his shoulder. I thought about Grandma Lily.

"Bleach kinda strong, don't you think?" I said, pinching my nose.

"I'll just lift the windows. The fresh air will take the strong scent away. I'll be done in a little bit. Wanna go grab breakfast afterward?"

"Sure. I'm hungry, and I'm sure the kids are starving," I said, turning to go check on Anna and Michael.

"Do they have to come? I mean, we could just bring them something back," Jeff suggested.

"Make them wait until we eat first? No. The kids are hungry now. I'm not one of those mothers that feeds her belly first," I said as I walked off. His suggestion had irritated me. I was beginning to detect a pattern, because it wasn't the first time Jeff had suggested leaving the kids behind. I was beginning to wonder if he even liked children.

Anna and Michael were still asleep when I went into their respective rooms. A light sleeper, Anna woke up just as I was attempting to walk out of her room.

"Good morning, Ma."

"Good morning, sweetie. How did you sleep last night?" I said, turning around to face her.

"I slept good," she said, forcing a smile.

"Did you?" I asked, trying to gauge her nonverbal cue. That was one thing about Anna and Michael; their nonverbal cues always revealed how they truly felt. I returned the smile. I knew our current living arrangement was just temporary. I was sure I'd own another home soon; it was just a matter of time. In the meantime, however, living in Charles-slash-Robert and Delores's house took the ease out of wondering on which day and at what time the sheriff might show up and put us out of the other place and toss our belongings out on the street. It was one of the most horrifying feelings, especially the thought of having to subject my children to such a terrifying experience. But as the old folk used to say, "But thanks be to God that it all worked out in my favor."

"Yes, I did," Anna said, peeling away her covers.

"Well, get on up, brush your teeth, and get yourself together. Mr. Jeff is gonna take us to breakfast this morning."

"Mr. Jeff … Oh, he's still here," Anna said, putting two and two together.

"Yes, he ended up staying the night again, so he can finish helping us get settled in," I said, offering some form of an excuse for Jeff's second overnight stay. I felt guilty about exposing my children to this lifestyle, but I needed Jeff's help, and he was ready, willing, and able to take care of me and my children's needs.

"Is he gonna be your boyfriend?" Anna blurted out.

Caught off guard by the question, I swallowed hard. Silence crept in. I didn't know how to answer her.

"Is he?" Anna asked.

"He's just my friend … for now," I said, turning to exit the room. I knew Anna would have fifty more questions for me if I stayed in her room.

Six months later, Jeff was still my "friend … for now." In his mind, we were in a committed relationship. But in my mind, I was in a relationship of convenience. I needed Jeff's generosity, his kindness, his physical help, his money, and even his companionship, at times. If I could have just taken his good qualities and created a new man, one I was physically attracted to, I would've had the perfect boyfriend. The fact that the sex was horrible, if that's what you'd call it, was another reason I knew it wasn't going to work with him. Nevertheless, I took it for what it was worth and made the best of it. After all, the relationship, for the time being, was working, for the most part.

The day I invited Jeff to go to church with me was the day I thought he was going to buck. But to my surprise, he didn't.

"I thought you said you didn't like going to church," I said inquisitively.

"That's not what I said, Latwaina. I said, I didn't like being in church all day on Sundays," Jeff corrected.

"So you mean you don't have a problem going to church with me and the kids?"

"No, Latwaina. My parents didn't do the church thing. They were too hungover from partying on Saturday nights. Getting up early to go to church the next day was the furthest thing from their minds, so I didn't grow up having to go to church on Sundays. If it wasn't for my grandparents, I wouldn't have even gone to church on Easter."

"You mean, Resurrection Sunday," I clarified, suggesting the non-paganistic term for the celebration was incorrect.

"Easter … Resurrection Sunday … whatever," Jeff said, throwing up his hands. "The bottom line is that I went to church on that particular Sunday."

"Okay," I said, trying to diffuse what I sensed was mounting agitation in his voice.

"Do they dress up at your church?" Jeff asked.

"The Bible says to come as you are. So, if you want to wear jeans, wear them. If you want to wear a suit, wear it."

"Cool. I got it," Jeff said.

We did the church thing the following Sunday, looking like a loving family. But the reality was far from what was being portrayed. Through my peripheral vision, I watched Jeff's facial expression various times throughout the service. He seemed to be pretty engaged, but I couldn't be certain.

After church, we headed straight to the parking lot. I waved at a few people but did not stop to speak with anyone, not even my mother. Apparently, Jeff noticed, and he didn't hesitate to bring it up on the drive home.

"Didn't you say your mother attends the same church?"

"Yeah. We go to the same church," I said matter-of-factly.

"Was she there today?" Jeff said inquisitively.

"Yeah, I saw her."

"Saw her?"

I nodded. The last thing I wanted to do was go into details about why I didn't introduce Jeff to my mother and vice versa. I had given him the skeleton version of my relationship with my mother. I was growing up and learning that every man in my life didn't deserve to know the intimate details about my life, not until he proved he was going to be there long term.

"So, she was there?" Jeff asked again, expecting me to elaborate.

"Yeah, she was there. Look, Jeff, the kids are in the back seat. I don't like going into detail about what's going on with me and my mother, period. And I especially don't like going into detail in front of my children."

"You don't think they know? You don't think they deserve to know that something's wrong?"

"Jeff, please. Not now," I begged, holding my hand up.

"Okay. If you say so," Jeff said, huffing.

"What are we doing about dinner today?" I said, changing the subject.

"I can't afford to feed four people every time we go out," he said in a curt tone.

"You don't have to. We can eat at home. I took some steak out. I just need to pick up a few things from the grocery store. Can you swing me by Kroger right quick?"

Without responding, Jeff made a quick U-turn, spinning the vehicle around from the middle lane. "Whoa, Jeff! You're gonna kill us!" I said, turning around to check on Anna and Michael.

"We just passed the store. Why didn't you say something beforehand?"

"Because we just decided what we were going to do about dinner," I said in a forced calm voice. I knew Jeff was irritated, not because I asked him to go to the grocery store, but because, in his eyes, Anna and Michael were "in the way." He would have much more preferred that I didn't have children or that their fathers were in their lives. Either scenario would have given us more one-on-one time.

"Okay, well, we're on our way to the grocery store now. It's all good," Jeff said, trying to act as if he was unbothered.

I sent Anna and Michael in the store to pick up the items I needed while Jeff and I waited in the car. Neither one of us spoke. Jeff turned the radio on and focused his attention on listening to sports radio. Me? I watched the many patrons as they walked in and out of the store, some couples holding hands, others holding the hands of their children, mindful of the busy vehicular traffic in the parking lot. Finally, I spotted Anna and Michael walking out of the store. My eyes followed them until they reached the car.

"Got everything?" I said as they got in the car.

"Yep," Michael said, closing his door.

"Any change?" Jeff asked, turning down the volume on the radio.

"Yes … a dollar and forty-three cents."

"Do you mind handing it to me?" Jeff said, holding his right hand up for Anna to drop the money in it.

Trifling, I thought. He asked my baby for a dollar and forty-three cents. If I didn't need him so bad, I would have cut him off right then and there. But I did need Jeff … at least that's what I thought. And since I did, I had to muzzle my mouth and grin and bear it.

We drove the rest of the way home that afternoon in silence. That is, until we pulled into the driveway of the house and spotted Charles's vehicle parked on the street in front of the house.

"What is he doing here?" Jeff said as he slowly crept up the driveway, peering at Charles through the rearview mirror.

"I don't know," I said, leaning over to look at Charles. Our eyes met. He had a blank stare as if he had been blindsided.

"You know, it's illegal for landlords to just pop up like this unannounced. And he definitely shouldn't be going in the house when we're not here," Jeff said, putting the gear in park.

"I know," I said, reaching for the car door handle.

The driver side door of Charles's Cadillac opened, and from where I was now standing, I could see his long legs emerge. He was dressed in a suit as if he, too, had been to Sunday service.

"You guys go on in the house while I talk to Mr. Charles," I said to Jeff and the kids. I waited until the three of them went into the house before I headed down the driveway to speak with Charles-slash-Robert.

"I'm sorry, did we schedule a meeting today?"

"I wanted to surprise you and take you out to dinner. But to my surprise, I didn't know there was a man around here. If

I had known a man was going to be shacking up in here with you, I could have sold the house or rented it to someone who really needed a place to stay," he said with an obvious attitude.

"What makes you think I didn't need the place? I told you that when we were on the chat, remember?" I said, jogging his memory.

"But you conveniently left out the fact that you have a man."

"I didn't have a man at the time," I corrected him again.

"Well, seems like you have one now. I guess you no longer need the reduction on the rent."

"That man is my friend, Jeff," I lied.

"Does he live here?"

"No, he doesn't," I said defensively. I knew where he was going, and I wasn't about to let him back me into a corner.

"No?"

"No, he doesn't," I said, folding my arms.

"He's here all the time," Charles said, challenging my defense.

"How would you know that?" I said, now shifting my weight to one side.

"Oh, you don't get it, do you? You needed me, and I agreed to help you, right?"

I nodded.

"We made an agreement, didn't we?" Charles continued.

"Yes, you said you'd charge me four-hundred and fifty until I got on my feet."

Charles chuckled. "Bad choice of words," Charles said, shaking his head.

"Look, Charles, I'm only working fifteen hours a week. I don't make that much money. I'm raising two kids all by myself. I can't pay more than four-hundred and fifty dollars a month for rent."

"Well, then you'll have to consider our original arrangement."

"Arrangement? What arrangement?"

Charles smirked.

"What arrangement?" I repeated once again.

Leaning over and whispering in my ear, he said, "You take care of me, and I'll take care of you."

His cheap-smelling cologne traveled up my nostrils, prompting me to begin coughing. "Now, you go on in there and enjoy the rest of your Sunday," Charles said, smirking as he walked off.

It didn't take a genius to know what Charles-slash-Robert was insinuating. I was already in a relationship of convenience with Jeff, and I had no intentions of trading sex for rent with Charles. So, even though Jeff wasn't my preferred cup of tea, I knew I was going to have to keep him around for the time being, at least until my circumstances changed.

Before I knew it, a whole year had passed, and not much had changed in terms of the way I felt about Jeff. Sure, he was still hanging around. We were still going to church together, even though we were "shacking." I was still trying to land a better job, and I was still warding off Charles's unwanted advances toward me. Deep down, however, I still knew my circumstances were temporary.

Jeff took me by surprise one Saturday when he suggested that we go ring shopping.

"Ring shopping?" I said, swallowing hard. *Marriage? Does he really want to marry me?*

"Yeah. Let's just do it," Jeff said, holding my left hand up in the air as if he was trying to determine my ring size.

"Well, let's see what Pastor says," I suggested. Getting my pastor's input was important to me.

"The pastor?" Jeff challenged.

"Yes. It's what we do in the church."

Jeff chuckled. "Wait a minute, wait a minute … You telling me we gotta go *ask* the pastor for his permission to get married?"

"It's not necessarily permission," I said. "The pastor is our spiritual counselor. We are supposed to consult him on these types of decisions."

Jeff shook his head in disbelief. "We can still go ring shopping," he countered.

And so we did. We went to Halstone Jewelers in Downtown Detroit. Jeff didn't mind spending money on me, for the most part. But whenever he couldn't get his way, he'd hold back giving me money to help pay my bills. This day, he didn't seem to have a budget.

"Pick out what you like," he said, holding his arms out as if he was advertising the entire store inventory.

"Do I have a cap?"

"Pick out what you like. Don't worry about the cost."

Of course, I had to use common sense no matter what came out of Jeff's mouth. He was a security guard at the bank, not a bank executive. I tried on several rings before finally settling on a one-and-a-half-carat pear-cut diamond. It was just my taste.

I made the mistake of wearing the ring to church the following Sunday, pretty much announcing our engagement prematurely. I knew it would only be a matter of time before I was summoned to the pastor's office, so I went ahead and scheduled a meeting with Pastor King.

The following Tuesday, Jeff and I drove to the church to meet with Pastor King.

"Can I help you?" Sister Felicia, Pastor King's receptionist, greeted as we entered the front part of the pastor's office.

"We're here to meet with Pastor King," I said, looking at Jeff and then back at Sister Felicia.

"What time is your appointment?" Felicia said, eyeing Jeff.

"It's at two o'clock," I said, positioning my body in front of Jeff.

"Your name?"

"Latwaina Tyler and Jeff Carson."

Scanning the large calendar in front of her, Sister Felicia said, "Okay, I see you here. Have a seat. I'll let him know you're here. He'll be out shortly," she said, with a half-smile.

"What's the deal with her?" Jeff said as we walked away.

"I don't know," I said, stupefied by Sister Felicia's behavior. I was beginning to wonder if the two of them knew one another in a past life.

Before we could sit down good, I heard soft music coming out of Pastor King's office. He'd opened his door and was motioning to Sister Felicia that he was ready to see us.

"Pastor is ready to see you two," Sister Felicia said, standing up.

Pastor King was tall, standing about six-foot-five or taller. He sported dark skin and deep, wavy hair. He was well dressed and wore very expensive cologne. I could tell because I could still smell his cologne on him even after he'd preach three sermons on Sunday. I lifted my head to inhale the smell as Jeff and I walked past the receptionist's desk and into Pastor King's office.

"Praise the Lord," he greeted as he walked over to his oversized cherrywood credenza. I wasn't used to seeing Pastor King sporting just slacks, a white tee, and a sports jacket, because he was always dressed in a suit and tie or wearing a clergy robe.

"Praise the Lord," I greeted back.

Jeff didn't repeat the age-old greeting. He said he could never get used saying it. Instead, he just asked, "Close the door?"

"Yes, please," Pastor King said as he sat down at his desk. "Have a seat here," he said, pointing to the chairs in front of his desk.

Jeff and I sat down in the two chairs as invited. We didn't really know how to start, so it was a good thing Pastor King broke the ice with preliminary chatter.

"Hot out there today, isn't it?"

"Yes, indeed," I said, fanning my face with my right hand.

"Thank God for the invention of air conditioning," he said, chuckling.

I chuckled too, and Jeff offered a partial smile.

"What can I do for you two?" Pastor King said, leaning back in his chair.

"I want to marry her," Jeff blurted out.

"Well, I must say that marriage is an honorable thing. But …"

"But … what?" Jeff challenged.

"But it's not to be entered into too lightly."

"I love her," Jeff declared.

"Okay, okay, hold on a minute. I'm not challenging your love. I've been married for nearly thirty years, and I've been pastoring about half of that time. So I think I know a thing or two about love and marriage," Pastor King said, folding his hands into each other.

"So, what are you telling me?"

"I'm talking to both of you. How old are you?" he asked, looking directly at Jeff.

"I'm thirty-six," Jeff said.

"And you?" Pastor King said, looking at me.

"Twenty-six," I said.

"And how long have the two of you known one another?"

"A little more than a year," I said.

"Well, that's really not a lot of time to know a person, especially when you don't live under the same roof," Pastor King said, eyeing Jeff and me as if he knew we were shacking part time.

"Just what are you suggesting?" Jeff said, cutting to the chase.

"I want you both to wait six more months. Then, if you both are ready to walk down the aisle, we'll start your premarital counseling sessions."

"So you want me to wait to marry the woman of my dreams?" Jeff said, agitated.

"If you want to *stay* married to the woman of your dreams, yes. But look, you're free to do as you please. However, you came here to receive wise counsel, and wisdom says give it six more months before saying, 'I do.'"

After going back and forth with Pastor King a few more times, Jeff finally agreed to wait six months. And the next six months revealed who Jeff truly was.

 They That Wait

I was certain that Jeff and I weren't going to make it the day he suggested the kids go live with their dads.

"You know, you should really let that boy go live with his father."

"*That boy*?" I questioned, giving him the side eye.

"Michael. Young boys really should be raised in the house with a male."

"And what are you?" I barked back.

"But I'm not his father. There's but so much I can say to your kids, Latwaina, without you jumping down my throat."

"Because my kids are good kids, Jeff. They don't give me any problems. I think I'm doing a darn good job being Mommy and Daddy around here."

"That's the thing, Latwaina. It's not necessarily the kids; it's you."

"Me?" I said, putting my hands on my hips.

"Yes, Latwaina. You don't know how to draw the line from smothering them and giving yourself space as a parent."

I chuckled. I sensed all along that Jeff was jealous of my kids.

"And you think it's funny, don't you?" Jeff said, squinting.

"Well, kind of. I've never seen a grown man jealous of kids."

"You think it's jealousy? I'm not jealous of your kids. I just don't get how you keep putting them before me," Jeff said, swinging his black duffle bag over his shoulder.

"So where are you going?" I said, pointing to the duffle bag.

He didn't answer. Instead, he gave me the "none-of-your-business" look. "So, you're just gonna walk out on us like that?" I said, walking up in his face.

"Us? Us, Latwaina? You can't be serious. There's no us, and you know it," Jeff said, pointing at my bare ring finger.

"I took it off when I was cleaning the other day," I lied.

"Latwaina, just stop," Jeff said. "I can count the days you've worn the ring. You don't love me. You love my hand, not my heart," Jeff continued as he opened the front door and began to descend the front steps.

His comment felt like a hard blow to my gut. But it was the coldhearted truth. If I had to be honest with myself, I kept Jeff around because of his generous hand. He kept food in the house. Kept the lights, gas, and the water on. Kept my hair and nails done. Paid the fees for the kids' extracurricular activities at school. Yeah, he had a very generous hand all right, one I wasn't prepared to let go of at this point in time.

"Don't go, Jeff," I begged, following him down the steps.

Jeff descended the last step and kept walking to his truck. "I'll be back for the rest of my stuff," he said as he swung his duffle bag in the bed of his white F-150, got in it, backed out of the driveway, and sped off down the street. It was over … in *less* than six months.

I got Rose to watch the kids that night, even though Anna was thirteen and Michael was nine. I just wanted to be alone. Just me and God.

I lay in my bed that evening, questioning God—*God, I'm tired of living like this. When is it going to be my season?*

I heard nothing but chirping crickets outside my bedroom window. If I had to tell the truth, I was angry. I was angry with God.

"What if God is moving people and things out of your life to replace them with someone and something better?" Those were the words Pastor King had spoken in one of his sermons.

I contemplated … meditated on the words.

Yeah, what if? I thought. And I could hear the faint voice of Grandma Lily reading First Corinthians 9:24—"Don't you know that those who run in a race all run, but one receives the prize? Run like that, that you may win." And this scripture was followed by Isaiah 40:31—"But they that wait upon the Lord shall renew their strength; they shall mount up with wings as eagles; they shall run, and not be weary; and they shall walk, and not faint."

Endurance. Waiting. Patience. Blessings. Something was right around the corner, and I was sure of it. I just had to walk those traits out.

Nearly three weeks later, on September 10, 2011, I attended my niece's wedding. When it was time for the bride to toss the bouquet, I stood in the line along with all the other anxious hopefuls, hoping that if I was lucky enough to catch the bouquet, my knight in shining armor would miraculously appear. To my surprise, my niece threw the bouquet in my direction as if she intended to throw it to me.

"Uh oh," the crowd of women said in unison.

"Somebody's about to meet their husband," my niece, Kierra, chanted.

"Girl, that's an old wives' tale," I said, fanning her away.

"Oh, not really. I caught the bouquet at a wedding and met my husband shortly thereafter," an older woman by the name of Olivia Raines said as she winked simultaneously.

"Oh, I'm sure it was just pure coincidence," I said, making light of the occurrence.

The very next day, September 11, 2011, I'd forgotten all about the festivities of what occurred at the wedding the previous day. I went about my day, running a few needed errands. But while at a red light, I heard the incessant sound of a beeping horn. Looking over to my left, I spotted a handsome caramel brother who'd pulled up in a black Tahoe truck on the side of me.

"Mama, that man is looking at you," Anna said, smiling.

I smiled, noticing that the stranger's eyes seemed locked on me. He was smiling as well.

"Call me," he yelled out, trying to raise his voice over the sound of an approaching ambulance.

"Huh?" I said, motioning with my hands and pretending not to hear what he'd said.

"Call me," he repeated, gesturing with his hand near his ear.

"I can't," I yelled out.

"Why not?"

"My phone is broken," I said. At the time, my cell phone's screen was shattered, and I could only take incoming calls.

"Then, what's your number, beautiful?" he said, prepared to type my number into his phone.

Although I was attracted to this stranger, I was still a little reluctant to give him my number. After waiting a few seconds, he continued. "You gonna give me your number?" he said, holding his phone up.

As if someone had taken over my voice box, I gave him my phone number without further contemplation.

He called my cell phone right away. "Pick up. It's me," he said, winking.

"Hello," I answered as if I had no idea who was on the other end.

"Hello, beautiful. Now, are you gonna gimme your name?"

"Latwaina," I said, smiling from ear to ear as I pulled off from the light, which had turned green by this time.

"Latwaina? That's different. But I like it. Not common … like you."

"How do you know I'm not common? You just met me two-point-five seconds ago. You don't know me."

"I know your type."

"My *type*?" I said, challenging him to go into details.

"Yes, I know your type."

"And what's that?"

"A good woman."

"Oh, really?"

"Yes, really. And I want to get to know you."

"Well, we'll see, Mr. Stranger."

"Mr. Stranger? I have a name."

"Well, what is it?"

"Cliché."

"Cliché?"

"Yeah, that's what my mama told me."

"Like, in the word cliché?" I asked inquisitively.

"Yes, as in the word cliché. But if you give me a chance, this won't be no cliché," he said, winking, proud of his comeback line.

Interestingly enough, it was that infamous date, September 11—the date the world will forever remember, especially Americans. In that moment, I felt as though God was saying, "I am answering your nine-one-one emergency; I'm sending this man to the rescue!" But within moments, the feeling of excitement seemed as though it was beginning to melt away like a withering snowman on a sunny, hot day. I began to feel undeserving. I shook my head as if I could shake the self-sabotaging thoughts from my mind. I grew quiet.

"You all right?" this Cliché guy asked.

"Yeah, I'm all right. Why do you ask?"

"'Cause, all of a sudden, you got quiet on me."

"Oh, never mind me. I was just thinking about something. I'm good though," I said sort of embarrassingly.

"You sure?" he questioned as if I didn't sound too convincing.

"I'm sure," I said, blushing.

Cliché and I continued the conversation as we both drove off in separate directions, he, turning right onto Six Mile Road and I, going straight down Southfield Freeway.

"So, are you gonna let me take you out?"

"When I get to know you," I said, picking up my speed on the freeway.

"That'll be pretty soon, 'cause I like what I see. And I go after what I want."

"You just met me three minutes ago, and you already know that you want me?"

"Yes, I do," he said.

"Well, how do I know you're not married and out just to get a side piece?"

"You don't. But I'm not that type of man. I have a lot of lady friends, and I'll be up front about that."

"Hmmm … lady friends? Is that what they call them now?"

"Well, none of them are my wife, so I don't know what else you want me to call them."

"Well, I am definitely not interested in joining the circle of women club you got going on over there," I said defiantly. Any hopes I had about being with this brother long term was beginning to dwindle away.

"Who said you had to?"

"I'm just letting you know. I've been played before, and it's definitely not a place I want to revisit," I said, standing my newfound high and moral ground.

"I think you got me twisted, beautiful. I'm not that guy," he said. And that's when I heard it—something different in his voice. I couldn't explain it. I only grasped it in the spiritual realm. I did not have the intellectual capacity to articulate this "feeling" with words. But even though I knew I heard something different beyond the words this Cliché man spoke, the voice of my low self-esteem began to rise. *What does this attractive guy want with you, Latwaina? What do you have to offer him? You're just a thrown away, retarded little bitch. What does he want with you?*

Cliché was handsome. His thick, wavy hair could cause motion sickness, as if you were riding against a billowing sea. I knew if I was attracted to him, plenty of other women were attracted to him as well. *What do I have to lose?* I thought. The least I could do was go for it. See what would become of it. After all, he blew his horn at me; I didn't blow mine at him.

Let's see if he can put his money where his mouth is, I thought to myself. And with that, the challenge was on. I was open to see what this "Cliché" dude was all about.

As I turned the corner to pull onto my street, I noticed a strange vehicle parked in the driveway. My first inclination was that it was Jeff, driving someone else's vehicle. I slowed down, creeping down the street toward my house, barely driving fifteen miles per hour. I stopped at the foot of the driveway, waiting to see if someone would emerge from the parked vehicle. Slowly, the driver side door opened, and a leg swung out from the car's interior. Next, the other leg emerged and stepped onto the driveway's asphalt. Slowly, the figure revealed itself. It was Chad. My jaw dropped.

"You look like you just saw a ghost," Chad said after walking up to my car and leaning over into it as I put the gear in park.

"I did. You are a ghost ... to me and especially to your daughter."

"Don't say that. I've come back home to my family," Chad said, trying to plant a kiss on my lips.

"Don't kiss me. I'm taken," I lied.

"Not for long," he said, opening the car door for me.

"I got it," I said, pushing his hands away.

"No, you don't, Latwaina," Chad said, looking me over.

Although I shouldn't have been. I was embarrassed. Because of my financial situation, I hadn't had my hair or nails done in nearly two months. I'd kept both up when Jeff was around. But now that he was on the "you're-not-gonna-play-me," mission, I was on my own. I couldn't afford personal upkeep. "How did you find out where I live?" I said, trying to throw Chad off.

"I have connections; you know that."

"Oh, yeah ... I forgot," I said facetiously.

"Look, Latwaina, let's go inside. I know you're mad, and you have every reason to be. I haven't held up my end of the bargain, but neither have you."

"Excuse me?" I said perplexed.

"You heard me. You and I made a vow to never leave one another. We're a family."

"We're a family when it's convenient for you, Chad. Where were you when our lights were out? Where were you when I was losing my house? Where have you been?"

"I'm not going to stick around when you have another man smelling around you and Anna. That's *my* daughter."

"Then you should act like it," I said, getting out of the car, storming past Chad and walking up the front steps.

"I don't compete with other men for what I know belongs to me," Chad said, following me up the steps.

"You have a lot of nerve to come here with this slick talk as though I did something to push you away," I said as I put the key into the door. I'd forgotten all about the hot water and the lights being off. But then again, Chad needed to see how we were living without his financial help. I pushed the front door open and stepped inside. It was sweltering hot inside.

"Put on the A.C.," Chad said, fanning his face.

"Ain't got none," I said.

"Then turn on the ceiling fan," Chad said, walking over and plopping down on the sofa Jeff had bought before he left.

"No electricity," I said, handing him a folded piece of newspaper to fan with.

"No electricity?" Chad said with disbelief.

"No. I lost my job some time ago," I confessed embarrassingly.

"Why didn't you call me?"

"Call you for what?"

"I would have come," Chad said.

"Well, you're here now. What are you gonna do about it?"

"Where's Anna?" Chad said, changing the subject.

"She's not here."

"Where is she?"

"She's at my bonus mom's house."

"I want to see her."

"You can see her when she comes home," I said, sitting on the opposite end of the sofa.

"When is that?"

"They'll be here in about forty-five minutes."

Chad nodded as he stood. "Bathroom?"

"Down the hall to your left," I said, pointing him toward the direction of the main bathroom.

While Chad was in the bathroom, my mind traced the events that occurred earlier that day. I smiled to myself.

"What's so funny?" Chad said, walking back into the living room.

"I'm not laughing," I said, looking up at Chad, who was rubbing his hands against the sides of his denim shorts.

"No clean hand towel either, huh?"

"Gotta go to the laundry," I said.

"Well, I see there's shaving cream, razors, and men's cologne in the bathroom cabinets. So tell me … how are you living like this if there's a man around here?"

"He's no longer here," I said, shocked that Chad had the audacity to try to check me like that.

"Doesn't seem like it to me. I took a peek in your bedroom. He's got his stuff all up in the closet and everything. I was coming to get my family, but you look like you've already replaced me."

"I said, we broke up," I said, getting up from the sofa. "You were gone, so what did you expect … for me to sit around, twiddling my thumbs, hoping and praying you'd come to your senses?"

"That's that bull you women play. You don't remember hanging up in my face that night, do you?"

"Yeah, I remember," I said, rolling my eyes. "You called me for a booty call."

"Booty call? That's what you call it?"

"Yeah, that's what it was. We hadn't seen you in a month of Sundays, and then you come calling in the middle of the night, asking me if you could come over. I don't know what they call it on your side of town, but on mine, it's called a booty call, no ifs, ands, or buts about it," I said, doing a hard eye roll.

"I'll tell you what … I'm not about to share you or Anna with anyone else. Check for me when you put that dude out for good," Chad said, heading for the front door.

He wasn't making any sense, and I wasn't going to spend any more of my breath going back and forth with Chad and his three-legged argument. I let him walk out of mine and Anna's life that day. After all, I'd just met another potential guy … Cliché. And if he was even half the man he said he was, I knew I'd score big, and my children would score big as well. It was all good.

I closed the door behind Chad and locked it, locking him out of my house, heart, and mind for good.

CHAPTER 19

Conflict of Interest

The ping on my cell phone woke me up that morning. With squinted eyes, I reached for the phone and entered my passcode.

Jeff: Can I come by?

Jeff … I took a deep breath before texting him back.

Me: U don't have to ask to come get your stuff.

Jeff: That's not why I want to come by.

Me: Then why do u want to stop by?

Jeff: Umm … to talk.

Me: Talk about what?

Jeff: Us.

Me: Us? U said u didn't want this.

Jeff: I didn't mean it. I was talking out of frustration.

Me: Got a lot going on, and u know it.
Jeff: So … is that a yes or no?
Me: I'm not making any promises, but u can come by.

My body tensed up when I heard Jeff's footsteps walking up the front steps. I wasn't ready to deal with him. Plus, I liked the new Cliché guy. But I was still struggling financially, and Jeff had already proven that he would help me if I needed it.

Before Jeff could knock, I swung the door open.

"You must be happy to see me. I didn't even have to knock," Jeff said in a boastful tone.

"I heard you coming up the steps," I said, bursting his ego.

"Oh, so you're not happy to see me?"

"Jeff, you said you wanted to come over and talk, so let's talk," I said, walking over to the sofa. Jeff followed me.

"Look, Latwaina, I just want to make it work. Can we just start over?"

"What's gonna change?" I said, plopping down on the sofa.

"Both of us," Jeff said as a grin formed.

I cracked a half-smile, my way of letting Jeff know that I was willing to give "us" another shot. After all, I really didn't have a choice, at least not yet. I still needed him.

"Can I have a kiss?" Jeff said, puckering up his thick lips.

Reluctantly, I puckered my lips and leaned over to kiss him. His lips were wet, as if he'd just licked them. After the awkward kiss, an awkward moment of silence crept in.

Finally breaking the silence, Jeff said, "Are you good?"

"The lights are still out," I said, holding my hand out.

"Here. This is all I got on me," he said, reaching in his front pants pocket and handing me a roll of crumpled bills.

I didn't want to appear like a fiend, counting the money right then and there, so I just smiled and said, "Thank you."

"I'll be back a little later. I gotta make a quick run," he said, getting up.

I stood and followed Jeff to the door.

"I missed you," Jeff said, turning to face me before exiting.

"Missed you too," I lied. I was getting used to this lying game; it got me what I needed. *Too bad he isn't the new guy, Cliché*, I thought. I watched Jeff descend the front steps and closed the door once he got in his vehicle and began to back out of the driveway.

I ran my hands through my long, braided extensions. *I need to get my braids redone*, I thought as I did a self-assessment of my hairdo in the bathroom mirror. I'd agreed to go on a date with the new guy, Cliché. Not only was my hair a mess, but I was driving an old, raggedy green van that kept stalling and cutting off on me. My nails and feet needed to be done, too. The money Jeff gave me was sure going to be put to good use.

Although I had no intentions of letting this Cliché dude in my place, I tidied up, nonetheless. I knew the ole "Can I use your bathroom," ploy all too well. People, both men and women, use the line when they want to inspect your place … to see how you're living … to check to see if you live alone … or to simply prolong their stay in your presence.

With the money Jeff had given me, I made an appointment to get my braids redone. Getting my braids done always took four to five hours, so I made the appointment for ten o'clock the next morning. My date with Cliché was at five o'clock, giving me enough time to get my hair done, drive back home, take a shower, and get ready.

Peering through the kitchen window, I spotted his truck as he turned into the subdivision. I felt the pebbles pop out on my forehead as I watched him slowly drive toward the house.

"He's here," I said to Anna.

"Your new boyfriend?" Anna said gleefully.

"No, he's not my boyfriend … just a friend," I said, smiling.

"You like him already, Mama?"

"No, I'm just going on a date, that's all."

"But you have a big smile on your face," Anna said, totally taking me by surprise with her comment.

"I *do*?" I said, trying to erase any semblance of a smile on my face.

"Yes, you do, Mom," Michael said, taking his attention away from his homework.

I looked over at Michael. Seeing Michael rush to complete his homework before the sun went down made my heart sink to my stomach. The lights were still out, and there I was going on a date. I knew it didn't make sense, but there was nothing I could do. I owed too much money to get the lights turned back on. And what Jeff had given me wasn't enough. And as if he could read my mind, Michael said, "I'm almost done, Mom."

I forced a smile, but inside, my heart was bleeding. Emotionally, I was succeeding at parenting, but financially, I felt I was failing. I headed for the front door, so I could meet Cliché on the front steps. Anna followed me.

"So, do I look all right?" I said, twirling around like a ballerina.

"Yes, Mama. You look beautiful."

"Okay. I'll take your word for it," I said, opening the front door.

I stood at the top of the steps until Cliché pulled into the driveway. Under the assumption that he was going to park, I began to head down the steps.

"Where are you going?" he asked, rolling down his window.

"I thought we were going out to dinner?" I said, stopping on the last step.

"Not so fast, cutie pie," Cliché said, now getting out of his truck.

"By the way, that's a nice truck you have," I said, admiring his Chevy Tahoe.

"Thank you. But you've seen it before."

"I know, but it looks extra shiny today."

"Yeah, got a wash this morning," Cliché said, walking toward me. I tried to disguise my excitement. I was turned on by a brother. He looked good, and his cologne had traveled up my nostrils, causing him to look even more appealing. "Are you going to invite me in?" he said as he walked up on me.

"Do you have to use the bathroom or something?" I said, trying to gauge his reason for wanting to go in the house.

"No … but I'd like to meet your children, if that's all right with you."

"Well … um, I usually don't introduce my children to men until I know it's serious."

"Cutie pie, it's gonna be serious soon enough. Let me meet your children."

"Well …" I said, hesitating.

"Well, what?"

"I have a little problem."

"A little problem?" Cliché asked inquisitively.

"Come on, I'll show you," I said, leading him up the steps.

I opened the front door and let Cliché in. He looked around and looked back at me. "So, what's wrong?"

I flipped the light switch. "My lights are out."

"How long have they been out?" Cliché said, looking around.

"A few weeks," I admitted, embarrassingly.

"A few weeks?!" Cliché asked, shocked.

"Really, it's been a little over a month."

"Well, obviously you don't have the money, or else your lights would be on. But don't you have family you could borrow the money from?"

"No … I mean, I have family, but we're kind of estranged. They treat me and my children bad and don't really want us around, so I just stay away," I confessed.

"Wait … when you say family, do you mean your parents?"

"My mom, yes. My dad is deceased. But my mother and her side of the family."

"Why?" Cliché asked in disbelief.

"It's a long story. I can't get into it right now, but one day I will," I said, fighting back tears.

"Well, we're gonna do something about these lights today. Hold on, I'll be right back," Cliché said, walking past me and heading for the door.

"I thought you wanted to meet my children?" I said, not wanting him to leave so soon.

"I said I'll be back. I'll meet them when I get back."

"Well, where are you going?"

"I'll be back, cutie. Just wait," Cliché said, exiting the front door and closing it behind him.

I sat down on the sofa bought by Jeff. I was ashamed and sad. Poverty. I was living in poverty, and it had probably cost me a relationship. I wondered whether Cliché even had any intentions of returning. *What if he never comes back? What if he thinks you're a bad mom? What if, what if.* I knew I couldn't do anything about my circumstances. I knew I worked hard. I was once a homeowner. I had a good-paying job in the past. I drove a nice vehicle. I was sure I'd recover one day; I just didn't know how long the recovery period would be.

I was on the verge of trading my dating outfit for my pajamas, wiping the makeup off my face and throwing my braids in a bonnet, when I heard the sound of a car pulling into the driveway. Peering through the side window of the living room, I saw that it was Cliché. *He came back.*

I watched as he got out of the driver's side of the car and retrieved a large box from the back seat. When he started up the steps, I ran to the front door and opened it.

"You came back," I announced from the doorway.

"Of course. I told you I'd be back. "I'm a man of my word," he said as he landed on the top step.

"What's that?" I said, referring to the huge box he was carrying.

"It's a generator … so you can get some electricity going on in here," he said, walking past me and into the living room.

"You bought me a generator?" I asked, both shocked and happy by the gesture.

"That's what you need. You need that more than a meal at some fancy, dancy restaurant, don't you think?" Cliché said, putting the box on the coffee table. "You got a knife so I can open this?" he continued.

"Sure," I said, heading for the kitchen.

Once I handed Cliché the knife, I sat on the sofa and watched him as he opened the box, retrieved the generator, and set it up.

"I need to hook this up outside," he said, picking up the generator.

I followed him outside and watched as he worked the wiring and set the generator up.

"Lights should be on now," he said, clapping the dirt off his hands.

Looking up, I could see the lights on in the living room. I couldn't help but smile from ear to ear. Finally, we had electricity again. I wanted to jump into Cliché's arms and kiss him. But I knew I didn't know him like that. Plus, he'd probably think I was some crazed lady. So instead of jumping into his arms, I simply asked, "How can I repay you?"

"Cook me a nice dinner on our next date," he said, winking.

"Date? You call this a date? You've been helping me the whole time."

"That's what a man is supposed to do. If a man can't help you, he shouldn't be around. Remember that." I offered a smile. "So, do you think you can do that … cook me a meal?" he continued.

"Sure," I said. "Do you have anything in particular you want?"

"Chicken. Some good ole fried chicken."

"You got it," I said.

"But for tonight, let's go pick up some pizza for dinner. Have the kids eaten?"

"I picked them up a sub earlier."

"They're probably hungry again. Let's just get enough for everybody," Cliché insisted.

He's including the kids. I recognized Cliché's selfless concern and behavior … something absent in Jeff's psyche. He had to be reminded that I had children, because he almost never included them as part of his conversation or quest for adventure. But this Cliché dude … he'd just scored major brownie points with me.

Cliché and I left for Happy's Pizza, where he'd ordered two large pizzas, sausage, which as Michael's favorite, and Anna's favorite, supreme. During our drive to Happy's, we engaged in the typical "get to know you" conversation.

"So, tell me, what made you give me your number?" Cliché said, looking at me and then at the road.

"I thought you were cute," I said.

"Ha," he laughed. "And I thought you were a chocolate queen."

"*Really*?" I said, blushing.

"Yes, really." He paused and then continued. "Can I ask you a question?"

"Sure," I said, looking over at him.

"Why is a beautiful lady like you single?"

"That's the million-dollar question. I've wondered myself."

"No, serious. Why are you single?"

"It's just timing, I guess." This question often makes women uncomfortable. I mean, the question sort of puts us on the spot, as if we're supposed to know why. Sometimes, we do … sometimes, we don't. I don't think I'd ever really thought about what input I might have had in my singleness. Perhaps I had unrealistic expectations when it came to relationships. Then again, maybe I had some flawed characteristic that either allowed men to take advantage of me or a quality that communicated my low self-esteem, which drove the good ones away. Heck, it could have been a combination of both. I wasn't sure. But I repeated, "It's just timing, I guess."

"Is that the answer you want to stick with?" Cliché said, taking his eyes away from the road and looking dead at me.

"Yeah," I said, feeling even more uneasy. He was digging too deep … in areas of weakness, shame, and pain. "Why are *you* single?" I said, directing the same question back at him.

"Well … I'm not really single. I mean, I don't have *one* girlfriend or lady friend."

"Oh, so you're a playa?" I said, sucking my teeth.

"No, not that. I just don't have one lady right now. I'm dating."

"So, I'm just one in the number, huh?" I said, sucking my teeth again.

"No, I wouldn't say that. I haven't found the woman of my dreams … that is, until I met you," he said, winking.

"Please spare me the sentiments," I said. "Does a woman of your dreams really exist?"

"Sure, she does."

"Well, I only deal with one-woman guys."

He chuckled.

"Is something funny?" I said, trying to disguise the humor in my voice.

Cliché cleared his throat. "Latwaina, finding the right lady takes time. But I can already tell that we're gonna go far."

"Is that what you tell *all* the women?"

"No, but I do tell them where we stand. The last thing I want is to come outside and see my tires slashed. I don't have time for that. So, I'm upfront with women on where they stand. Until it gets serious, we're just kickin' it."

I heard Cliché clearly. One thing my dad taught me was to respect the truth that a man speaks. At least he was being honest. It let me know how I should move as far as Jeff and my own love life were concerned. I wasn't about to give up my financial support system … i.e., Jeff, at least no time soon. One thing I'd learned over the years was to keep my emotions on the back burner until a man showed me that I was number one in his life. So, I was good with kickin' it with Cliché for the time being. In my eyes, what was good for the goose was good for the gander.

We picked up the pizzas and headed back to the house, where Anna and Michael were eagerly waiting. And there you have it—our first date became a family affair. And you know what? It was probably the best thing that could have happened. No mushy kissing. No lies being told. No unreasonable expectations. And most importantly, no sex. Just a laid back, casual evening.

I sat back and watched Cliché interact with Anna and Michael. He asked Anna questions about her plans for the future while playing a quick game of UNO with the three of us and then playing video games with Michael.

I must be dreaming, I thought as I lay in bed that night. I had electricity in the home after several weeks. I'd met the most generous man that I truly liked. Unlike Jeff, I was attracted to this Cliché guy. He turned on every button in me that I could think of. He was sociable, friendly, funny at times, and just genuinely nice … at least that's what he showed me—us—that night. I could already see myself in a committed relationship with him. The only problem was there were two things in the way—Jeff and other women.

CHAPTER 20

Tug of War

squinted, trying to zero in on her face. It was "her." Her, being Alisha Davis, an old classmate from the all-girls' school I'd attended. She must've spotted me because our eyes met and soon locked in on each other. She smiled. I waved. Then we both walked toward each other.

"Alisha? That's you?" I said, eyeing her from head to toe. She'd gained at least fifty pounds since I'd seen her last. She used to be skinny like Popeye's wife, Olive Oyl. Even having had one child at the time, Alisha was still pretty darn skinny back then. We both fell into each other's arms once we got close enough.

"Oh, my goodness! Where have you been?!" she said, squeezing me tighter with each uttered word.

"I've been around," I said, gasping for air.

"Girl, it's been forever since I've seen you!" Alisha said, finally releasing her firm embrace.

"I know … same here. It's been forever since I've seen you. And speaking of it, when was the last time we've seen one another?

"Graduation?" Alisha said, trying to jog her memory, because she didn't need to jog mine. I'd dropped out of school long before graduation. So graduation wasn't the last time we'd seen each other; it had to be long before then.

"No, it was way before graduation," I said, correcting her.

"Well, it don't matter. It's been a long damn time, that's all I know," she said as a bright smile swept across her face.

"Yeah, long time," I agreed.

"So, is this your baby girl … what's her name, again?"

"Anna. Anna Nichelle."

"Oh, that's such a pretty name. How's baby daddy doing, with his fine self."

"Baby who?" I said, trying to act as if she'd just cursed.

"Chad. How's Chad?"

"Anna, go on over there and sit down until I get finished," I said, fanning Anna away. I didn't want her to hear my response. Once Anna had walked over to the sitting area, I resumed my conversation with Alisha. "You mean the sperm donor?"

"Don't say that. I take it y'all are not together."

"Nope … and by his own choice. He chose not to be in his child's life because he can't be my man."

"But y'all were such a great couple. He loved you, Latwaina."

"You got that right … lov-ved," I said, placing emphasis on the past tense of the word.

"Well, I guess that's water under the bridge now," Alisha said, brushing her bangs to the side.

"I almost didn't recognize you. What have you been up to?" I asked.

"It's the weight, I know. You're not used to me this size. I'm sixty-three pounds heavier since high school. Sixty-three pounds and three children later."

"Three? You have three children?" I said, shocked. I couldn't have imagined my life with three children. Anna and Michael were more than enough for me.

"Yes. Courtney is my first born, and then I had twins, Aiden and Asia."

"Well, where are they?" I said, looking around.

"They're at my mama's house. I can't handle them in the mall. They want too much," Alisha said, laughing.

"So, what have you been up to?" I asked, making conversation.

"Working and doing a little playing on the side," she said as she burst into laughter.

"You're still crazy," I said, giving her a slight nudge. Alisha was a no-holds-barred type of person. As a matter of fact, she and Keisha didn't get along, because Alisha felt Keisha was coming between our friendship.

"Look, I gotta hurry up and get back to my mom's to pick up the kids. Let me get your number. And let's hang out … just the *two* of us," she said, whipping out her cell phone to lock my number in her phone. "I'mma call you, and we can plan something. Maybe even let the kids meet up at some point," she said.

"Okay. Sounds good."

"I'll be seeing you soon," Alisha said, rushing off.

I watched Alisha until she was completely out of sight. Then I motioned for Anna to come back over to where I was standing.

"Who's that lady?" Anna asked.

"Somebody I know from school."

"Well, what did she want?"

"Nothing. We just happened to bump into one another. We haven't seen each other in years. Gonna get together soon."

"Sounds way too cool. Now you have a friend," Anna said, smiling. I could tell she was genuinely happy for me. Although I wanted to smile, I was sad. Anna was correct. I didn't have any friends. Even though our children were cousins, Keisha and and I were estranged. It's not that we didn't like each other; we were older and living in separate worlds. Me? I was still trying to make the best out of a tragic past. I had put most of my energy into my children; they were my whole world. I wanted friends, but the rejection I'd experienced with my own flesh and blood held me back from trying to form friendships. In my mind, there was always the possibility of that friendship causing me to experience feelings of rejection and isolation once again. I didn't even want Anna to know that I was afraid of reuniting with Alisha. But to mask my fear, I pretended I was excited about the run-in with Alisha.

"Yeah, I know … way too cool," I said.

Jeff was waiting at the house in the driveway when Anna and I returned home from the mall.

"Uh oh … guess who's here," Anna announced, looking at me.

"I know. It's Jeff," I said, cringing on the inside. I'd promised him we'd go out, but I wasn't really in the mood to go out. I had to make up an excuse to keep from having to go out with him. I had to think fast. Then, it popped into my head: *I'll pretend my cycle is on. Yeah, that's what I'll do.*

"We still on for tonight?" Jeff said, getting out of his car.

"I'm cramping," I lied, holding the bottom of my stomach.

"Sick enough to go out on a date with me but not sick enough to spend my money in the mall? Tell me, what's wrong with that picture, Lawanda?"

"It's Latwaina," I corrected. "And for your information, my cycle started once I was at the mall."

"So, I'll just stay here then. We can watch movies here," Jeff countered.

"You can stay here all you want," I lied. I didn't want him to stay. I wanted him to turn right back around, get in his car, and drive off.

"Cool. I'll order food for us to eat."

"What about the kids?" I said, motioning for Anna to go into the house.

"They didn't eat?" Jeff said, trying to act oblivious.

"You never include the kids. Why?"

"I don't mean no harm. I just didn't mention them."

"But you do that all the time, Jeff. You never include the kids," I said, agitated.

"Lawanda, I give you money for the kids, don't I?"

"It's Latwaina, Jeff. Latwaina. You give me money, yeah. But you never give me money and say, 'Here, this is for Anna, or here, this is for Michael.'"

"Okay, thank you for reminding me. Next time, I'll make sure to mention the kids' names. Is that what you want? I just can't win with you," Jeff said, throwing up his hands.

"Don't worry about it, Jeff. Don't do them no favors. They can already tell you don't care about them."

"Because you've put that in their heads."

"I don't say anything to my children. They're smart. They can think for themselves," I said, sucking my teeth.

"Isn't your stomach hurting? Can we just go in the house and stop arguing? I didn't come here for that," Jeff said, storming past me and up the front steps.

I followed him into the house and headed straight for my bedroom. But I could hear Jeff and Michael's conversation from my bedroom.

"We're gonna order in for dinner. Anything in particular you have a taste for?" Jeff asked Michael, who was preoccupied, playing on his gaming station.

"Anything but pizza or Chinese rice."

"Do you like Thai?"

"It'll do," Michael responded.

"What about your sister? Does she like Thai?"

"Why don't you ask her?" I said, now walking back into the living room.

"She likes Thai," Michael said, giving me the ole "don't-be-so-mean" look.

Jeff ordered the food, and we sat down, watching Michael play his gaming station until the food arrived, making small talk. I was irritated with Jeff. I'd much rather have been out with the new guy, Cliché. That's why when he called my phone, I was surprised. I pretended it was a call from my mom.

"I'll be back. It's my mom," I lied. I went into my bedroom and closed the door. "Hey, you!" I greeted Cliché.

"Hey, beautiful. What are you up to this evening?" his velvety voice said from the other side of the receiver.

"Just chilling with the kids."

"You want some company?"

I broke out in a hot sweat. Of course, I wanted *his* company. But Jeff had already paid for my company that night. So, the same lie I'd told Jeff, I had to tell Cliché. "I'm actually not feeling well. Got cramps."

"Do you need me to get you anything … soup, medicine … whatever?"

"Nah, I'm okay. It's just that time of the month," I lied. I wanted to kick Jeff out of the house, but I knew he'd suspect something if I told him I needed to leave for a so-called emergency. Jeff had been around long enough to know my family dynamics.

I reluctantly ended the call with Cliché and returned to the living room where Jeff had stretched out on the sofa. The pretend game was beginning to make me irritated with Jeff. He loved for us to snuggle up together on the sofa, which made my skin crawl every time. I couldn't wait until my financial circumstances changed and I could dump Jeff. But until that time came, I had to play this little game for my financial survival.

"I'm confused. So, which guy do you like, Latwaina?" Alisha asked between sips of her Long Island iced tea. We had agreed to meet up at Starter's Sports Bar just to hang out and catch up.

"I like the Cliché dude," I said, smiling.

"So, what's the problem?" she said, taking another sip.

"Well, I feel sort of trampy because I'm seeing them both."

"And what's wrong with that?"

"Well, you know girls ain't supposed to be out here playing the field," I confessed.

"Says who?"

"It goes without saying. It's just the way it is," I said, twirling a fallen ring curl on the right side of my head.

"Look, Latwaina. You don't owe nobody jack. Until you start treatin' these niggas in the street like they treat us, they'll never learn. You want a man to sweat you? Start ignoring his butt. Do what they do to us. They can't handle the heat. I watched my older cousins do it. They get what they want too. Play by these crazy rules if you want, you'll get crazy results," she said, chuckling. She'd obviously humored herself with the mini-sermon she'd just rendered.

But she was right. So, for the next several months, I played the game that men had taught me all too well. I dated Jeff on the weekends and saw "my favorite guy," Cliché, Monday through Friday. Talk about being pulled in both directions like the rope in a tug-of-war competition. That was me.

PRE-FORECLOSURE. The words were printed in big, bold letters at the top the letter from Wachovia Bank. Charles was losing the house. And what it essentially meant for me was one word: eviction. Then, there was that feeling again—losing the place where I laid my head every night. I felt a surge of heat creep up my spine. *Calm down, Latwaina.* I grabbed my cell phone and called Charles. He picked up on the second ring.

"Hey, beautiful. Everything all right?" he said in a cheery voice.

"No, not really," I responded.

"Something break down over there?"

"The mortgage."

"Ohh …" he said, figuring out what I was referencing. "Oh, don't worry about that. Delores and I got that taken care of on our end."

"Why would they send a pre-foreclosure notice to the house?"

"Don't worry about that. It was just a mix up."

"Are you sure?" I said, detecting skepticism in his voice.

"Sure, baby girl. I'm sure. Just keep paying your rent. Everything will be fine," he said. But for some reason, I didn't believe him. "Latwaina? Are you there?"

"I'm here," I answered.

"Well, you're quiet. I said don't worry about that letter. Matter of fact, I'm gonna stop by and get it, so I can call them about it. You home?"

"Of course, I'm home. I just pulled it out of the mailbox a few minutes ago."

"Well, isn't it addressed to me and Delores?"

"Tell you the truth, I didn't pay that no mind. It said 'time sensitive information enclosed' on the envelope. I've been through foreclosure before. So yes, I opened the letter."

"That's a federal offense, you know. You can go to jail for opening someone else's mail."

"Mailbox, not mail."

"So, I'mma head your way and come grab that letter in a few minutes."

I was the least bit happy to see Charles when he arrived. Happy and cherry to see me, he reached out to hug me, but I pushed him away.

"Don't be like that, baby girl. I said I have this all under control. You're so used to men lying to you that you don't know how to let one love on you."

"Charles, you have a whole wife at home," I said, sucking my teeth.

"I told you when we first met, she and I have an arrangement. Delores is none of your concern. Let me handle Delores."

"I never told you I wanted to handle her."

"Just pay your rent as we agreed. Give me a little time and attention, and we're good. You know …" Charles said, pulling me into his chest with force.

"My kids are here," I said, trying to loosen his grip on me.

"Shh … just give me a little hug," he said, pulling me tighter. Before he could plant his crusty lips on mine, we heard footsteps walking up the outside steps. "You expecting company?" he said, looking around, disappointed.

"Not really expecting company. It might be my friend, Jeff."

"You mean, your nigga, huh? The dude you got living up in my house, playing house with you," Charles said, letting my hands loose so he could fix his pants in an attempt to disguise his erect penis.

"He's just a friend."

"Yeah? Well, I'm just a landlord. It's about time we modify the special rental agreement we have. Don't you think?"

Knowing both Jeff and Cliché had my back, I didn't hesitant to agree. I mean, come hell or high water, I'd get a little money from both of them and add it to whatever I made from my job and the little odds and ends money I made whenever I went to help Mama with her clients. "If that means I don't have to be your slave, then so be it."

"Expect the new agreement to come in the mail in the next few days."

"Okay," I said, following Charles to the door.

Jeff was just about to put the key in the lock when Charles opened the door to leave. The two of them did the head nod, acknowledging each other, but neither one spoke. Charles dashed down the steps and jumped in his car so fast, I couldn't stop him to give him the letter from the bank that he'd left behind.

"What's that all about?" Jeff asked when I walked back in the house.

"Oh, nothing. Just a piece of mail for him."

"Must be an important piece of mail because you almost knocked me down trying to flag him down to give it to him."

For two and a half seconds, I debated whether I should go into details about the pre-foreclosure issue with Jeff. Ultimately, I decided not to. Cliché was around, and the last thing I wanted was Jeff using his financial help as leverage for why I should be with him and not Cliché. But I was digging Cliché and didn't want to bring any unnecessary drama into the picture. Plus, Jeff had been good to the kids and me, so I owed him a certain level of respect.

"It's nothing," I said, folding the envelope up and tucking it in the back pocket of the jeans I was wearing.

I knew my feelings toward Cliché were strong the day Cliché called me when I was out with Jeff. I didn't hesitate to pick up.

"Where are you?" Cliché asked.

"At the mall," I replied.

"Oh, with who?"

"Me, the kids, and my friend, Jeff."

"*Jeff?* Who's Jeff?" Cliché said with a hint of jealously in his tone.

"My friend, Jeff," I said, not offering any further details.

"Well, I want to come over tonight."

"I don't know what time I'll be back home," I lied. I had every plan on returning home once we left the mall. I just didn't want to let Cliché know my plans.

"What about tomorrow?" Cliché said, this time, with a little desperation in his voice.

"Church tomorrow. And after church, I have plans," I said. I did have after-church plans. I was stopping by to see Rose. She had carpel tunnel surgery on her left wrist, and I promised to come by and fix dinner for her.

"Guess that leaves me for boring Monday," Cliché said, settling for Monday.

It took everything in me to continue to proceed with this game I was playing. I so desperately wanted to see Cliché, but I wouldn't have ever been able to get rid of Jeff so easily. Plus, I didn't want to expose the kids to my raggedy lifestyle …

at that moment in time. You see, I was doing Latwaina and nothing but Latwaina. The way I moved was for the benefit of Latwaina.

When Monday rolled around, Cliché came over just as he'd said he would. But he was acting different, a little edgy … pacing back and forth.

"What's up with you?" I said, having never seen this side of Cliché. He didn't readily answer. "So, am I talking to you, or am I talking to the wall?" I added.

"That Jeff dude—"

"What about him?" I said, cutting Cliché off.

"Are you gonna keep seeing him or what?" His eyes were fixed on me; he didn't even seem as though he blinked.

I remembered the words of Alisha. Everything she'd said seemed to be unfolding right before my eyes. Cliché—the one with at least fifteen other women—was in my house, jealous of me and little ole Jeff. If he only knew … I didn't like Jeff at all. He was a person of convenience in my life. I didn't like anything about him, not his smile, his conversation, his sense of humor, his sex—nothing. Only his money.

"Aren't you dating other people, yourself?" I responded, playing tough. "I mean, how do I know I'm not just another notch on your belt?" I lashed out.

"Ms. Lady, I don't want none of them other women," Cliché said, pulling me into him.

"Yeah, that's what you say."

"I want you. And so, things are about to change around here," he said, squeezing me tight.

"Oh, really," I said, taking what he'd just uttered with a grain of salt.

"Let's go get married," Cliché said.

"Married?"

"Yes, let's get married."

"When?" I said, anticipating he'd throw out a ridiculous date so far down the calendar that you'd need a telescope to see it.

"Tomorrow."

CHAPTER 21

Cliché

"Whatever." I said, brushing him off.

"I'm serious as a heart attack, Latwaina."

"Married. You wanna get married?"

"Yes," Cliché said, not even batting an eye.

"Tomorrow?"

"Yep. Tomorrow."

"How do you suppose we do that?"

"I have it all planned out," he said with a big smile on his face.

I burst into laughter. "You're joking, right?"

"No, I'm not joking. I'm serious."

"Umm … what about bridesmaids? Groomsmen? Flowers? My dress? My hair? My nails?"

"I got you. But we ain't doing that formal kinda stuff. No bridesmaids. No groosmen. Just us. Just you and me. And I got money for your hair and nails. We'll go out later, and you can pick out a nice dress you like."

"And where is this wedding supposed to take place, downtown at the Justice of the Peace?"

"Don't worry about the details. I have it all planned out to the tee. The only thing you need to do is get your pretty little self all dolled up for your husband-to-be."

A wide smile swept across my face. He was serious! He wanted to marry little ole me. Latwaina. The outcast. The girl-turned-woman with low self-esteem. The used and abused girl. The one they tried to lock up and throw away the key. Me. Finally, when my nerves had calmed some, I spoke. "You're serious, aren't you?"

"Yes. I told you."

"Can I ask you a question?"

"You can ask me anything you want."

"Why me? You're paid well and work in the plant. You're handsome. And, before meeting me, you were dating doctors and lawyers. You could have any woman you want. Why me?"

Cliché cleared his throat. "You don't get it, do you? Why *not* you?" I hunched my shoulders. Cliché continued. "Listen, I need to admit something to you. When we first met, it was your beauty that attracted me. But when we began to get close, I started falling in love with your soul. And then, God told me you would be my wife."

The moment was surreal. Standing in front of me was the man I was crazy in love with, even though I'd played it off many times. After all, no one wants to appear as though they are digging a person if the feelings are not reciprocated. I felt so much, but my mouth couldn't form the words to articulate what I was feeling. But I tried. "I feel …"

"Like what?" Cliché said in a soft whisper.

"Like I'm—"

"Dreaming?" Cliché said, cutting me off.

"Yes, like I'm dreaming."

"Baby, you're not dreaming. This is for real. I am asking you to be my wife."

"Are you sure?" I said, wondering whether he was going to blurt out, "Joking!"

"Look, I wrestled with this for a while. Trust me, I didn't want to give up the way I was living. But God told me that I had to … in order to be with you. You are a woman of value. You are dedicated, and you love hard. I watched you struggle with your children, oftentimes, not asking anyone for help. And even when you were struggling, you maintained a beautiful heart the entire time. I love your laugh and your sense of humor. But to be honest, your wrath has scared me a couple of times," Cliché said, letting out a light chuckle.

I burst into laughter. He was referring to the few times our paths crossed, and he was out with another female. One time, I followed them around town, trailing a few cars behind them. Of course, he knew I was stalking him, and he ended the date early. The second time, we bumped into each other at the mall. There again, he had some scallywag on his arm. When I saw them sitting down in the food court, I politely walked over to their table and threw my cold cup of iced tea at him and the chick he had been parading around the mall with. "Those chicks deserved it. They were with my man," I joked.

"You gone marry me or what, lady?" Cliché asked.

"I have one last question."

"Shoot."

"Well, you said I was the one for you. But what did you do about all those other women?" I just had to ask the question. Cliché had enough keys on his key ring to make think he was the maintenance man in a high-rise residential apartment building. But his were keys to the homes and apartments of the many women he was seeing.

"They're gone. Don't worry about them. They don't matter anymore," Cliché said, chuckling as he retrieved his keyring from his pants pocket. There were just four keys on the key-ring—the key to his house, his car, his post office box, and golden a key—the key to my house and heart. "See? Gone. They're all gone. I either gave them back their keys, or I threw them away."

"You did what?" I deliberately asked. I wanted him to repeat himself.

"I gave them their keys back. I only want one woman … and that's you. Now, again, are you gonna marry me or what?" he said, digging his hands in his opposite pants pocket and pulling out the most gorgeous piece of jewelry a man, besides my dad, had ever given me. He held it up to the light. "This, my dear, is a two-and-a-half carat cushion-cut diamond ring."

Tears began to flow down my cheeks. I could feel my knees buckling. "Oh, my goodness!" I screamed.

"Will you marry me, Latwaina?" Cliché said, now getting down on his knee.

"Yes! Yes!" I said as I walked closer to him and nearly collapsed on top of him.

Helping me catch my balance, Cliché placed a soft, wet kiss on my lips. "Give me your hand," he said, holding the ring out.

I was so nervous that I held out my right hand.

"No, baby, your left hand," Cliché said, enjoying a humorous laugh at my gesture.

If you've never been proposed to, you're missing out on one of the most magical moments in life. It literally felt like time stopped for a moment, and when it did start back up, everything seemed to move in slow motion. Teary-eyed and all, I watched Cliché slide the cushion-cut platinum diamond ring on my left ring finger. The sparkling color not only lit the room up; it lit up a dark, empty space in my heart—the place that knew no love, only abandonment, shame, and castigation. It had become my dwelling place. But no more. I knew from that moment that I was going to take back my life and invite love into my heart. The only love I knew was the love of my children. Their unconditional love kept me from taking pills or walking in front of an oncoming train. Those thoughts were never too far from my mind before I had my children. Once they came into my life, I knew I had to live for them, even if I didn't want to live for myself. But now, I had someone else to love on and be loved by. And it felt good!

"You must have a big date coming up," Michael said between chews as we ate dinner that evening.

"Why do you say that?" I said, wanting to explore his line of reasoning.

"'Cause it's Tuesday, and you've been to the hairdresser and the nail salon. You only do that closer to the weekend. You know, like when you're about to go on a hot date with Mr. Cliché."

I smiled. I couldn't help it. Just the mention of Cliché's name lifted my spirits. "Well, it's something like that," I said, examining both Michael and Anna's faces.

"What is it?" Anna said, trying to decipher my facial expression.

"He asked me to marry him," I said, turning the engagement ring around on my finger, so the diamonds were readily apparent."

"He did?!" Anna said, nearly jumping up from her seat.

"Yes, he did," I said, flashing my ring finger back and forth, so they could get a good look.

"It's beautiful, Mom," Michael said. He paused. "So?"

"So … what?" I said.

"You gonna marry him?" Michael said, looking at me, Anna, and then back at me.

"Well, what do you think?" Although I'd already said yes, I wanted to make Anna and Michael feel as though I took their opinions and feelings into consideration. After all, they'd be living in the house with the man they'd call Mr. Cliché … or even "Dad."

Anna whispered into Michael's ear. He smirked.

"So? What do you guys think? I repeated.

"How soon are we talking?" Michael asked.

"Yeah, how soon?" Anna chimed in.

"Soon … as in tomorrow," I said as I looked down at my food.

"Well, to tell you the truth, we don't know why y'all took so long to get married. This has been a long year and a half. Marry him, Mom. He makes you happy. We see how you smile when he's around," Michael said.

"And we see how happy he is when he's around you. And not to mention, you feed him like a king. He loves your cooking," Anna said, wiping her mouth with a napkin. She leaned back in her seat as if she was gathering her thoughts.

"What?" I said, inviting her to express her thoughts.

"Do it. It's about time you enjoy true love and happiness," Anna said.

"You have our blessings," Michael added.

And that was all she wrote. With my children's blessings, Cliché and I were getting married the next day.

Before we headed to Toledo, Ohio the next morning, I went to get my makeup professionally done. Cliché had scheduled the ceremony for later that afternoon, allotting for the time to get my makeup done and drive to Toledo.

To my surprise, when Cliché showed up, he was sitting in the back seat of a Lincoln Navigator. He'd rented the vehicle and hired a chauffeur to drive us to Toledo. Anna and Michael helped Cliché load my luggage into the truck, and the chauffeur placed it in the trunk for us. Off we went.

The plans were executed flawlessly. Cliché and I were married outside of the courthouse in a beautiful garden on July 15, 2013.

Later that evening, I made the official announcement on my Facebook page. But if I was expecting my family or those around me to be happy for me, I was sorely wrong! When they read the words, "I's married now!" on my wall, all hell broke loose.

CHAPTER 22

When All Hell Breaks Loose

I knew what my mother was calling about the moment I saw her name pop up on my cell phone. I took a deep breath before answering. "Hello?"

"Tell me it's a joke!"

"Tell you what's a joke?" I said, trying to act oblivious.

"Latwaina, you know what I'm talking about," Mama said between what I assumed was gum pops.

"Nope, Mama, it's no joke. I got married," I said, coming clean. I felt light … free. I owned my actions. I didn't have second thoughts about my actions, and I was most certainly prepared to defend my actions.

"Latwaina, you've barely known the man. How are you gonna marry somebody you don't know?!"

"Cause God told him I was his wife, and he told me Cliché was my husband," I said unapologetically.

"Oh, here we go bringing God into this. Latwaina, stop it with that foolishness! God ain't told you to marry a complete stranger."

"Mama, we've known each other almost two years now. We're hardly strangers. He's a stranger *to you* because you don't regularly see your own daughter. Therefore, you don't know what's going on in my life."

"Where's Jeff?"

"Jeff and I broke up."

"And you're ready to marry someone else?"

"Like I said, Cliché and I have known each other for about two years now," I said, rolling my eyes, even though I knew she couldn't see me do so.

"All that man wants is to fleece you out of your money and have a place to stay," Mama said with a slight chuckle.

"Like y'all, huh?" I shot back. "Just like y'all, huh? That 'takes one to know one' thing, Mama?"

"What in the world are you talking about, Latwaina?"

"My money. My money that somehow mysteriously disappeared out of my bank account," I charged.

"I don't know what you're talking about. And stop changing the subject. We're talking about you running off and getting married."

"I didn't run off. We had a private wedding ... just the two of us."

"Why would you not include me or ask me"

"Ask you or tell you?"

"Latwaina, I just don't think that was a smart thing to do."

"Mama, can I ask you a question?" She didn't answer. "Can I?" I repeated.

"Go ahead, Latwaina," Mama said with agitation in her voice.

"Why do you think no one can love me?"

"That's not what I'm saying at all. And where do you come off with that accusation anyway?"

"Because you don't, Mama."

"Latwaina, I'm just saying this for your own good. You have two children that you're raising by yourself. Isn't that clue enough?"

"Mama, I'm no longer raising them by myself. I have a husband now. You don't know Cliché. He's not like any other guy I've ever met. He's not Chad. He's not Eric. He's Cliché. And by the way, he doesn't ask me for a dime," I said.

"For now. For now," my mother said, before dead silence crept in. Finally, Mama continued. "Now, can I ask *you* a question?"

"You can ask anything you want."

"Tell me, what do you know about marriage? About being a wife? About pleasing a man? Nothing. You don't know anything. All you know is how to—" Mama stopped mid-sentence. I think we both knew where she was going with her comment. "Oh, never mind. Just … what do you know about anything?" she continued.

"Mama, I know a lot. I've been through a lot in my little lifetime. One thing I know for sure is what true love feels like."

"Really?" she said sarcastically.

"Yes, I do," I said, standing my ground.

Mama paused for a moment before speaking. "And by the way, did you consult Pastor?" she asked.

"For what?"

"Because that's what you're supposed to do. He's your spiritual father. You're supposed to get his input."

"I didn't. I didn't get his input."

"Why not? You went to him about Jeff. Why didn't you go to him about this Cliché guy?"

"I didn't think I needed to. This just felt right. I know he's who God sent me."

"All right. But remember, you owe the church some form of accountability."

She was right, but I didn't elaborate on it. I could see the conversation would have been never ending if neither one of us were smart enough to just let it go. But I was tired of being the "bigger" person. I had to be the "bigger" person for years. And even then, nothing ever changed. And even though I wanted to go toe-to-toe with my mother, I knew I had to honor the Bible and the Word—"Honor your father and mother, so that your days may be long in the land that the LORD your God is giving you."

"Okay, Mama. I understand you being upset. I get it. But I simply followed my heart. I just need you to understand that. At the end of the day, I followed my heart. I married the man I fell in love with. The man that loves me and loves my children, like they're his own."

Mama didn't say anything. I could tell my words were marinating. In a much softer tone, she said, "Well, it's a done deal now. You said yes and married the man. Ain't nothing anyone can do about it now. You'll have to live with that decision," Mama said. I could sense the anger in her voice was easing. If counseling taught me anything, it was how to diffuse a situation—sweeten your words, soften your tone, or simply stop engaging altogether.

My call with Mama ended with her requesting a ride to the doctor's office the following week. How could I say no? I agreed.

"How do I look?" Cliché said, adjusting his tie.

"You look dapper … just like I like you," I said, winking and catching a pinch of his muscular left buttock as I passed by. It was the first Sunday Cliché was accompanying the kids and me to church. No doubt the word was out that I'd gotten married, so I was trying to mentally prepare myself for the stares, curt remarks, and so forth. What I didn't want to happen was for Cliché to bear the brunt of the backlash, however.

Spotted as we pulled onto the church grounds headed for the parking lot, the pointing of fingers began. Nevertheless, Cliché drove past the cluster of spectators and straight to the parking lot. Before we could park good, Sister Thompson made her way over to our vehicle. She waited for us to get out of the truck.

"I heard the news. Congratulations," she said, looking past me at Cliché.

"Thank you," Cliché and I said in unison.

"You gonna introduce me to your—"

"Husband?" I said, finishing her sentence. "Yes, this is my husband, Cliché."

"Yes … husband," she said, taken aback by my frankness.

"Cliché," Sister Thompson said, echoing me. "Well, praise the Lord, husband. Nice to meet you," she greeted, extending her hand.

"Hello," Cliché said, extending his. He purposely avoided repeating the churchy greeting.

"Hope you'll like it and join us," she said.

"We'll see," Cliché answered, not making any promises.

"See y'all around," Sister Thompson said as she flagged down another church member.

As we proceeded to walk through the parking lot to the front of the church, it felt as though I could feel heat from all the stares.

"Oh, is that how they do at church?" Cliché whispered in my ear.

"Yeah, this is what they do at church sometimes," I confessed.

Anna and Michael veered off in their own directions, meeting up with their friends. I only hoped they didn't catch any heat from my decision to get married. By nature, I was a feisty mother hen. If you came for my children, you were in for a fight. I was super protective of Anna and Michael, and I made no apologies for it. I had long ago decided that I wasn't going to be anything like my mother when it came to protecting my children.

Of course, as we entered the front vestibule of the church, we were stopped by sincere well-wishers, those who were fishing for details, or those who were just downright nosy. Surprisingly, however, both Cliché and I managed to keep our cool. That is, until it was time for the sermon. What was Pastor King's sermon topic? "Seeking Counsel." And of course, it didn't take a genius to know who he was referring to. If we had walked out of the sanctuary in the middle of the sermon, it would have signaled our sense of guilt. I knew Cliché was bothered by the pastor's sermon, because he fiddled with his watch off and on throughout the sermon.

When service was over, we made a mean break for the door. Serving on the Hospitality Group that Sunday, Grandma Lily was already in the church vestibule when we entered.

"Latwaina," she called out.

"Yes," I said, turning to face her. She smiled at Cliché. Grandma Lily liked Cliché the moment she met him. Like the old folk would say, "She took to him." Said he had a genuine smile and reminded her of her dad, my great-grandfather. Said he was sent by God.

"Don't worry about what anybody says. That man was sent to you by God," Grandma Lily whispered into my ear.

"Really, Granny?" I said.

"I ain't down on my knees every morning just for the heck of it. I'm down there talking to Jesus for real. And if there's one thing I know, it's good and bad people. And that man standing right there next to you … he's a good one. Keep him close too. You hear me? Cause you got a lot of rats looking for cheese 'round here," she said, laughing at her own joke. I guessed it was a figure of speech old folk used to say as well, 'cause I hadn't heard Grandma Lily say it until that day. "Why don't y'all come by the house for dinner today?" Grandma Lily invited.

"Not today, Granny. We have plans," I said. I didn't want to put Cliché on the spot like that. Plus, I wasn't quite ready to confront the entire family. "How about next Sunday?" I suggested.

"Then, next Sunday. I'll see you two next Sunday."

"Okay," I said.

"And bring the kids too," she added.

"We will," Cliché said, giving Grandma Lily a goodbye hug.

With the exception of Grandma Lily, we barely spoke to any members other than saying a quick hello, making a brief introduction, or waving goodbye. We had one agenda, and it was to get outta dodge fast!

"So, how was it?" I said, finally addressing the elephant in the back seat, if you will.

Cliché rubbed his beard with his left hand, keeping his right hand on the steering wheel. "You really want to know?"

"Yes, of course."

"I think we should start looking for a new church. I don't like the way the pastor disrespected you. Now, he can disrespect me all he wants because he doesn't know me, but it took everything in me not to approach him after church and have a man-to-man conversation."

For me, the thought of leaving that church was like the thought of cutting off a limb. All I knew was that church. I'd gone to that church since I was a child. And when I stayed with Grandma Lily, church was practically our second home. But Cliché had long told me that when we got together, I'd have to get adjusted to changes. I was a married woman, and when I said, "I do," I was saying I would trust the judgment and direction of my husband.

"There are plenty of churches out here. We don't have to find one tomorrow. But I don't think you or I should attend this church. Plus, I just think you need a clean slate from everything. Like, don't worry about the foreclosure proceedings on the house. I'm already working on getting us our own home."

I must be dreaming. Our own home. I don't think I heard anything else Cliché said during our ride home. The fear of being kicked out of the house and having nowhere to go literally disappeared the moment Cliché uttered those words.

"How long are you gonna be gone?" Cliché asked, looking up from the sports section of the newspaper he was reading.

"Not long. Maybe about a couple of hours. Gotta take my mother to the doctor's office and then drop her off at Grandma Lily's," I said.

"You sure you want to go over there? You know the clan's gonna be there."

"Well, it's now or never. I can't hide forever. Plus, it'll be good for me to test the temperature before having dinner at Grandma Lily's."

"It's not now or never. You don't owe those people over there anything. They deserted you when you needed them most. I haven't even laid eyes on more than half of them. If you asked me, going over there is asking for trouble," Cliché said, folding the newspaper up as he stood.

"I know. I get it. But I'm not the same Latwaina," I said. Truthfully, however, I felt my heart sink to the pit of my stomach. Something inside stirred up the old feelings of hurt and loss. Why was I going over to Grandma Lily's to be tortured? I couldn't answer the question, but I knew I needed to go. Maybe to free myself from their bondage. Maybe even to prove a point to myself—that I was no longer going to allow them to intimidate me.

"Do you need me to go with you?"

"No, I'm good. I can handle them," I said in a somber tone.

"You sure?" Cliché said, raising his eyebrows.

I nodded.

Sensing my changing emotions, evidenced by a tear that had escaped its tear duct, Cliché said, "Look, Latwaina, do what you feel you need to do. I'm not trying to tell you not to see your family. That's not what I even want to do. But you and I both know how things can pop off. You're my wife, and it's my job to protect you. So, if they start acting crazy, pick up your cell phone and call me."

Cliché walked over to me and wrapped his muscular arms around me. The smell of his jasmine musk aftershave lotion penetrated my nostrils. I closed my eyes. I wanted to melt into his arms and allow him to just hold me … forever.

"You don't have to do this if you don't want. You got me and the kids, and we love you unconditionally. You don't have anything to prove. You hear me?"

"I hear you," I said, opening my eyes. "But I need to do this. I need to do this for me. It's long overdue." Cliché released his hold.

"If it's what you want to do, then I support you one-hundred percent."

I grabbed my purse from the coffee table, and Cliché escorted me to my car."

"Why don't you take the truck?"

"Cause, I didn't know if you needed to go somewhere."

"Take the truck, baby," Cliché said, handing me the keys. "It's more reliable than your car. The last thing I want is for you to get stranded over there, and they're looking at you like you're crazy."

I chuckled as I took the keys from him. As he'd always done, Cliché opened the car door for me and saw me off. Glancing through the rearview mirror after I drove down the street, I could see Cliché standing in the same spot, watching me as if he were a parent, watching their child drive by themselves for the first time. I smiled to myself.

I popped my favorite CD in the player and listened to the soothing sound of Anita Baker's "Rapture." It was one of Cliché's favorite songs too. I was so caught up in the music that before I knew it, I was turning onto my mother's street. She was standing outside, waiting when I pulled up to her house.

"Who's truck?" Mama said as she got in the truck and pulled the seatbelt to strap herself in.

"My husband's," I said with pride.

"Hmmph," she said. And that was all she said. Surprisingly, she didn't have much more to add about the marriage ordeal. It was a done deal, like she said.

I took her to the doctor's office, let her run a few errands, and then headed for Grandma Lily's house. I deliberately slowed my speed when we pulled onto the family block. I could see what looked like a mob of folk on the front porch area. I parked in front of the house.

"You gonna get out?" Mama said, unbuckling her seatbelt.

"Should I?" I said, still contemplating whether I wanted to deal with the drama.

"Do what you want," Mama said.

I took it as a challenge and unbuckled my seatbelt. No matter what Cliché had said, in my mind, it *was* now or never. Confront them now or never.

"Look who the wind blew by here," my cousin Skylar said facetiously.

"Where is he?" Ebony said, getting up from the wicker chair she was sitting in.

"He's at home," I said, my eyes still casing the faces of those standing close.

"For now," I heard Mama mumble underneath her breath.

Laughter rang out in the air. And in that instant, it blew a fuse in me. I turned to face my mother. "I guess it feels good when I'm the laughing stock, huh?"

"Latwaina, get some thick skin, will you?" she said, making light of my feelings, which made me even angrier. "Everybody is asking the same questions: 'What do you know about pleasing a man? And what do you know about marriage?'"

"Mama, you wanna know what I know? I know I haven't felt this way ever in my life. I know that I've never felt this protected in my entire life. Yeah, my dad was a good man, and he loved me with every breath he had in him, but Cliché is not a just good man; he's *my* man! He's my lover and protector. He doesn't disrespect me."

"Yet," my cousin Cecil mumbled as he walked past me and groped my crotch on the sly.

Cecil wasn't really my cousin, just like Nick wasn't really my uncle. Cecil was Uncle Mike's first cousin. The families were so close and intertwined, they just claimed kinship. Anyway, Cecil was a notorious drug dealer from around the way. He'd stop by Aunt Lisa and Uncle Mike's after making his pickups and drop-offs in the area. It was obvious that he, like Uncle Mike and the rest of their family, felt some kinda way toward me ever since Nick went to jail.

"Did you just touch me inappropriately?" I yelled.

"You're imagining things. Maybe you want me to … just like you wanted Nick to," he said with a sinister grin on his face.

Before I realized it, I turned around and swung on Cecil.

"Grace, get your daughter before she goes outta here on a stretcher!" he yelled, backing up to dodge the blow.

"Latwaina, stop!" Mama yelled.

I looked at my mother. "So, you gonna just let him say that to your daughter and not say anything … and he touched me inappropriately!"

"Don't pay him any mind," Mama said.

The lightbulb came on. She didn't get it. And in that moment, I finally came to the sad conclusion that she probably never would. She didn't possess that feisty mother hen spirit like I did and many other mothers, for that matter. She was a different breed altogether. And as much as the realization crushed my spirit, I knew I had to accept the hard reality.

"But that's the problem, Mama!" I screamed. "You never defend me!" All my life, you've let people walk all over me. Talk about me. Abuse me. Kick me to the curb." I tried to hold the tears back, but I couldn't. I felt the anger and hostility brewing on the inside. The kind that makes you scared of yourself … of what harm you are capable of committing.

"And while I'm here, let me just say this one last time. In case you're wondering why I got married without telling any of you guys. It's because you don't care anyway. When I needed my family, you guys were never there. When I was losing my home, no one came to my rescue. When my lights and water were off, no one came to my rescue. No … wait, yes, someone did. My husband. My husband, Cliché, saw to it that my lights and water got restored. My husband made sure me and my children ate breakfast, lunch, and dinner. None of you guys were around! None of you! So, if I wanna marry the person who has shown me love and respect, so be it. And I want you all to get a real good look at me, because you don't have to worry about seeing Latwaina Kelley—not Tyler. It's Latwaina Kelley. Get a good look now, because it'll be a cold day in hell before you see me again.

"Baby, don't say that," Grandma Lily said between coughs.

"No, Granny. That's the way I feel."

"I still want you guys to come over for dinner," Grandma Lily said in what seemed like a hopeless tone.

I didn't readily answer. I was too immersed in my anger.

"Come over for dinner next Sunday, like we agreed," Grandma Lily said, looking at Mama and Aunt Lisa, almost daring them to challenge the invitation.

"I don't know, Granny. I'll think about it," I said, turning to walk towards the truck.

He was right. Cliché was right. I shouldn't have gone over there. I had nothing to prove. But I did find out that no one had really changed. Maybe Grandma Lily, since she was getting older. Maybe getting older and tapping into her mortality had something to do with it. I mean, still a church-going woman, Grandma Lily knew better than anyone that what was going down in our family wasn't right. The drug dealing, the drug addictions, the incest, and a slew of other family secrets was tearing the family apart, and most of my relatives had no clue. We weren't close, as they believed and our community perceived. Instead, we were a group of people connected by blood only. If anyone dared peer inside of our family dynamics, they would see that we didn't really love one another; we tolerated one another. We didn't really trust one another; we were highly skeptical of one another. We didn't have a strong bond; we were woven together by the very things that were eating us all from the inside out, just like cancer. Hatred. Jealousy. Self-hate. Dark secrets. And the insatiable desire to remain woven together in that cancerous web called "family." And God forbid if one decided to break free, like me. Luckily for me, I didn't have a choice. I was forcibly isolated from the pack. And this day was the first time I recognized that my rejection was actually a blessing. I saw my family for who they really were. I knew I'd have to give Grandma Lily's dinner invitation careful thought and consideration.

I could barely turn the key to open the front door before Cliché opened it. He didn't have to ask how the visit went; my eyes told the story. I fell into his arms. "It's all right, baby. It's all right. You got me. You got your kids. This is your family. We are your family. We're here. We love you," he said.

As if I were an infant, Cliché helped me get ready for bed that evening. He held me in his arms, gently rocking me back and forth. My mind began to race. He was right. It was the dawn of a new day. There was gonna be no more looking back for me. I realized, even after all those years, that I was still yearning and desiring to be accepted by people who would never see me for who I am. Who would never accept their culpability for what happened to me when I was a teenager. Who would never apologize for introducing me to the world of drug dealing, forcing me to hold their drugs when the police raided the property. Who would never apologize for being too stoned out to realize I was becoming withdrawn right under their noses. Who would never apologize for turning me into a modern-day Cinderella by forcing me to cook and clean up after my siblings, my cousins, and the adults after parties.

Somewhere in the wee hours of the morning, I finally drifted off to sleep.

CHAPTER 23

Farewells and Goodbyes

When I turned the key to unlock the door, something in me leaped like a spark of joy. Cliché pushed the door open wide. The smell of fresh paint saturated the air and traveled up my nostrils.

I took the first step into our brand-new home.

"Oh, my gosh!" Anna said, admiring the glistening chandelier hanging in the foyer.

"Isn't it beautiful?" I said, twirling around.

"All I want to know is where is my room?" Michael said, brushing past us and bolting down the hallway.

We must've spent the next hour or so going from room to room, admiring each and discussing ways in which we wanted to decorate. Once the movers showed up, the hard work began. Unpacking, something I didn't necessarily enjoy. But I had to admit, it was a bit different this time. I was unpacking and moving into a "home," not just a house. I was moving in with my husband and my children.

We took a break about four hours in and went out to grab something to eat at a nearby diner. It was there that I ran into Jamel. His eyes almost popped out of their sockets. I waited to see how he was going to respond. He was staring, with that "you still standing" kind of expression on his face. *Absolutely, I'm still standing.* I was not just standing by myself; I was standing with my husband—my anchor, my lover, my protector, my provider—and my children … happy, healthy teenagers by this time. I offered a half-smile. Jamel nodded. If he expected me to roll my eyes and confront him about the aged-old debt he still owed, he was sadly mistaken. He owed it, sure, but I was in a totally different space and place. And I understood why he was standing there so perplexed; I was happy and healed and not bitter and broken.

"Who's that?" Cliché asked.

"No one," I said. "No one important," I added, just as the hostess came to seat us.

We enjoyed a delicious meal at the diner, killing some time before heading back to the house to resume unpacking. That is, until we just couldn't do anymore. Zonked and tired, Cliché and I showered and went straight to our bedroom.

"You know you're not going to sleep tonight, right? We're christening our new bedroom … our new mattress," Cliché said, pulling back the covers.

"Oh, I know. I was hoping you weren't anticipating going to sleep right away. It's mattressmony time," I said, jokingly.

Cliché slid in the bed next to me, cuddling me in his muscular arms and planting soft kisses on my neck. Everything about the day was perfect thus far, and the lovemaking that had just begun was the icing on the cake. Yes, I was married, but I knew that inside, I was changing. Something was happening both in and around me, and God was allowing people to witness the change, without me even having to mumble a word. Showing that his blessings were stowed upon me like he'd done earlier that evening with Jamel, and it was just the beginning.

I had long wondered whether I would ever move past the trauma of my past, to be able to give my husband all of me without experiencing flashbacks of the violent sexual assaults. Somehow, God allowed Cliché's love to overshadow the traumatic experience. As we'd often done, Cliché and I enjoyed a night of wild, passionate lovemaking … in our new house, our new bed, and with renewed covenant to each other.

Our residence, 234 Camden Place, was more like a house of refuge. My children's friends would hang out at our house all the time. Cliché and I were like neighborhood parents. Many of the children in the neighborhood could confide in us. They saw us as extensions of their real parents. And Cliché and I gladly assumed the roles and responsibilities. As the years went by, Grandma Lily became more attached to Cliché and me, more so than her own children. She'd often come over and climb in the bed with me until Cliché came home after working second shift.

"Granny, Cliché's home now," I'd say.

"Well, good. You done fell asleep on me. Now I can have some company," she'd say, sitting up on Cliché's side of the bed. Cliché had spoiled her, so she seemed to much more prefer sitting up chatting with him than with me. I couldn't blame her though. Cliché was a people's person, very warm and caring. And he was funny too. But things changed after Granny had a stroke. She couldn't speak all that well. But somehow, because of the special bond we shared, Cliché and I were able to communicate with Granny in our own unique way. I will never forget the day of June 16, 2016. I walked into Granny's hospital room, and she was lying there, a bit incapacitated due to the heavy doses of medication she'd been given. Nevertheless, she was able to engage in one last, meaningful conversation.

"Baby, you know Granny appreciates all you've done for me, right?"

"Oh, Granny, I'd do anything for you. You're my granny," I said, choking back tears.

I could read between the lines. Grandma Lily didn't have to spell it out. She was in her last days and felt it in her heart to make peace with me. That's the amazing thing about love; it communicates in inaudible ways.

I reached over and placed Grandma Lily's hand in mine. God had healed me, and I was no longer holding anything against her. I felt a calm and a peace in that moment.

"Aunt Le … Le," Granny said.

I could tell she was trying to say something about Aunt Lisa, but she just didn't have the strength to do so. "It's okay,

Grandma Lily. I'm good. Don't worry about me. Don't try to talk. You need your energy so you can get well," I said as I ran my hands through her curly bangs, carefully moving the dangling curls from her face. And although I wasn't a song-bird by any stretch of the imagination, I remembered one of Grandma Lily's favorite songs, "God Has Smiled on Me," and began to sing it to her. I sang it until Grandma Lily drifted off to sleep. Slowly, I bent over and gave her a soft kiss on the lips. "Goodnight, Granny. See you in the morning."

I had no idea that when I said, "See you in the morning," to Grandma Lily the evening before, I would be referencing that "Great Gettin' Up Morning," we call the rapture.

Granny went to heaven on June 17, 2016. Saying goodbye to Granny was almost as difficult as it was saying goodbye to my daddy. Our last conversation is etched in my heart and will never be forgotten. To hear someone admit their wrongdoing and apologize, even if it's years after an offense has occurred, heals wounds you might not realize still exist.

So just how does a damaged crown still shine? Interestingly enough, the very natural design of a diamond bears a crown-like image within it. The diamond crown, as it is called, is the portion that spans across the top of the stone towards the outer side of the stone. Looking from above, the diamond crown would look exactly like an actual crown that's placed upside down. It is no coincidence that God designed this natural gem in such a manner. When God looks at us, no matter how broken or battered we are, he sees the diamond crown within us. This is why it is also important to surround ourselves with people who will see our value. And the only way they can see our true value is from the correct vantage point.

The crown of a diamond is what influences the light or brilliance of the diamond. It is because it's the part that handles the largest amount of light entering or leaving the stone. The crown of a diamond has two fundamental aspects that determine the fire and brilliance of the diamond—crown height and crown angle. A diamond's crown height refers to the straight distance between points on the top of the diamond to the outer side of the diamond. The crown angle is the most significant factor that influences how light enters the crown, and, subsequently, how the entire structure of the diamond handles that light. This is interesting because when we see ourselves as precious gems—diamonds—how we position ourselves determines the reflection of love and light. We are created with such meticulous design by our Creator. Like diamonds, when we are in the correct position, light and brilliance can exude from within. This then attracts others to us.

The very nature of cutting a diamond is what gives a diamond its uniqueness. If you've ever gone shopping for an engagement ring or any type of diamond jewelry, you'll notice that the brilliance of each cut, or style, radiates differently. Whether it's the marquis-, princess-, oval-, pear-, emerald, or cushion-cut diamond, each shines with its own unique brilliance. It doesn't matter if you take a sledgehammer and crush a diamond, it will still shine.

God crowned women with precious diamonds. It's what we are made of. You can't destroy the brilliance of a diamond with force. Only we can destroy the brilliance of our light shining in the world from the inside out. We dull our own light when we allow external factors to hide our light from the world. Again, I pronounce and declare, no matter who does what or what happens in our lives, damaged crowns still shine.

This final chapter is titled "Farewells and Goodbyes" because not only did I have to say goodbye to my dad and Grandma Lily; I've had to say goodbye to the old Latwaina and the burden of that pain I carried around. I realized it would keep me from being the best wife and mother I could be. I had to give up looking for role models and become one myself. Become the woman young girls and some women look up to. Saying goodbye to a version of your old self is a process; it doesn't happen overnight. And while it is sometimes easier to hold on to your pain as an excuse, it's unhealthy and toxic. So, I said goodbye to the old Latwaina and welcomed the new Latwaina … a woman who is evolving with each passing day—learning, loving, and laughing through all things.

EPILOGUE

People often ask me what made me decide to write this book. The answer isn't simple, but I'll try to explain. I was chosen to write this book. There's nothing glamorous or exciting about my childhood that would make me want to share my story. Rather, it is the exact opposite. My childhood is tainted with stains of hurt, loss, pain, and trauma. While I know I am not the only person who's been sexually assaulted, I recognized that most of us (those that have experienced this type of trauma) go through life with feelings of shame and guilt. Some of us hide our pain through being super-dedicated at work or becoming a workaholic altogether, materialistic things such as jewelry, cars, clothes, etcetera, or even through relationships or false relationships. I wrote this book so I could share the story of a broken girl-turned-woman who has now overcome the pain of her past and is living a loving and ful-filling life. No, things are not perfect. There are still some kinks to be worked out. There are some relationships that need healing. But as long as I'm alive, the opportunity to do so still presents itself.

My road to recovery wasn't easy. No walk in the park for sure. And it won't be for the vast majority of sexual assault victims. Just the reason God allows us to experience trag-edy can seem like an eternal mystery. The reality is, however, that some painful things can never be explained or under-stood. This can cause us to continuously lament in sorrow and discouragement. But it's fascinating to know that in some of our lowest moments in life, we can find solace. Picking up the pieces of your life after trauma can seem daunting. Interestingly, however, this is where courage and strength spring up from within. In fact, finding consolation and com-fort in yourself and your own thoughts is a strength in and of itself.

Some may not believe this, but my life is a testament that you can indeed find solace or comfort in your sorrow. In some of your deepest and darkest days, a simple word or phrase or even scripture can be the spiritual food you need to pick your-self up, dust yourself off, and keep striving forward. Strength and courage are already in us but can lie dormant until we summon them forth. And sometimes, it's only through hard-ships and trials that we discover what truly lies deep within us. Power. We have power to overcome anything in life, except death. Look at how phenomenal and powerful God made us!

For me, I believed Psalms 147:3 –"He healeth up the bro-ken in heart, and bindeth up their wounds." Scripture is pow-erful; it's the uttered Word of God through man. Just like this book, it is God-ordained to spread God's love, His promises, and His healing power. There's no way I could have overcome the tragedy (double tragedy) without God having a hand in it. You can indeed find comfort in sorrow and tap into your internal reservoir and unveil a monumental reserve where courage, strength, and forgiveness all dwell.

RESOURCES

911 – Emergencies only

What is **Sexual Assault?**
Sexual assault is an act in which one intentionally sexually touches another person without that person's consent, or when one coerces or physically forces a person to engage in a sexual act against their will. It is a form of sexual violence, which includes child sexual abuse, groping, rape, or the torture of the person in a sexual manner.

If you are someone you know has been a victim of sexual assault, call your local 911. For additional assistance, contact the **National Sexual Assault Hotline** at 1-800-656-HOPE (4673).

You can also contact the **Rape, Abuse, and Incest National Network**

Rainn.org
Rainn.org/get-help

If you are someone you know is experiencing thoughts of suicide, contact the **National Suicide Prevention Lifeline** at 1-800-273-8255.

If you are a victim of domestic violence and need help, contact the **Domestic Violence Hotline** at 1-800-799-7233 or TTY 1-800-787-3224.

To receive mental health services, contact the **Mental Health Assistance** service line at 1-888- 844-6026.

For free **Mental Health Treatment**, contact 1-877-819-2152.